A. D. Bergin was born in No:
Tyneside. He graduated from (
first class degree in History, since when he has worked as an
archaeologist, historian, researcher, postman, roofer, builder
and barman. *The Wicked of the Earth* is his first published
work of fiction.

Follow A. D. Bergin @adberginwriter

The Wicked of the Earth

SPECIAL EDITION

A. D. BERGIN

Northodox Press Ltd
Maiden Greve, Malton,
North Yorkshire, YO17 7BE

This edition 2024

1
First published in Great Britain by
Northodox Press Ltd 2024

ISBN: 9781915179432

This book is set in Caslon Pro Std

Dedicated to the memory of:

Elizabeth Anderson;
Elizabeth Brown;
Margaret Brown;
Matthew Bulmer / Bonner;
Jane Copeland;
Katherine Coulter;
Elizabeth Dobson;
Elianor Henderson;
Alice Hume;
Jane Hunter;
Margaret Maddison;
Janet Martin;
Margaret Muffet;
Mary Pots;
Elianor Rogerson;
Ann Watson;

and to the many other unnamed victims
of the Northumberland and Durham
witch hunt of 1649-50.

Praise for The Wicked of the Earth

'Excellent, a fascinating, thrilling,
and tense historical crime novel.'

Trevor Wood, author of *The Silent Killer*

'Fans of S. G. MacLean and Andrew Taylor will enjoy this
pacy, twisty novel. Fascinating.'

Naomi Kesley, *author of The Burnings*

'Well plotted, memorable characters. I found myself rushing
to the very satisfying - and moving - conclusion. An excellent
addition to the genre.'

Robert J. Lloyd, author of *The Bedlam Cadaver*

'Brimming with atmosphere and suspense,
The Wicked of the Earth is a stunning debut and in James
Archer we have a hugely compelling character.'

Chris Lloyd, author of *Banquet of Beggars*

'Loaded with atmosphere and great storytelling.'

Paul Burke, author of *Crime Time*

Cleverly weaves a tightly-plotted novel. I love the
characterisation, in particular James Archer. You feel for him
as he is dragged into a power struggle where danger lurks,
conspiracy abounds. One to recommend, a perfect blend of
character and historical fiction.'

Andy Wormald

'What a read! A deep dive into the human psyche perfect for
those who like their historical fiction with a side of mystery
and dash of the macabre.'

Nessa's BookTok

For in the hand of the Lord there is a cup, and the wine is red;
and He poureth out of the same;
but the dregs thereof, all the wicked of the earth
shall wring them out and drink them.

Book of Psalms 75:8

England, 1650

The King is dead, executed at the hands of a Parliament purged and controlled by its own New Model Army. The Monarchy and the House of Lords are abolished. The Commonwealth of England is a new-born Republic.

Fearful that the enemies who beset it on all sides might unite around the late monarch's eldest son, young Charles Stuart, the Council of State has viciously repressed Royalist support in Ireland, launched a full-scale invasion of Scotland, and spies endlessly upon its own people.

Across England's towns and villages, men returning from the wars seek certainty in a changed world, scrambling for position, fighting for power, and looking to reassert their authority over women, who had found new freedom in managing without them during the years of violence.

Abigail Walker

On the Newcastle quayside, at the times of budding and of harvest, when the tides run at their lowest, there comes that most dangerous point known only as the breek.

Not long after the river turns and the thin black edges of its oozing mud begin to show, the out-flow of water makes a sudden acceleration. An unwise onlooker sees this only as a slight increase in the disturbance of the stream, for the real pull occurs several feet beneath the surface. The Tyne vomits up quantities of coal gas. The air chills. A dead stink overpowers the ordinary rot of the chares, the steep steps and alleys which lead up to the old town.

The people have learned to avoid the lowest parts of the quay at these moments. No work will be done under the bridge, by the water gates, nor near the water line of the tall ships clustered along the mooring, the breek bringing, as it may, nausea, delusion, even death.

Abigail Walker sensed the change. In the midst of her fear, she took from it new courage. The breek was a reminder that she knew the maze of passages running between the chares in a way her pursuers could not.

In that lay her only hope.

Abigail's fitted boots slid upon the worn stone of the steps. Winter had, once again, come on early. Under a quarter moon, the damp already threatened to turn to frost. She skidded and came close to falling as she reached the next precarious landing, losing precious seconds in righting herself. Before scrambling into the tight cleft presenting itself on the right, she risked, however, a single upward glance.

The men hurtled towards her down Peppercorn Chare, even closer than before. She could see the malevolent glint in the dark eyes of the smaller of the two, his face hollow, the workmen's clothing hanging off a meagre frame. But it was the cold emptiness in the gaze of the other man, the blond giant, which scared her back into flight.

Feet scraping against an earthen floor packed dense by centuries of use, Abigail disappeared into the cut-through. Tears rolling down her cheeks, she lunged forward to take the next, hidden turn, exiting into a narrow, rising ginnel. Ignoring the first two openings, she pressed upwards for a few more strides, hurling herself left into the even more constrained crevice of Wilson's Wynd. Flattened against its steepling side, the pain in her chest steadily mounted as she laboured to remain silent.

Close behind sounded mismatched footsteps, the one rapid and eager, the other deep, slow and heavy. They hesitated, then stopped. An indistinct volley of words passed between the two men, their voices rising.

A fine thread of excitement tugged inside her and she had to stifle an urge to cough, digging deeper into the crumbling, coal-greased plaster. The men began to move again. She tensed at their greater purpose and urgency. Their steps echoed louder ,then slowly, almost imperceptibly, began to recede.

Abigail waited. Her heart felt as if it may burst. The sounds did not return. She let out a sharp gasp and sagged away from the filth of the wall. Her gamble had worked; the giant and his short, dark companion would have disappeared into one of the many other paths leading across the bank. Now, she must again move fast, before they had time to double back.

In two minutes, she would be in her family's house on Trinity Chare. Before her father and her brothers, she would, finally, tell all: about the secret meetings on Tuthill Stairs; about her involvement with Elinor Loumsdale and the Newgate women;

about these two foreign men, sent first to tell her to leave the town but now pursuing her for her life.

The overhang of tall buildings kept out what light the moon offered. Here, no lantern was ever lit. The way was shrouded in an absolute darkness, but she stepped forwards smoothly, knowing, without the need for sight, every turn needed to reach her home.

'You ought to have heeded the warning, you know. You were told that there would not be another.'

The voice was as easy as it was calm. Abigail began to back away, but the shadow, which had been no more than an extra layer of depth to the blackness, overtook her and became a man. Behind, she could hear the approach of the others, closing off any possible escape. She began to scream, although she knew that in this place, a woman's cry would draw no attention.

The sound was cut off by a soft glove placed gently against her trembling lips, an even softer voice, whispering her name, and the sight of the long, silvered blade.

Chapter 1

The low sky glowered overhead. Smoke struggled out from the clusters of tall, dirty, red brick chimney stacks which rose from the disparate wings of the old palace. Their smuts and sludge fell in great globs to the open walks and courtyards below, greasily spoiling the shabby provincial best of the crowds of waiting supplicants long before they had even stepped within the precincts of government.

One man strode purposefully through the confused throng in the most central court. His broad, stiff-brimmed hat, heavy burgundy leather cloak and high boots kept out almost all of the filth of the air and the mire of the ground. The sword swinging by James Archer's side, along with the coldness of his manner, caused the people to part before him as he swept towards an anonymous corner staircase whose guard barely glanced at the officer's sunken face, an ugly scar running long down its left side, before allowing him through and up to the first floor.

He emerged into a mean, low-ceilinged corridor. Along its unadorned length, a row of small doors lined the left-hand wall. To the right, just by the top of the stair, was set a wider double doorway. Archer passed this by, shivering with the knowledge that beyond it, and through other more ornate rooms and galleries, the Council of State was in session.

Confident despite the dim light, he moved along the passage to stop outside a door near to its mid-point, one no more or less distinct than any other. His knock received a curt response, less a word than an echo of the dull tap his knuckles had

7

made upon the thick wood. Removing his hat, Archer paused fractionally before taking the handle.

'Ensign Archer, you are late.'

He had been expecting this. No, Captain Richard Deane, newly appointed clerk to the newly appointed keeper of the Council's archives, would not intimidate him today.

Deane stood from behind a table piled with documents and thick-bound ledgers. He seemed to ponder for a minute before selecting from among them a single, folded paper. The captain stepped back to open the small window a few inches, allowing reeking tendrils of smog to enter into his cell.

'You should be happy. You are required in Newcastle. You are going home.'

All of Archer's nurtured poise fell vertiginously away.

In the months since they had trapped him with the choice, which was no choice, to work for them without question or to be thrown to the waiting jackals, Archer had turned his hand to bribery and to theft. He had intimidated and killed for them. He had become buried deep into the morass of corruption, greed and brutality which sustained the newborn republic. And none of this had touched him. Not after all he had seen and done in the wars. Faced, however, with returning to the town, family and duty he had abandoned, a clammy nausea formed, joined by a gathering pain across his brows.

'I am ordered to report to the Lord General, in support of the Scottish campaign.'

'It is the Council which rules in this Commonwealth and not my Lord Cromwell. Are you arguing with that?'

Archer wrestled to control a flicker, which tugged at the right-hand side of his face. Deane, stepping closer, affected not to notice.

'There is arisen a matter which concerns the Sergeant-Major General, so it concerns me, and now it very much concerns you.'

Major General Philip Skippon, member of the Council of State, keeper of the Tower, self-styled Christian Centurion.

Deane's master and the ultimate arbiter of Archer's toils. How like him to insist upon retaining his old, unique, wartime title.

'A Newcastle merchant wishes to communicate with us. You shall establish the contact.' Deane's thin fingers stroked the folded sheet, but he did not hand it over. 'You understand that this is quiet work, do you not? It remains between us and between us alone.'

Archer immediately apprehended the significance of such 'quiet work', the illicit tasks assigned to Skippon's network of private intelligencers, used to intimidate or spy upon any who might potentially prove useful to its master.

'The details are in here,' Deane continued. 'They are to be learned, as usual. Signs, tokens and the like.'

The mission was commonplace, most likely no more than the receipt of cheap information from some wavering Royalist, but to choose Archer seemed near to madness.

'Do not make me go back. You know I am loyal. I defied my family and my master to join the cause.'

'Your cowardly town cleaved to the King to preserve its monopoly over the coal trade. There are many in it who would still mourn that man of blood, your own family included. But this merchant has requested you specifically. We would be foolish, even negligent, to ignore that. You do not suggest that Master Skippon is foolish, do you?' Deane's thin lips quivered. 'Besides, there is quite another reason why you will want to return.'

The pull upon Archer's face quickened. 'Skippon garrisoned the town for two years. He must retain a dozen eyes and ears there. What could I possibly add to that?'

'You do not know? Do you keep no correspondents from your own hometown? Is your estrangement truly so very deep?'

'It is more than six years since I left. I was a boy of seventeen. I know nothing.'

The captain glowed with some twisted pleasure. 'Then, listen. You understand that in Scotland a great many women have been killed as witches? Last December, the corporation brought in a Scot, a notorious witch pricker. There have been accusations, inquisitions, and executions. But among the women put to trial, some were drawn from Newcastle's most important families. Such as they are.'

Deane waited for a reaction, which Archer determinedly refused to give.

'Through its own means, the Council cannot discover what this may signify for the safety of the coals. That, of course, touches upon the safety of the Commonwealth. Your commission is to investigate these occurrences and to uncover what lies behind them.'

The captain lowered his tone, nauseatingly. 'Several women were hanged last month. One of those devilish Jezebels may have been known to you very well. Very well indeed. Your loving little sister Margaret.'

Archer's guts writhed. His head pounded as a shivering weakness spread down each of his limbs. The room darkened.

Deane's smooth features erupted into a terrible, detached smile. 'Meg, I am told she is known as. Meg is named as one of the accused. Was she a witch, Archer? Would you not like to know the truth about your own sister, whether she supped with the Devil? Whether she lives, or is already burning in the fiery torment of Hell where you shall, surely, soon join her?'

Chapter 2

Archer's raucous yells echoed from the bare walls and ceiling of his Holborn chamber. Upright, silenced, sweat pouring from him, he searched its darkest depths for the dead.

They emerged softly, some regarding him with insubstantial anger, more with sorrow, a very few with loose, distracted smiles. Men he had known, men he had fought with, now become eternal comrades alongside those he had killed.

There was Thomas, who had taken a bullet to the brain at Lyme, his one remaining eye glistening with a bright good humour. Next to him, father and son together, stood the pair from the barricades upon Gabriel's Hill at Maidstone. Always together.

Slowly, every one of the apparitions turned away to face the back wall. Following their gaze, between the grey and tan and dullest red of their coats, Archer caught a flash of brighter colour. As he strained forwards, it became the movement of a girl, stumbling as she ran, a mane of fair curls cascading behind her.

Meg, fleeing from the hideous cadavers. Meg, fleeing from something worse, something behind him, sensed but unseen. Meg, fleeing from Archer himself.

He made to speak, but no word came. The room was still, and all were gone.

Cautiously, he rose from the bed. Step by uncertain step, he approached the window, violently opening its shutters to lean out into the night. Over the farthest rooftops, only the slightest thinning of the deep blackness was evident. Below, Rose Fields was shrouded in a dense, low mist. Archer's breathing slowed.

The trembling in his limbs gradually diminished.

The nightmares were becoming more frequent, chasing him out of sleep and all too often pursuing him throughout the day. Meg's appearance in them was chillingly new.

Faint sounds began to reach him from the activity of servants in the surrounding stables and out-houses. From within his own lodging, there remained only silence. The other residents of the tenement had long since ceased to rouse themselves for his nocturnal shouts. Nor would Parker, or any of his fellow orderlies, by now surely awake and busy with their earliest tasks, be bothered to investigate the disturbances resounding from the topmost floor.

Archer gripped hard at the window's frame. The visions had finally burnt away only to be replaced by clawing guilt and the same shivering fear and flashing anger which had burst forth upon Deane's revelation. Anger at Skippon and his vicious minion. Anger at the Council. At Meg. Anger, most of all, towards himself.

He closed his eyes and leant out further. When, eventually, he was calm enough to look again, the mist was all but gone, the ground shimmering in the earliest light. Directly before him, there in the very middle of the fields, the single solid thing in the whole ethereal scene, stood one lone, uniformed man staring steadily back.

'Good morning, Ensign.' It was a gentle, educated, Durhamshire voice, retaining its north country breadth but softer and slower than a Newcastle accent. 'My name is Wilkinson, Captain under Colonel Lilburne. I hoped that I might prevail upon you to walk with me.'

Captain Wilkinson had removed his hat to reveal greying, close-cropped hair above a thin, pale face. A neatly maintained, still-dark beard did little to hide a network of scarring far more extensive than Archer's own. He knew Wilkinson, like Deane, to be a Baptist. Had Skippon's bloodhound alerted his fellow sectarian to Archer's mission? To which one, the official investigation into the witches, or the quiet work involving the Royalist?

Halting a few paces away, Archer took time to quarter the silent fields and confirm that they were alone. Only then did he return the man's greeting. Replacing his hat, he was disconcerted to see the captain looking beyond him, back towards the tenement.

'It is a strange lodging you have taken. It seems you are not the only one, among its residents, to rise so early.'

Archer turned to see a dark silhouette hunched in one of the window seats of the ground floor, appearing to watch them. 'That is Captain Antonis. He sits there in the bay of his room very regularly, like this, in the mornings. Whatever he sees, it is certainly not us.'

The lines around Wilkinson's soft eyes creased further.

'The captain,' Archer explained, 'left his sight, along with his right arm, at the last siege of Pontefract. I do not believe there is anything in his presence to concern you.'

A hint of hesitation came into Wilkinson's response. 'That fellow is Antonis, who was Fairfax's Captain of Horse? The man with the trick to quieten the most disturbed beast? Antonis the Moor?' Wilkinson took a step closer to the lane.

Archer moved fractionally across to stall the captain's progress. 'General Fairfax furnishes a pension to the Savoy to keep him. This is one of the hospital's properties, housing a number of officers for whom there can be no further treatment but who lack other refuge.'

The Durham man curled his top lip, taking in a deep draught of the frigid air. 'And lodged together with those unfortunate gentlemen, we find one solitary, but intact, ensign.'

From another man, it might have been taken as a barb. Archer found Wilkinson's sombre compassion to be oddly disarming. Besides, the man's surmise was correct. After Archer's disgrace at Colchester; after his return from Ireland, more distant and severe than ever; still less after the fatal brawl in The Ship Tavern; no officer in Barkstead's regiment would share lodging with him.

He had entered the Holborn inn, seeking shelter in a tankard, to find only a clutch of drunken fools. Provoked, his first blow had landed too well. It was Deane himself who had fetched Archer from the hole of a military prison where they had thrown him. Deane, too, who had revealed to him the dead man's elevated position, had detailed the influence of his friends, their ability and intent to exact revenge. Archer faced discharge, indenture, and a journey in irons to the plantations of the Indies, a journey from which none returned.

It was then that Deane had made the offer of Skippon's protection, in return for enrolment in the Sergeant-Major General's quiet work. And it was Deane, finally, who had found the little attic room amidst the maimed and the mad of Lewknor's Lane.

Archer stepped forwards to take Wilkinson's offered hand.

Here, where Drury Lane rose to meet Holborn, investors had snapped up parcels of Rose Fields for development, competing to meet the ever-growing demand for London housing. Together, they crossed what open space was left, towards the old Rose Inn, entering into its enclosed kitchen garden. In one corner, a brazier glowed deepest orange. A small table had been set with bread, meats, and a steaming jug. Two troopers stood in the shadows. A third man, short, muscular and broad-faced, took up a position surveying the fields.

'Sergeant Clark will ensure we are neither seen nor overheard.'

Wilkinson offered a slow and almost apologetic smile, pouring them each a small cup of warm, spiced beer. Here, in better light, Archer could see how haggard the man was, his hazel eyes red-rimmed.

The captain placed his drink down, untasted. 'Do you really know what it is you are heading into, when you get to Newcastle?'

'I know the town.'

'I wonder. You will be entering Heselrigg's fiefdom.'

The mention of Sir Arthur Heselrigg, hard-line republican, bitter rival to Skippon and the new governor of Newcastle, brought Archer's attention to a point of razor sharpness.

'The governor is corrupt. He uses his position to gather both riches and power. Colonel Lilburne was recently angered to hear of refurbishments to the manor of Norham, made only to help Heselrigg bring in his war booty from Scotland. The man has much to hide. He will be disturbed to have a Council spy enter into his domain. He will not be alone.'

Archer drank. 'I have no reason to fear for myself. There is come a more godly government to Newcastle.'

'Not least in the person of your old friend Henry Dawson?'

'Mister Dawson is an honest and a godly man.'

'Is he so, Mister Henry Dawson? Perhaps. I suppose you should know. It will help that he is become an alderman and that others of his faction, such as Bonner, are similarly favoured.'

'I know the Bonners. Better men than the old families.'

'Families like your own? Again, perhaps.' Wilkinson took a careful sip of his own small beer. 'Be warned. It is a cockpit you enter, and I fear your intelligence is out-dated. It is true that the new men, the godly as you would say, have ascended to unusual heights of power, but the old families continue to prosper.'

'The Royalists retain their influence?'

'For the most part, yes. Grey, Riddell, even old Carr. Any who can fill Heselrigg's coffers are re-established. The governor found that the trade could not prosper without them. But they plot constantly to overturn the Puritans. An uneasy armed peace, I have heard it called. I rather say they are all still at war.'

'You Durham men have always wanted to see the Newcastle

families brought low. Why should I believe any of this?'

'At last! There is a man in there. Let me be open with him. Of course, we would see the coal monopoly broken. That is our interest, just as it is our fate to contend with our richer neighbours to the north and to bear their condescension.'

A look of infinite weariness overcame the captain.

'I have not brought you here to impart gossip. There is something I would ask of you for myself. In the six weeks since the witches were hung, two of our baptised sisters in Christ have been slain. Help to find their killers. Bring them some justice.'

'Why would you ask me this? What would you do with such information? Surely it would be better to work through the town authorities?'

'What justice do you think I could expect from those who are like to have been the damned murderers?'

Sergeant Clark looked into the garden only to be dismissed by a few quiet words. Wilkinson turned back to face Archer.

'Abigail Walker. Their names were Abigail Walker and Sarah Turner. Sarah Turner was young and innocent enough. Abigail Walker was my sister's eldest girl. She was my own niece, but seventeen years old. Abigail was found cut open from neck to belly. What, Ensign Archer, do you imagine I would do?'

Chapter 3

Lean and solemn, Sophie Ord bent low over the intricate piece of machinery upon which she worked. The girl was lit with unusual white intensity by a full-bellied workbench lamp. To her watching father, Ephraim, she resembled nothing so much as some biblical figure, rendered in ungodly chiaroscuro, such as he had seen hung in the churches of the town during the years of persecution before the wars.

Ephraim Ord's eyes wrinkled with guilty pleasure at the observation, one which would surely have shocked Pastor Hobson. No thought of such Popish distractions would be allowed in the bare meeting room high up on Tuthill Stairs.

The pale young woman standing behind Sophie noticed Ord's look. In return, she wrinkled her small nose before bestowing a nod of encouragement upon the girl, who had glanced up from her work.

Ord's long face softened at this sign of Sophie's close bond with Elizabeth Thompson, the only friendship his daughter seemed able to allow. The wash of contentment was acidly dispersed by a wild hammering upon the workshop door, overlain with the urgency of a familiar voice. 'Engineer! Ord! Open up, man. Open up now.'

Sophie looked across calmly. Elizabeth's dark eyes shone. Ord gestured to them both to remain, easing back the bolts while the door shook under a renewed assault.

Fine features straitened dangerously. Upon the threshold stood the formidable figure of Captain Thomas Gower, his uniform jacket hanging open over the torn linen rag of a shirt. Behind him, teetering in the darkness of the small landing, two private soldiers carried between them the limp form of a woman. A glance at her bloodstained dress told Ord everything he needed. He stepped back, allowing them entry and directing them to a relatively uncluttered workbench, which he swept clear with a great clatter of falling parts.

Their burden laid down upon the space the engineer had created. The soldiers heeded the intrusion of Elizabeth Thompson's pointed chin, to withdraw to an open patch of wall. There, they slumped, eyes dulling, as the urgency of the tense journey across Newcastle gave way to a cold acceptance that their part was now done.

The injured woman's head coverings had been lost. Long strands of dark red hair draped across a round face which showed bone grey in the lamplight. Ord checked the pale lips and felt under the neck before looking down towards the rough dressing which had been secured about her middle.

Without her father speaking or appearing to summon her in any way, Sophie moved noiselessly across the room and recovered a heavy cloth bag. The girl placed it upon the bench, unhooking its sides and rolling it flat to reveal a set of carefully arranged, shining instruments. Unhurriedly, she went off, first to open one of the windows overlooking the yard before continuing to the rear of the workshop.

Ord selected a pair of long-nosed scissors, speaking to Gower even as he made his first incision into the linen. 'Another?'

'It is Rebecca Weaver. Can you save her?'

'How is it that she still lives?'

Gower took a deep breath before addressing his reply to the watching Elizabeth Thompson. 'Your mother was worried. She asked me to seek out Rebecca and to escort her home. We found her too late.'

Ord peered more closely at the fragile movement under the bloody dress. He moved his head back to examine the deep knife wound he was progressively uncovering. 'We are perhaps too late. Perhaps not.'

His daughter had returned to the bench bearing a large bowl

of steaming water with a series of clean cloths laid around the rim. Ord took one, beginning to dab at the exposed, lower part of the cut. The cloth at once turned crimson. He deposited it into the water bowl and reached for another. 'Did you see them?'

'Shadows. No more than shadows. Our concern was for Rebecca,' replied Gower. 'She was still breathing, still speaking.' His voice wavered. 'We were trying to save her.'

'Why didn't she get out? Why didn't you get her out?'

Gower fell silent, stepping out of the light. Elizabeth, knowing that she could offer Ord no help, which his daughter would not better provide, gave the only support she could, in the form of silently voiced prayers. The captain and the woman stood together, watching the engineer's delicate work. The girl Sophie remained alongside her father, passing him equipment before he asked for it, slow and serious in her assistance.

Ord raised his head. He looked over at his daughter before turning away from Rebecca Weaver's body. 'She had lost too much blood.'

Gower's tall form sagged. He had not dared move for the past half hour, as the pair had sought to stem the bleeding and close the wound. Now, he watched Sophie Ord move straight into collecting up the bloodied instruments, placing each in turn into the stained bowl. '"Then shall the dust return to the earth as it was",' he began.

The two soldiers detached themselves from the wall and came upright. The girl continued with her work as if he had not spoken. Ord glared across at Gower. The captain held his gaze and completed the verse. '"And the spirit shall return unto God who gave it".'

A keening sound, more animal than human, broke in from outside. Only Elizabeth Thompson's quick eyes caught the suggestion of fear, which flickered briefly across the engineer's brow.

'It must be the yard dog, escaped its leash,' said Ord. He strode across to close the window. 'Sophie knows the beast. She can handle him.' He looked at Gower challengingly. 'You and your men can best help to clear up here. And do what you can for Rebecca.'

Before they could respond, he had walked his daughter across to the door and out.

On the open top landing, another wail reached them. Ord dropped his voice to the slightest whisper. 'Go to her. Soothe her. Silence her.' Sophie looked narrowly at her father. The girl's lips parted as if she were about to reply, but she simply eased away down the wooden steps into the darkness. He waited a few moments, alert for any other movement, closely scanning the black slit marking the passage through to Heath Court.

Re-entering the workshop, Ord secured the door behind him. Rebecca's body lay fully wrapped in Gower's uniform cloak. The two soldiers stood ready to take her away. Nearer the doorway, the ashen captain was helping Elizabeth to put on a layered, green winter cape. The engineer felt a low twinge of something approaching pity for the diminished Gower. It proved no match for his anger. 'Why can you not stop this?'

'You know we cannot move.' He indicated the shrouded body. 'We do not know who is behind the attacks, and Paul is watched constantly. I can barely trust more than these two men.'

'You mean Heselrigg cares more for lining his purse than for the killing of women.'

'One is coming. You know this.'

Elizabeth turned abruptly about. 'Then he had better hurry, and he had better be worth it, before none are left, before they come for us in our turn.'

She drew the cape's hood up over her head so that Gower spoke only to a shadow. 'It will be soon. Wilkinson took boat from Leith nearly two weeks ago. He will have made contact by now. Be assured, Ensign Archer will already be well upon the road.'

Chapter 4

The serving girl was young, perhaps near to the age Meg would be now.

Strands of light brown hair, working themselves loose from a fraying cap, shadowed her face as she approached. They failed to hide an all too evident distress. Her cheeks burned. Her eyes darted between his pursed lips, the pale scar and his hands, loosely coiled upon the table. Trembling as she put down the bowl, the girl spilled some of its mushy contents across the scuffed planks. She seemed about to weep.

Does she think that I am about to reach up and grab her?

Archer's gaze followed her hands as they withdrew. They were small, their pale fingers unnaturally long and thin. Above them, the wrist bones stuck out with painful clarity. Her forearm was near-white and almost fleshless.

He looked down at the watery sludge of roots and grey leaves she had brought, then towards the gritty bread set on a small platter. For him, for his uniform and his warrant, this thin stew would be the best they had. What, then, passed as sustenance for the inhabitants of Doncaster, for this girl, after the years of war, after another failed harvest?

What might it be like to take those fragile hands in his?

He was shocked to find the girl's expression turned to one of open fear. She glanced over her shoulder to the door, then back towards him with widened eyes. Her mouth, pale and dry, opened, only immediately to shut again. Before he could make any move to reassure her, she had fled. After a few seconds, he heard the anguished, high cry signifying that she had reached the sanctuary of the kitchens.

Archer stared at the empty doorway while his face twitched and the food chilled. What had just happened? He had thought all of that was shut off from him.

He pushed the bowl away, all weariness and hunger forgotten. The ill-kept room only further depressed his spirits. There were uneven cracks in the joins of each of the walls. A bare patch, pale next to the stained expanse around it, showed where some large painting, or mirror, had once hung. Under the long settle bench which stood below this clustered several piss and vomit pots. Archer contemplated them for long seconds, tension mounting in his brows, wondering if he needed to walk the few paces over to retrieve and use one.

He pulled the unappetising stew back towards him. How could he leave it untouched for the ill-fed girl to see when she returned to clear the room?

Over the long days spent traversing the bleak edge of the fenland, he had done his best to focus solely upon coaxing, bullying and dragging forwards his mounts. In many places, the levees protecting the old road were so far worn away, and the track itself thereby inundated, that he had been forced to traverse widely in order to find a passable route.

Four days, since leaving Hitchin, of hard riding through a flat, half-submerged landscape. Four days together of driving ruthlessly on into the cutting north wind, across the very bleakest and coldest part of the whole worn-out country. But even now, in the silence of the neglected parlour, he ached for morning, for the renewal of the tortuous journey, for each slow, mud-caked step that would bring him closer to Newcastle, and to Meg.

Yet he also knew beyond doubt that he could not pass on without making this one detour, to the makeshift shrine established in Doncaster's market square to Thomas Rainsborough, the great martyr of the Leveller cause. The same cause Archer had left behind, just as he had abandoned his only sister.

The pounding in his head grew stronger as he picked up his field spoon and set to the task of swallowing each formless mouthful.

During the first war, Parliament had, in desperation, built up a newly professional soldiery. That New Model Army's succession of victories, founded upon the harshest discipline and most rigorous training, were fuelled also by a faith before God in the righteousness of its great cause, seeking justice and freedom in a world made new.

Those now contemptuously called 'Levellers' had seen the potential of that faith.

After the war had been won, the peace had steadily been lost. The lawyers and merchants who sat in Westminster wanted the army disbanded, to quell utterly the swell of dangerous ideas it had fomented. Each man had been ordered to choose, between service in Ireland, or to go home without pay to their old servitude, in a world unchanged.

When Williams, with his blazing blue eyes and fiery oratory, had come to the regiment from London, he found the ready kindling of the disheartened soldiers all too easy to ignite.

'See,' he had said to the gathered men as the shadows lengthened, 'how the Parliament has become every bit as tyrannical as the King and is now just as zealously engaged against the faithful army. We were this much deceived. The soldier has fought to enslave himself.'

Sergeant Archer had remained behind, around the dying campfire. As the glow from its embers faded, and the darkness closed in, Archer had felt his mind soar and his heart open.

The men of Lilburne's regiment of foot trusted their sergeant. Having heard little from his lips but terse orders, or the sharp battlefield instructions which kept them safe, when Archer began to talk alongside Williams, more soldiers had listened, more took note. Soon, the sergeant had become something of an agitator himself, leading his men all the way to the muster at Corkbush Field in Ware, where it was said that Colonel Rainsborough was waiting, the only senior officer to remain steadfast to the cause.

But Rainsborough never came.

Cromwell himself had ridden alone before them, one man against the whole regiment, a terrible fire burning in his eyes. The sunlight had glinted viciously off his drawn sword as he ordered the men to back down. Something in him had compelled that obedience.

Williams had stepped back through the panicked mass of their company and slipped quietly away, while the soldiers, Archer among them, had torn from their hatbands the slogan declaring, '*England's Freedom, Soldiers' Rights*', begging the Lord General for mercy.

The main ringleaders had been arrested. Three of them were condemned to death by an improvised court-martial, allowed to throw dice for their lives, and the loser, Private Arnold, had been shot, there and then, while the rest of the regiment watched on. As Arnold's buff coat was stripped from him, his hands tied, and as he refused the offer of a blindfold, Archer had been able to think only of how easily it could have been him.

He had stood and watched, unable to break away from Arnold's pale eyes, which stared out, defiant and accusing, scanning the ranks of his former comrades until the volley of musket fire had ended his life.

The parlour felt colder than ever. Leaving his bowl half-empty, Archer took off the inlaid *memento mori* he wore on his left hand. Still unused to its chafing grasp, he stretched out his sore finger, all the time turning the ring over. Before he replaced it, the light caught its tiny inner inscription, "*vita terr. est sed umbra*". Our earthly life is but a shadow.

A sudden elation overtook him, showing in the briefest of smiles. The next moment, his neck prickled with the sense of being observed. Around the edges of the doorway, a shadow lightened, as if someone had taken a step away.

Was the girl set to watch him?

The image of her skeletal hands returned. His mouth dried. He felt dizzied. Looking down in dull incomprehension, he was startled to find that his left leg had begun to shake.

Standing up so swiftly that the table jerked forwards with an agonised screech, he strode out of the parlour leaving the spilled stew to congeal upon its wooden surface.

Catching the Devil-stench of the surrounding bog as it reached to suffocate Doncaster, Archer was surprised to find his headache had eased. He had spent enough time exposed on the nearby moors, during the long siege where Antonis had lost his eyes, to respect the dead lands of Elmet and greatly to fear them. For now, however, he was able to find some comfort in their encroaching presence.

The twisting alley protecting his approach had been shrouded in darkness. Here, crossing the marketplace, Archer fell instead under the light of a waxing moon, cleanly illuminating the site of Thomas Rainsborough's murder.

Two-stories of bent timbers, dirty, darkened windows and crooked door frames, topped by four leaded attic windows in a gapped slope of loose tiles, the inn festered like a decayed tooth on the cold north side of the town's central square. At least he wouldn't have to sleep here tonight. Presumably, the colonel had been presented with no other choice.

Above the main doorway, a sign, little more than three boards roughly wedged together, still bore the painted image of a crown. Its colours were faded, and further obscured by a series of violent gashes which had stripped away the wooden surface at the centre.

The door, by contrast, seemed to pulse and shimmer in the moonlight. Fresh branches of rosemary rustled in the breeze.

Rosemary, for faithfulness. They were woven into bright ribbons of the same sea green colour which had adorned Rainsborough's personal standard. Someone was taking good care of the memorial.

He sensed movement across the square behind him, but when he looked, he could find nothing. Perhaps, simply a rat?

Delicately, Archer took the strand of herb he had preserved close to his skin from out of its wrapping. Drawing near, he selected a protruding strand of ribbon at shoulder height. Carefully, he threaded the fragile branch through its loops. He breathed in the faded scent, along with the dampness of the night air, before retreating a few short paces. There, he waited in contemplation of the battered door and its halo of offerings.

His being here was not entirely a lie. Once, out there in the dark, he had believed.

He tried to tell himself that he was far from alone in abandoning the faith.

Each of the acknowledged Leveller leaders had come to accommodate themselves to the new Commonwealth. Overton, without hesitation, had loyally taken the engagement oath. Wildman had accepted an army commission before resuming his practice at law. Even the incendiary John Lilburne, younger brother to Archer's old colonel, had retreated back to his soap making.

Death, in the brutal second war occasioned by King Charles' falsehood in negotiation, had saved Colonel Rainsborough from having to make any such compromise. It had also left him as an inviolable lodestar for the disappointed and disaffected.

Williams alone was said to have remained true to the colonel's vision of a just power, with authority bestowed only by the consent of the people.

That great cause could no longer be Archer's. Not after the viciousness of the renewed conflict. Not after Colchester. Not after Ireland. Such hope was now quite beyond him. Yet here, nevertheless, he was.

Even were his presence no more than a meaningless act of

defiance against, he knew not what, there was both respite and satisfaction in it.

He could not have said why, but he found, in these few breaths before the rustling ribbons and dried-out herbs, a kind of succour, a strength which he would need to confront the return to Newcastle and the uncovering of Meg's fate. His earlier animation returned as he realised that these short moments belonged neither to the Council nor to Deane, not to Wilkinson nor to the many other ghosts of his past, but to him and to Meg alone.

Taking a further step backwards, with a slight incline of his head in silent salute, Archer contemplated the blank windows of The Crown for a last time.

Halfway back across the marketplace, he stopped dead at the suggestion of movement in the outer shadows. A shard of ice probed between his ribs. If Deane or, even worse, the Council's own intelligencers, Scott or Bishop's men, came to know of his witness at Rainsborough's shrine, he could expect, at the best, a firing squad. Most likely, his would be a quieter, more hidden dispatch.

Backing away, he watched the movement become two separate figures. They waited, observing him in their turn, standing carefully out of clear sight beyond the stark moonlight.

Straining to make out the taller and broader of the two, Archer's skin crept with an intimation of recognition. Something about the man's stocky shape, the manner in which he had planted himself full and foursquare upon the earth, brought with it a curdled memory of blood and woodsmoke. Even, however, as the certainty grew that he was squinting back at Williams, his attention was inexorably pulled towards the more disquieting second figure.

Short, slight, at such a distance it was difficult to tell whether this was merely a boy or the smallest of men. He had an otherworldly impression of coal-black hair, wide-set, equally dark eyes, and of flat, un-formed features in a face which showed ghostly-white in the gloom.

Before he could move nearer, both forms retreated into the darkness. He stood, tautly alert for any hint of their return. The flicker returned to the side of his face. He tried to push away a rising unease.

All remained still. Archer was left alone in the deserted square.

Chapter 5

After the low night clouds had fully dispersed, the morning emerged crisp and clear.

At first, the slanted light fell only upon the highest towers of the tallest buildings. The finely wrought crown of Saint Nicholas' Church glowed golden. The steeple of All Saints and the very top stones of Saint Andrew by Newgate were lifted temporarily above the tawdry foulness of the streets below.

The advancing day began to reach the lower town. An orange warmth tipped the line of masts on the ships berthed along the quay. For a few moments of calm beauty, the whole of Newcastle, from grandest mansion to lowest hovel, was preserved in a silent perfection it did not deserve.

The great bell in Saint Nicholas' tower sounded its first, harrowing note. It was joined by a dozen more pealing from the other town churches, the old Jerusalem hospital and the many guild houses. Alongside the moored ships, such harmony was uncomfortably accompanied by the discordant, high-pitched tone of the Guildhall bell in its little archway.

The light moved on. The beautiful illusion was broken. People of all stations emerged into the travail of another weary day. Some to labour, some to beg, some to pray.

Some few, to the long-awaited news of Archer's arrival.

In one of the larger houses, two-thirds of the way along a broad garth favoured by some of the town's most important merchant families, a fashionably dressed, hawk-eyed young man emerged from the back stairs and slipped through an inconspicuous panelled door on the sleeping floor. Without knocking, he entered the dressing room of the head of the family, waiting there in the darkness, letter in hand, while the old man pulled on his breeches.

High above the faded luxury of the dressing room, on the second floor of a teetering structure set back from the western-most, and least desirable, of the principal chares, two men sat comfortably together. Each was wrapped up tightly against the unseasonal cold. Eyes lowered, black-clad shoulders hunched in joint prayer, their faces were lit only by the single candle flickering on the table between them. Next to it lay a letter, its broken wax seal impressed with the same motif the younger and taller of the two bore on a small signet ring.

'He will come then?'

The other man, ruddier and more powerfully built, spoke with an ease resting upon years of familiarity. 'Exactly as expected, Thomas. The young ensign arrives soon. Go now and inform Mistress Thompson and Elizabeth, would you?'

Thomas Gower half-stood, looking into the soft grey eyes of his companion as if seeking further guidance. Seeming to think better of it, he rose properly.

'Oh, and Thomas?'

'Paul?'

'When he arrives in the town, I look to you to keep a good watch over Archer. We need to know how the man proceeds, who he meets, where he goes. See to it, if you will.'

Bidding a quiet goodbye, face drawn with concern, Gower passed through the door, down the creaking stairs and out into the cold of the steps.

On the administration floor of the castle keep, the town governor was already busy in his high-ceilinged study. Two servants were occupied in opening the shutters of its huge windows and in dowsing the lamps he had worked by for the past, pre-dawn hour.

Heselrigg's young secretary, Pearson, new to the role but pleasingly intelligent and efficient, entered, bringing with him the overnight dispatches from Whitehall. At a gruff nod from his master, these he proceeded to outline. Among them he passed over a letter, its ornate official seal already broken, addressed in Deane's clear and careful hand.

'There is one more thing, Sir Arthur,' began Pearson. 'The Council agent, an ensign named Archer, will arrive in the town shortly. He is commissioned to investigate the deaths of the women.'

The governor leaned back from the growing pile of papers, which threatened to slip across the desk. He flexed his broad neck and the skin surrounding his deep-set eyes wrinkled in concentration.

'Then, Anthony, we must ensure that the ensign receives a proper welcome. You can arrange that, can you not?'

Chapter 6

Archer sat high in the saddle peering anxiously back along the open length of the Great North Road, dwindled to little more than a plain cart track as it ran level along the eastern edge of the wide Team valley.

In the days since he had departed Doncaster, he had made sudden stops. He had regularly turned off into stricken hamlets where the only people to be seen were thin children with the deep-set eyes of hunger, who watched on as he waited, patient and alert, before making his loop back the main route. He had, on occasion, doubled back entirely. Not once had he found anything to support the constant sensation that unseen eyes were upon him.

If that oppressive feeling was more than just another devil's trick, some weakness of his mind, pursuing him out of his nightmares, whoever it was knew their job well.

It would not be beyond Deane to have set his own watch upon Archer's mission. He could only pray it was not one of Scott's men. Perhaps some Leveller sent by Williams. Had it truly been the formidable agitator that he had seen in the shadows of Doncaster's market square, or was that, too, no more than a figment of his own shame and guilt?

Turning the horse about, Archer crested the final rise above Gateshead township. Immediately, a broad and unexpected smile stole over his face.

Before him, the Tyne gorge slashed the landscape in two. In its depths, the river itself, flat and grey on its early ebb tide, rolled lazily in from the Elswick curve, bisecting the long oval of King's Meadow

Island before continuing upon its seaward journey. The brown and green of low hills rose to the north. In between, Newcastle squatted uncomfortably, girdled by its walls and gates, dominated by the foursquare castle keep and the delicate lantern tower of Saint Nicholas, perched together atop the high bank rising from the river and its long line of quay. This, the centre and source of the town's wealth, bristled with ranks of tall ships' masts.

As he looked more closely, his features sank into a thin-lipped grimace.

Twice, Newcastle had been attacked by Scots' armies. General Leslie's brief 1640 campaign, chasing King Charles' poorly trained levies back over the border, had left little enough mark. It was evident that the same could not be said for the great siege of 1644, before which, at barely seventeen, Archer had quit the town to avoid conscription by its Royalist defenders, trekking instead south to volunteer for Parliament.

The laced stonework of Newcastle's church towers was, in several places, broken and powder marked. Its proud walls and fortified gates showed regular, jagged-toothed gaps, evidence of the effectiveness of the Scots' heavy guns. The pall of coal smoke that lay always over the town took on a darker hue.

It seemed as if he were high up on some gun platform, overlooking the breached walls of another besieged citadel. Taunton, Bristol, Drogheda, it was all the same. He knew what the inhabitants could expect once the defences were overwhelmed, wondering anew how he could ever have left Meg to face that alone.

Cracking the reins, he set the horse into a brisk trot down the steep, winding track towards the river.

Slowly, they walked into the crowded street of ramshackle houses comprising the length of the covered bridge. Above its entrance arch, Archer could not miss the statue of old King James, along with the coat of arms of his son Charles, both still firmly set into the stonework. For how much longer would such images be tolerated under the town's new rulers? What pressures must have been brought to bear to preserve these symbols of Stuart royalty? As if he needed one, it was just another reminder of the morass of conflicting interests awaiting him when he crossed to the north bank.

Halfway over, he passed the large blue stone which marked the town boundary. Finally, whatever it meant, he was home.

Emerging through Bridge Gate, the town rose steeply before him. Its chares dropped vertiginously down, twenty and more of them opening out along the two lengths of The Close, to the front and left of him, and Quayside, on the right, towards which he set the horse.

Tightly packed with warehouses and the grand dwellings of wealthy merchant families, the view was so familiar that he was shocked to see two empty plots, crude, ugly gaps in the otherwise grand prospect. One space stood wholly vacant. In the other, courses of new brick had been laid and wooden scaffolding erected for the next phase of building.

Crossing Sandhill, the open space of reclaimed land set between the town and its quayside walls, he was further surprised to see how quiet it was.

The day's work along the quay was done, but Newcastle's most important public space had always remained bustling late into the evening, crowded with people talking, drinking, singing, moving between stalls and pausing at street entertainments. Now, it was sparsely populated, only a few solitary men to be seen making their way home. No drinkers spilled out from the taverns; no players filled the air with noise. Not even the whores from the western steps were to be seen about tonight.

Despite this, the shadow which had passed over him on the Gateshead heights had lifted. The distinct smell of the Sandhill, a pungent mix of rotting fish and horse dung, of old leather and damp wood and, laid over everything else, of coal burning from a thousand fires, overtook all discomfort. It was the scent of his boyhood, as if the past six years had never been.

Dismounting, he walked the tired mare past the weathered stones of Saint Thomas' chapel, stripped of its old statuary, its adjacent water gate rotting with lichen. They reached the arched entrance, neat clock tower perched above, of the courtyard around which clustered the Guildhall and Town Court, both of which he would need to visit soon.

Across from the Guildhall complex, where The Close formed Sandhill's northern side, a long, conjoined row of merchant houses drew his attention. Each had been remodelled to boast three stories of clean, flat glazing, offering them a unity further underpinned by the white-painted wooden panels running at second floor level across the whole span. Archer allowed his eyes to wander over the clean facades, following their ordered lines up towards the deepening purple of the evening sky.

He searched his memory, seeking to recall the names of those families who had held property on that part of The Close. Maddison, Nicholson, Cock and Jenison, all from the town's Puritan faction. Together, it seemed, and recently, the very fabric of their dwellings had become a public display of order, harmony and light; the light of God itself, opening up the very heart of the dark, old town.

As a lad, long before this new decorative work had been performed, he himself had run messages for Henry Dawson in and out of more than one of those houses. The near prospect of a reunion with his old mentor coursed warmly through him.

Such feeling was swiftly dampened as he looked beyond the row of grand houses towards the jagged series of steps and alleys leading upwards and away from The Close.

Somewhere in the heights above would be found the killers of Abigail Walker and Sarah Turner. Somewhere, those who had initiated the witch hunt would be sitting in front of a warm fire, taking an evening draught. Did the foul practices of witchcraft linger even now, somewhere out there in the gathering dusk?

Chapter 7

Invisible in the shadows where Butcher's Bank met Sandhill, Elizabeth Thompson and Thomas Gower together watched Archer lead his horse along the front of the remodelled houses and away down Quayside.

'I said my men were reliable.'

'You said that Archer was reliable,' Elizabeth replied. 'I saw only a scared boy.' She had also seen the young ensign's pleasure unfurl, once he had dismounted upon Sandhill. That brief moment had moved her, lifting attention as it had from the man's terrible scar and softening his hollow face.

'You were the one who insisted upon being here.'

'I needed to see him. Now, I can contrive to meet him.'

Gower looked at her in exasperation. 'Or you could just leave the town, let him do his work and get away from here.'

'Please, do not think to tell me or my mother what we may do.'

'But...'

'None has come to threaten us. Now that this man is here, we need to stay, to share with him what we know.'

Gower knew better than to try to prolong an argument either with Elizabeth Thompson or, worse, her formidable mother. Besides, the dark was rapidly closing in. 'We must go. I will get you back to Castle Stairs.'

'I am not a child, Thomas. We should not be seen together. This is risk enough.'

Gower lingered uncomfortably.

'Go,' she said. 'Keep your watch upon Archer so I may see him tomorrow.'

A squat figure emerged from an alley on the far side of the bank and trotted over. Elizabeth recognised the man as one of the pair who had brought poor Rebecca Weaver to Ord's workroom.

'He's stabled his horse at the Blue Anchor, Sir,' said the soldier. 'Laing's waiting there to keep an eye, but we think that's where he's staying.'

'I'll come with you. Wait one minute.'

'Rest easy, Captain,' said Elizabeth, already three paces down the bank towards The Close. 'Go with your man.'

She turned away, glad to hear the sound of their heavy boots retreating. The captain was sweet, but over solicitous. One of the advantages she had found in being so plain, a woman men would not even call handsome, let alone beautiful, was that she was almost entirely spared the looks, and worse, which beset most gentlewomen, and which made it impossible for them to go about the town unaccompanied. In any case, her short route took her safely between the Guildhall, with its patrolling watchmen, and the open-faced, newly modelled aldermen's houses she had so recently seen Archer stop to admire.

Elizabeth found that she was glad, too, of the space, and of the cool of the evening. After the days of waiting, Gower's summons had brought with it only a renewed tension, one which her first impressions of Archer had done little to relieve. She had seen him clearly. Of middling height and no clear strength. Hesitant in his manner, he could not be much more than her own age. Could one somewhat underwhelming, apparently vulnerable young ensign really hope to uncover the truth behind what was happening in Newcastle?

Within a few minutes, she was at the junction with the entry to Castle Stairs. Elizabeth paused to look down The Close to where light showed from the family warehouse, only to be interrupted by a uniformed man passing out from the steps. Tall, strong in the shoulders, neatly bearded, his face was obscured by the low brim of his hat. Brushing far too close to her and lingering in the contact, making her skin creep, he drawled a languorous, possibly wine-sodden, good evening before slowly moving away towards Guildhall, as if he were tracing her very footsteps.

Pulling the cape tighter about her, Elizabeth hurried now up the well-lit stairs. Anxious to be away from the boorish officer, she was also newly eager to be back with her mother, to take, perhaps, a warming posset.

Approaching the polished front door of the Thompson house, her attention was taken by a giant of a man who had stepped out onto the next landing but one. Blond haired, piercingly blue eyed, he was dressed in the common breeches and rough, grey blouse of a wage-servant or day labourer.

She turned about at the sound of a loose stone being kicked away on the steps below, to find the contrastingly lithe form of a short, sallow, dark-haired man, whose teeth showed pale as he grinned up at her.

Neither made to move. Neither said a word. Elizabeth trembled, but held tightly to her determination not to show the pair any such fear. She knew who they were. She knew exactly why they had come. Still, they did not approach any closer. Each man remained where they were, as if to taunt her.

At last, life returned to her feet. Without apparent hurry, she walked the final few paces to her own door, pulled gently upon the long bellpull and waited, breath increasingly laboured, for the sound of the servant's deliberate traipse across the inner hallway. By the time its welcoming light streamed warmly out onto Castle Stairs, both men had disappeared.

Hastening up to the shelter of her bedchamber, Elizabeth Thompson's heart pounded. Her head gave way to a deep ache from which she could bring forth only one conscious thought.

If this James Archer was all they had to stand up to the big, blond man, his small, dark accomplice and whoever was behind them, then the young ensign had better be strong, he had better be calm, and he had better be quicker than he looked, in his wits.

Chapter 8

A strange and wicked silence enveloped Drogheda, after the gun platforms had fallen silent, after eight straight days and nights of bombardment.

The night firing had been one of Archer's own ideas, one he had first attempted at Sherborne. Deliberately pursued more haphazardly and less frequently than the constant thunder by day, it became all the more fear-inducing and sleep-depriving for the garrison.

The gunnery work done, and the walls breached in two places. Already the first pair of regiments had formed up to prepare their rush towards the southernmost of the weak points. Even as he descended to rejoin his company, before Archer's eyes, the lines of the leading storm battalions began to break apart. Men tumbled back down the blackened, shot-marked earthworks. The remainder crested the broken rise, wavered there for a dreadful eternity, then became separated, one from the other, so that the regiments began to be pushed back by the resolute defenders.

Despite the bombardment, despite all of the planning and the patient waiting and the prayers, the attack was wavering.

By the time he reached his own comrades, crouched in the shallow trenches, all were silent, their faces ghostly white, yellowed eyes fixed upon the harrowing sight above, where the Catholics on the Mill Mount bastion had re-filled the nearest breach with a stack of slack-limbed, red-coated bodies.

He saw another regiment to their left form up out of the trenches. The Lord General, sword drawn, stood at their head.

Cromwell himself was going to lead the second assault.

Archer's head was filled with the shrill south country voice of a preacher hurling the psalm at the lines of men: '"The Lord also thundered in the heavens, and the Highest gave His voice; hail stones and coals of fire. Yea, He sent out His arrows, and scattered them; and He shot out lightnings, and discomfited them".'

This was followed, after a menacing pause, by Colonel Venables' simpler, more brutal words. 'That bastard Aston said that anyone who could take Drogheda could take Hell. Well, today we take this Papist hell and the devils who hold her. For them, no quarter. Kill them, kill them, kill them all.'

With a great roar, both regiments charged. Their lines, too, were soon breaking, but now they broke forwards. Up they climbed towards the rampart, under a more scattered fire, most of the Irish having been pulled away from the high parts of the walls in their frantic defence of the breach. Up and on they ran. On and over the crest.

He fought with a blind fury during those minutes, which felt like hours.

This was unlike any of the other actions he had experienced in more than five murderous years of war. Knowing that they could expect no mercy, the defenders, Irish and English Catholic alike, responded with desperate frenzy. Faced with this and incensed by the wall made of the bodies of their friends and comrades, the attacking force cut and bludgeoned their way through the breach and into the fort itself.

A party of Cromwell's own regiment stormed over the drawbridge separating the strongpoint from the main town. There, a defending officer rallied a group of men and counter-charged, threatening to throw them back and render the attack thus far and all its bloody losses, meaningless.

Entering at the run, clubbing, slashing, butting, Archer threw himself into the centre of the Irish and, by some miracle, in his unheeding fury and fear, blunted their charge. At the price of a deep sword slash across his face, it slowed them enough for Venables' own company to come scrambling over the parapet, catching the defenders unprepared. They swept on into the exposed town, leaving him standing alone, gore-covered, bleeding heavily and roaring like a mad creature.

Wide-eyed, Archer darted looks into the corners of the top-floor room in the Blue Anchor, finding there only the familiar, haunting visions.

A small, dark man backed against a wall, pleading right up to the moment when the pikeman impaled him to it.

The pile of bodies rising high behind the altar of the Papist church.

A voice carried in the wind, 'God damn me. God confound me. I burn. I burn.'

The shrieks of a group of nuns, rounded up while fleeing their burning convent, herded down an alley by a squad of greedy-eyed soldiers. Archer looking on, long after they had disappeared into its rubble-strewn entrance, the secret, fierce joy which had sparked in him inundated by a tide of the bitterest shame as the cries of the women rose to terrified screams.

And for this he had been promoted Ensign.

Once General Cromwell, declaring the devastation to be God's work, had given his men their heads for sufficient hours to set the example he wanted, he had picked Archer out of the tired, scarred troops to commission him in that field of blood. Crushed in Cromwell's fierce embrace, Archer had numbly breathed in the Lord General's strange, clove-rich smell before returning alone to the cheering men he would now command.

It was then that Archer remembered the girl.

Just one more girl from another cluster of Ulster hovels loudly crackling as they burned behind her. A girl with jewel-blue eyes and untamed, curling hair that was strangely fair among those dark savages. A girl who looked so like to Meg and whose parting glare, right at Archer, had made him stagger, so that his men drew weapons again. Trembling in the dark, he felt once more the drained, hollow sense of God's withdrawal which had first come upon him under the leaden skies of that benighted province as the girl had fixed him with her malignant gaze.

The figure of the Irish girl faded. Her angry, cold eyes were replaced by others: softer, gentler, more afraid. He was left staring back at Meg. Red-eyed, skin blotched, defiantly keeping back her tears. She appeared exactly as he had last seen her on the family floor of the brewery house on the day he had left.

Jaw tight, slightly withdrawn from the chamber's single window, Archer observed the building activity upon the quay. Carefully, he poured water from the delftware pitcher into its matching bowl. Only gradually had the image of Meg faded, leaving behind it the customary headache, alongside an oppressive weakness in each limb. The shock of the cold water running down his face and neck began to soothe both. Taking time to savour the last of his clean linens, finally, he descended.

Once his main bag of coin had been stored in the Blue Anchor's strongbox, the woman in charge of the inn, Mrs Veitch, served Archer breakfast in a clean parlour. The bread, cold meats and small beer being laid out, she lingered, along with a round-faced serving girl.

'Your coat, sir. Nell will attend to it.'

'No, please, there is no need.'

Mrs Veitch remained unmoving, eyeing him with coarse disapproval. 'You must have that coat brushed and sponged, just look at the very state of it. Nell will take the clothes from your room as well.'

Sheepishly, he stood, shrugging off the coat, mumbling thanks, trying to remember the state of his chamber after the disturbances of the night. When the flushed girl had taken it away, Mrs Veitch again tarried, busying herself unnecessarily at a side dresser. He watched her for any sign of discomfort at whatever ranting might have resounded from his room, but the woman appeared wholly calm, neatly and methodically ,completing the small tasks before turning back to her guest.

'You have all you need now?'

'Quite everything, thank you.'

'You're from Newcastle. Have you been away long?'

Of course, she had caught his accent. What was good enough to hide it from southerners would not work now he was home.

He slipped back into his childhood speech with ease. 'I am, but have been away these many years.'

'You'll be glad to be home?'

'We are all happy to return. Is the town much changed? I have not been here since the beginnings of the wars.' He forgave himself the careful lie.

Now it was Mrs Veitch's turn to hesitate. He could see how cautious the woman was, in choosing what she might safely say.

'The wars have been bad for the town, but the trade is returned now, so all's well.' She coloured. 'Praise be to the Lord.'

'Praise His Love for us,' replied Archer, his voice, like his look, level and unyielding. 'Was it the fighting then, and the Scots, which took down the fine houses along The Close?'

'Those damned Scots did plenty damage, but that was never them,' she answered, unleashing the sharpest sliver of emotion, which was just as swiftly reinterred. 'All outside the walls was ravaged, mind, people's places torn down as if they never were.

Six years now and it's only just begun to be properly rebuilt, out there beyond Sandgate and even along the river by Newburn. But no, it was the corporation that ordered some of them big houses pulled down. Master Robert Liddell's place is gone and so is the Carr's fine town house. It's been put abroad that they were a common nuisance, but everyone knows it's because those gentlemen fought to defend the town of late.'

Mrs Veitch picked up an empty platter, beginning to mumble an apology. Determined to press home the successful breach he had made, Archer detained her.

'Sandhill and Quayside seemed quiet last night. I saw none of the ordinary gatherings, no music here or at any of the other taverns.'

'The new governor and the mayor have outlawed all that. They say nowhere in the Kingdom, I'm sorry, in the whole Commonwealth, has so many godly rules been so well made as in Newcastle, even including London.' Flushing lightly, she smiled back at him uncertainly. 'I mean, I wouldn't know that. You'd know London better, I'm sure. They say Newcastle will be a godly beacon to the whole people. A new Jerusalem.'

'And what do you say, Mrs Veitch? What do the people of the town say?'

She looked at him with fright in her eyes, and he cursed his misstep. A veil of caution descended. Hurriedly, she made ready and left.

Excellent work, he thought. Now they will think me a Council spy into the account. Well, was that not what he was? His breakfast tasted suddenly ashen.

By day, the Blue Anchor's cramped yard proved to be busy and well-ordered.

The thick-necked ostler who had taken Archer's horse the previous evening introduced himself as Jeremiah before accepting a reassurance that a new mount would not be needed. As the men spoke, a pair of stable lads slowed in their clearing of the night's befouled straw to sneak sideways looks at the officer's scar, only to be hurried on with the work by a sharp word from their master.

Neither boy so much as glanced up again, but the sensation of being watched persisted. Archer snapped his head around towards the right side of the yard gateway to find the new observer to be nothing more than a pinched-faced girl. Less than the marrying age, full of auburn-haired solemnity, she did not break off her stare as the boys had done, but continued to look directly at him with unblinking, green-grey eyes.

Beginning to walk east along Quayside, Archer remained dogged by the feeling that something about the girl had been wrong. Her dress, while simple, had been well-made, of fine cloth with a wide lace trim. How would a child of any substance come to be unaccompanied in such a place? For that matter, where was her outer garment, let alone any cap or bonnet? He looked back, wondering whether he should try to help, but already she had disappeared.

This time, he strode off, shivering as he came under the shadow of the river walls. Hurrying on all the faster, unsettled by the encounter with the strange girl, he failed to notice the slight, pale man maintaining a constant distance behind him, watching his every move.

Where Peacock's Chare joined Quayside, the yard of his Uncle Weston's brewery opened its gateway onto the main street. Careful to hurry past, not wishing any of those working there to recognise him, Archer was surprised to find how pleased he was to see the busy energy of the place.

Turning up the steps, he made his way through the miasma, which continually sullied the air outside the brewery house.

Nearing its familiar battered door, he was further gladdened to see that, all these years later, one of the panels on the left still required mending at the bottom. Not so many changes then.

Raising his head towards the dirty windows of the principal day room two floors above, guilt and anger equally coursed through him. Whatever had happened to Meg, it had begun fourteen years before, in that same room.

Plague had ravaged through the medieval squalor of Newcastle's old town, its talons reaching deep into the merchant homes teetering along the chares. Taking lives in its horrible wasting, shaking, sweat-soaked way, the pestilence made no distinction for place or condition. Masked men trooped through the streets waving burning fumigations of pitch, resin and frankincense. Long-beaked plague doctors walked through the night offering little more than a swifter death. The Dutch Plague, they had called it. By the end of that summer of 1636 near to half of the population of Newcastle had died of the sickness, a toll including James and Meg's small sister, Beth, three of the family's servants, and both of their parents.

Meg had stood, on that first morning, fidgeting and curious, all too distracted, at six years old, by the clutter of ornament and display adorning the room. Her eyes had eventually fixed upon the softly painted outlines of the feeding hummingbird, comprising the central motif, of a large Chinese porcelain bowl set prominently upon Weston's desk. Alongside her, nine-year old James, painfully aware of the need to show due respect, had worked earnestly to shut out the reek of the brewing yard and the tortured cries of the herring gulls over the quay, and so keep his attention focused upon their uncle's words of greeting.

Aunt Weston, again heavily pregnant, appeared confused, even scared. She looked on as her husband detailed the children's new status: 'In this household, but not of this family... courtesy and respect to your aunt and your cousin...expected to perform your household tasks every day, without complaint...'

until finally he lost control, slammed his fist down on the crowded table, turned to his wife and screamed. 'Take that girl away and teach her to stay still and listen. A few sharp strokes are necessary.' Weston had turned directly upon Meg, scaring her to rigidity.'You are nobody's pet here, girl, but I am your guardian, and you shall learn to conduct yourself in my house!'

Upon the chare, fixedly looking up at the same day room windows, the adult Archer felt a faint flicker of hope. Deane could have been mistaken, or pointlessly malicious. Meg might, even as her brother waited outside, be bent over some sewing work in one of the back rooms above.

The little flame guttered and died. What if she were gone, taken in the witch hunt? What if he had returned too late? He hesitated before taking the final step up to the battered door. With one last deep intake of the sour air, he tapped twice against the hilt of his sword with his left hand, then rapped the iron band of the knocker, again twice, with his right.

Chapter 9

Weston would see him. That was something. Left alone in the dark at the foot of the twisting stair, the smell of the old house, a combination of damp, coal smoke and the malt stench from the brewery, rendered Archer once more into the silent, withdrawn child he had been. It was almost a relief when the servant, a scraggy woman he did not recognise, tramped down the blackened wood to call him.

Upon entering the day room, the solid figure of the man who stood by the window overlooking the chare was still handsome, even imposing. But his uncle's bullish brow had wandered; Weston's eyes were become too deep set to convey their former strength; his body, always bulky, was now clearly running to fat. In truth, he looked much older than the years might reasonably allow. Nothing was said and no form of greeting offered. The brewer remained aloof long after the servant had gone her way, quietly closing the door behind her.

In the silence, Archer stood loosely, hat held low, and looked about the room. At first, it appeared just as he had remembered. The hummingbird bowl remained proudly upon the great desk-table, a double hand span of lustrous blue and white. All of the other surfaces were covered with bright textiles, each wall hung with woven scenes. Tall cabinets in between the tapestries groaned with glassware, elaborately decorated plates and bowls, or curiosities shaped from Baltic amber. These latter his aunt's favourite pieces. All, together, served as a carefully curated display of the Weston wealth, a means to promote their social aspiration.

As he continued to wait, Archer realised it was not quite as it had been. He found gaps among the collections of plate and glass. Some of the more ostentatious pieces of amber were missing. Many of the furnishings appeared worn and faded. He wondered if they had always been so. Looking more closely, he saw how a number of fine wall hangings and furniture covers were also gone, among them a woven tapestry of the judgement of Adam and Eve, and a richly coloured, filigreed ornamental throw which used to catch the eye behind Weston's desk. Each had been replaced by something older and duller.

Was this evidence of the depredations of the Scottish occupation, or did the Weston business prosper less well than it had, despite the activity in the brewery yard? He was just beginning to take a warming pleasure in such apparent misfortune when his uncle spoke, his voice rasping and hesitant.

'James. Commissioned. Well, good for you. Pretty too,' he said, indicating Archer's scar. 'Why, I wonder, are you returned here? Have you come to gloat over my difficulties?'

Anger, disgust, curiosity, even pity crowded Archer's thoughts. Reluctantly, he held fast to proper deference. 'I am not in the town by choice, uncle, but under orders. I desired to announce my presence to you first.'

'I am surprised you did not first announce yourself to Mister Dawson, who is so risen in the world, made alderman and member of the Hostmen in place of this poor brewer.'

The pull upon Archer's eye returned at the mention of the privileged group of merchants which controlled the coal monopoly. In taking in the orphans, the brewer had hoped to gain entry into those ranks. Despite such investment, Weston's longed for elevation never came. The same families, Carr, Grey, and Marley, foremost among them, continued to dominate the Hostmen's company. The men of the higher guilds were not prepared to allow in a mere brewer. He belonged with the lower tradesmen, the barber-surgeons, the bakers and butchers. So, in public, Weston had showed all due respects to the great men of the town. In the private rooms of the dark old house, with shouting and beatings and, worst of all, petty, small slights, he had continued to relieve his resentment upon the two unwanted children.

'I have not been to Spicer Lane, but am come immediately here.'

Weston turned away from his nephew and looked down into the chare. 'You did not think to offer such courtesy or respect when last you left this house. It is a wonder before God that you should have the courage to return. You fled before the Scots' army. You deserted your aunt, your lawful guardian, your master, your position, your friends, and your duty.'

The man finally met Archer in the eye.

'Then, aye, we know of your doings, we have had much news of your monstrosities. You joined with my greatest enemy. Lilburne, of all men. You went to Lilburne's son! The very devil. His trades are infinite: mercer, draper, collier and, yes, presumed brewer and all to one design, against your own city, your own society and your own blood! Yet you go to him, of all the rebel regiments you could find!'

Archer winced inside, not at the vehemence of the attack, but at his uncle's outspoken treason. He hoped the new town government did not think the brewer of sufficient significance to have bought any of his servants. He, of all people, knew how the Council of State worked, knew that it differed from the late king's network of spies and informers in scale and efficiency alone, and knew how fierce the punishment would be were Weston's words reported. He hurried to head off the older man's rant.

'No, sir, I did not seek out Colonel Lilburne. Only latterly did he take over command of my regiment. But he is a good and an honest man, a godly one. Did he give you any just cause for complaint in his time as governor here?'

'Other than those damned heretic lecturers? Do you have any idea what has been brought upon us? Sects, Baptists and schismatics multiplying daily, committing insolence and outrage against good people, preaching and railing against the truth of God and the civil government alike. Promoting riots, tumults and disturbances.'

He paused, snorting in more air, appearing to calm.

'Heselrigg, for all his Covenanter error, has at least stamped down upon the worst excesses unleashed by your precious Lilburne.'

Reaching for a cup of wine, Weston downed it in one gulp. 'Have you then come here to excuse or explain your desertion?'

'I need no excuse. I could not act against my conscience.'

'To the Devil with your conscience, boy! You owed your duty to your uncle. What has your conscience brought us but dissolution and despair? Do you know how it was here when your precious Parliament cut off the coal trade, when they opened up the Wear?'

'The wharf appears to be doing a brisk trade, uncle. I noted the activity in your own brew house. Business goes well for you and Mister Anthony.'

'My old partner is dead these four years past. Another thing you would have known, were you at all sensible of your duty?'

'I am sorry to hear it. He was ever a good man.'

'Save your pieties. What has been done here is a naked attack upon the Hostmen and the rightful worthies of this corporation, your own family included. Aye, and Anthony's. I have had to work hard to keep the business together and to protect both interests. Men whose families have served since before the old Queen died have been cast out from their rightful positions while rabble such as Dawson and Blakiston are preferred.'

'The trade will return to its former state, uncle. You, I am sure, will continue to prosper. It is not as if they would have allowed a mere brewer to rise.'

'You stand there, all mighty in your uniform and think to lecture me? The principal men of this town have long memories. Were you here when for three days and three nights a ring of fire burned around the walls, as if Hell itself had opened? Were you among the men forced to destroy their own town's suburbs to deny them to the Scots, no matter what suffering it caused? Were you there, where you were appointed to be, alongside Errington and Robson when the blue caps broke through the Pilgrim Street gate? Or standing alongside Sir Alexander Davidson, fighting to his last at eighty years, his son John, my own close friend, dead alongside him? No! You were part of the force hurled against your own comrades and kin.'

He gave Archer a sly look. 'They shall be glad to hear that you are once again come into the town, even if I am sick for it.'

'Do not presume to threaten me, uncle. It is many years since I was in the least bit intimidated by your bluster.'

'Think on your own back, boy, and be worried about more than me. There are none here who will look to protect you. You ought never to have returned.'

With the brewer's last sting resounding off the panelled walls, the door opened and Aunt Weston entered. Uncle and nephew stepped further apart.

The years had been kinder to Cecily Weston. Her youthful beauty had not faded, but mellowed into a warm vagueness of gentle eyes and soft features. The smile she offered remained uncertain, accompanied, as always, by a nervous glance towards her husband.

'Aunt, it is good to see you.'

The smile steadied and broadened as she accepted Archer's embrace. She looked him up and down with something akin to wonder and turned to Weston, now leaning with both hands upon the desk. 'Is he not grown fine, Ralph?'

'He is no concern of mine, nor of yours,' snapped her husband. She blanched and her face fell. 'You, boy,' the brewer said to Archer, 'were best begone.'

'I shall be, but before I quit your house for what I promise you will be the very last time, I would see Meg.'

His aunt appeared paler than ever. Weston looked at her and then straight back at his nephew, before hissing out a reply. 'Well might you think upon your sister, whom you abandoned so easily.'

'Sir, where is Meg? I must see her.'

Some of his former strength seeped back into Weston's expression. 'You have a fine opinion of yourself, to come back to this house, which you deserted, to make demands of me, to whom you owe respect and thanks.'

'I intend no disrespect but wish to be reunited with Meggie.'

'Your sister is not here!'

Nothing had prepared Archer for Weston's finality. He groped for a response; his mouth opened and closed but no words came.

'You return here after more than six years and expect to see nothing change? You unworthy, loathsome...'

'Ralph, please. This is not seemly.'

'Be quiet wife!'

The words resounded like a slap. The woman fell back, tears welling in her eyes. Weston ignored her.

'That headstrong girl is gone,' he said to Archer. 'We neither know nor care where.'

'Where is she? What has become of Meg?'

Uncle and aunt together visibly quailed as he moved nearer. The briefest spasm of guilt washed over him. Instantly, it was replaced by a cold anger.

'What is it you are hiding? Is she one of those hung for a witch?'

'No, boy, she is no witch,' blustered Weston. 'The devil to any who say it.'

'Then where is she?'

'She is gone. She left the town after the trial.'

'The trial? Then she was one of the accused?'

His aunt cried out, but the look in Weston's eyes was the only answer Archer needed. Until then, he had not realised how much he had hoped that Deane had lied. Put on trial as a witch. Even had Meg come through such an ordeal and lived, how could he have allowed this to have happened to his own sister?

'Where is she? Where has she gone?'

'We know not where,' replied Weston. 'But she will not return to Newcastle.'

The two men stood eye to eye, each equally still and silent.

'I shall find her, uncle,' said Archer. 'If she is not safe or perfectly well, or if your neglect and irresponsibility as a guardian has seen her harmed in any way, know that I shall return here for you.'

He turned, made a short bow to his aunt and left the room. Behind him Weston, having recovered his courage, sent against him a further torrent of invective.

Reaching the floor below, movement behind one of the half-open doors alerted Archer. Someone observing his descent had stepped back in an attempt not to be seen. In two steps, he had shouldered his way in. He was met with squeals and came to an abrupt halt in the doorway.

A young maid servant was cradling a girl child of not much more than a year, trying to keep the infant quiet. Flanking them were two other girls, dressed as young ladies with ringed hair and lace collars, each of them older than children but still far from full grown.

'Please, we mean no harm,' squeaked the eldest.

'Mattie? And is this my cousin Katherine?'

Both girls had changed dramatically in his long absence. Babies he had helped to coddle in arms when he was a lad and still childish nursery rats when he had left. His cousins would now, of course, be the one thirteen years, the other sixteen. And the toddler, presumably another new baby. A third girl, which must only further disappoint his uncle.

'Cousin James?' Mattie, the eldest, spoke nervously for them both. Katherine remained fixed upon James' scarred face.

'I mean no harm to you, cousins. It does my heart good to see you, and to see you grown into such fine ladies.'

Archer managed to force out a tight smile but was careful to remain half under the door frame, half on the landing.

'And my smallest cousin, she is equally fine. What is her name?'

The two girls glanced at each other, uncertainly. Archer strained to listen for steps from the floor above, for he had no wish to be found here. Of course, to his cousins he could look nothing like the boy they might vaguely remember.

'James, it is you!' exclaimed Mattie.

Archer felt his scar burn. 'Older and glad to be home, but not, I hope, so very much changed.'

He looked towards the child. The servant girl, eyeing him more in interest than fear, offered a short bob and moved the infant into the weak light the window allowed, puffing herself up with pleasure and pride. 'And this is Miss Emily, sir.'

Archer was near to going fully into the room when he heard the upstairs door open and with it his uncle's voice.

Whispering, 'I bid you good day, cousins. I am glad to have seen you so grown and now to have met little Emily,' he was down the final flight of stairs and gone.

Chapter 10

Meg was alive! Gone, but not dead.

Archer leant against the far wall of the chare, taking in great breaths of rank air as his inner turmoil slowly eased.

The burst of joy was clouded by the confirmation that in his absence she had been accused and put to trial as a witch. The last retort he had thrown at his uncle returned to him, mockingly. If Weston had failed Meg as guardian, what had Archer done as a brother?

There was something else. Throughout the whole encounter, in his bluster, in the way he had silenced his wife, even in his final outburst, there was more behind the brewer's anger. Weston had been holding something back. His uncle had been afraid.

Archer jumped back as two cloaked men turned into Peacock's Chare. No weapons, no sign they had noticed him at all. He stood, immobile, as the pair moved up the steps, came alongside, and continued on without a glance.

Looking down towards a thronged Quayside, he realised that already he had lost too much time. The military authorities at the castle would be sure to have learned of his arrival. He could not delay longer in reporting there. Reluctantly, he began to climb.

Hardening his face upon reaching the junction with Long Chare, Archer pressed upwards towards the Castle Stairs. Stalls and shops, for the sale of old clothes, shoes and clogs, pressed about on either side, their raggedly poor customers patiently moving from vendor to vendor in search of a cheaper or less worn-out item.

He side-stepped his way through the crowds of women and was thankful to emerge after a few minutes into the relative airy openness of Bank Side. From here, he ducked low as he took the foetid length of the arched-over Sheep Head Alley at a near-trot. Exiting the tunnel, he passed quickly by Dowey's Corner, a cluster of mean, leant-over buildings he knew as the home to prostitution, beggary and wretchedness. He was surprised to hear no solicitation from within, whether for trade or money, although he felt wary eyes upon him.

Archer turned away into King Street, striding ahead to leave the squalor behind, closing fast upon the Black Gate of the castle. The trio of regimental soldiers guarding its narrow drawbridge showed the looming tower gateway to be no longer leased out for civilian uses. Looking beyond them, he noted the notorious ground floor tavern of his youth had even been reconverted into a guard room, the windows to either side of its low doorway affixed with iron bars and solid, studded shutters.

Showing his warrant to the sergeant on duty, he was asked to wait and invited to keep warm by a large brazier, placed and maintained to keep the outer sentry positions bearable. A private was sent further inside to announce his arrival, while Archer stepped into the shadow of the gate itself.

Removing his gloves, just as he began to appreciate the thawing effect of the glowing coals, Archer saw a clutch of men emerge from the crowded confusion of Castle Garth, the crooked street linking the Black Gate to the squat keep, centre to the governor's administration. The delicate face, extravagantly groomed beard and curling, grey hair of old Carr was unmistakable. He was accompanied by his younger son, a more nervous, less substantial, replica of the father, along with three middle aged men Archer recognised as senior members of the Royalist Carr clan's wider affinity. Uniformly grim faces suggested that whatever the nature of their business in the castle, it had been concluded far from satisfactorily.

The men passed within a few feet of where Archer stood. Carr's son noticed him first, what colour he had draining from the young man's face before he spoke a few words to his father. Old Carr looked across and at once fixed Archer with a look of deepest loathing. One of Carr's companions stopped, shot across an equally frigid stare, spread his outer coats, and showily placed his hands upon the bejewelled hilts of sword and dagger. Then, at a single word from the old man, the group was gone.

Watching them pace away towards the Church of Saint Nicholas and disappear into the crowds of women and servants at the bottom of the Groat Market, the nagging pull returned to the side of Archer's face. The soot-darkened stones of the Black Gate hung all the more heavily upon him. He began to pace a short circuit back and forth between the cold of its open drawbridge and the heat of the coals, all the time trying to calm himself and refocus upon the coming interview.

At the end of his fourth lap, he stopped. Two fine greys had been led forwards, pulling between them a large, black-painted, ornately decorated coach. Vehicle and horses were matched in magnificence by three accompanying attendants, each tall and robust, resplendent in well-tailored, velvet uniforms and high, stiff hats.

'The governor's new carriage. Fine job, ain't she?' muttered one guard to another. 'Very pretty.'

The coach would not have looked out of place at the old King's infamously showy Court. This, Archer imagined, was the kind of additional information Deane, or rather Skippon, would be glad to receive. The last thing men in London would want was for a provincial commander to become too powerful. Leverage against them would always be useful. He returned to the warmth of the coals, calmed by the incident and wondering anew at the openness of Heselrigg's extravagance.

Eventually, the private soldier returned with a harassed-looking domestic servant.

'Please, sir. Ensign. If you please, this way. You will understand that the governor is busy with the affairs of the town. I am afraid the deputy governor, Lieutenant Colonel Hobson, is not to be found in the castle. The governor's secretary is available to receive you.'

'Ensign Archer. On behalf of the governor, it is my pleasure to welcome you to Newcastle.

Having delivered his initial greeting, the young secretary followed up with an uncertain bow, before continuing in a more strained voice. 'My name is Anthony Pearson, from the West Auckland Pearsons of Ramshaw Hall, lately of Christ's College. I have the good fortune to serve Sir Arthur, who has charged me to ensure that you are offered every assistance.'

Archer went to step forward into the cramped room, but the little man remained standing in its doorway, perhaps awaiting a formal response.

'Thank you, Secretary Pearson. I shall be glad to begin.'

This time, Archer attempted to edge left. Mossy green eyes blinking up at the long scar, the secretary remained in his way.

'I should like to see all records relating to the witches,' continued Archer. 'Alike for the accusations and the trials themselves.'

Pearson's gaze briefly shifted towards the outer landing. Archer determined to press ahead with his public demands yet more loudly.

'The same for the volumes of coal traded upon the river, the principal contracts for the London and Yarmouth trade and for export. The Council is most concerned to be satisfied regarding the security of the coals.'

The man's cherubic face appeared almost to flinch at this mention of the Council of State. 'The details regarding the trade, that, of course, I may help you with at once. There is no cause for concern, none at all.'

Archer managed to take the smallest of steps forwards, forcing Pearson to shuffle back against the leading edge of the overburdened desk which took almost all of the musty chamber's floor space.

The secretary's blinking only intensified. 'Please, sir, understand that the witch proceedings took place solely under the jurisdiction of the town corporation. There was no formal military involvement in any of it. The records you seek will be held down at the Guildhall. Alas, I cannot furnish you with such information here in the castle.'

Closing the door and noting Pearson's visible relief, Archer took another slow half step into the room. 'No matter,' he said. 'I shall go to Sandhill presently. Perhaps you can offer me your own recollection of the events surrounding these women.'

Casting a look over the desk's cluttered surface, the small man turned back to Archer, having apparently recovered some poise. 'I would be far from your best interlocutor on the matter of the witches, being new in my post. The previous man, Mitchell, has recently departed into Scotland with the army. I am afraid that I myself was far from Newcastle, even at the time of the executions.'

Archer controlled a spurt of anger. 'May we move on to the trade then, and the administration of the town?'

Pearson's small tongue flickered over rounded lips. 'Ah yes, of course. There is nothing there to concern the Council. Relations between the governor and the town authorities are, I must tell you, quite excellent. As providence has it, I have the details of the latest coal shipments just here.'

He scuttled back around his desk and began searching among its debris for the papers he needed. At last, he plucked one thick, folded sheaf from under several others, flicked through it and gave a grunt of satisfaction.

For the next few minutes, Pearson showed Archer the trade figures, answering questions with increasing detail and confidence. Shipment via the coastal route to London and Yarmouth was high and growing. The contracts already booked, to furnish the capital in particular with its fuel for the coming winter, showed a substantial and reassuring scale of business, conducted at a steady price. Sea-going exports to Denmark, Friesland and the Baltic were also increasing. There was no evidence here of the feared disruption but rather fulsome proof that the town, and its trade, thrived. The volumes involved even suggested the Hostmen must have been able to open up more coal measures than ever.

Archer noted with interest the names of the merchant families most heavily involved in this growth. James Maddison, the leader of Newcastle's Puritan interest, had become so greatly elevated as to rank first among all Hostmen by the value of his trades. Also risen in fortune were several other Puritans who had previously been excluded from office, principally Harrison, Henry Dawson, which pleased him most of all, and Blakiston. What he had not expected was to find names such as Riddell, Grey and even Carr, all former Royalist defenders of the town against Parliament, also apparently still involved at the very centre of affairs. Wilkinson had not lied.

A tinny bell sounded down in Castle Garth. The secretary's manner immediately retreated back to its former nervous confusion.

'You understand,' he stuttered, 'that this is decreed a special day of prayer?'

Archer hoped his lack of response indicated assent, even as he cursed inwardly. This meant delay, a delay which could only prove dangerous.

'That bell,' Pearson continued, 'signifies the principal officers of the administration to have finished their private prayer meeting. They will now be proceeding directly to service. I am most sorry, but I am required to hasten along with them. Would you, perhaps, accompany me? There is not much of consequence you can accomplish else. The town officials will be engaged in their contemplations and may not return to the Guildhall until after the dinner hour. Also, today will be a marvellous occasion. Dr. Jenison being infirm, Mister Woolfall from the All-Saints congregation has agreed to lecture. Together with the regular preachers, I can promise you several hours of godly exposition.'

Chapter 11

Crowding into the ancient, echoing stones of Saint Nicholas, Newcastle's principal place of worship, it took a few minutes for Archer's eyes to grow accustomed to the light. The church of his youth felt very far away. Having anticipated its mysterious, iridescent gloom, he was surprised to walk into airy brightness. All of the vivid stained glass had been removed. Pure, bleached streaks of light fanned out through the great apse window. Archer walked on alongside Pearson in silence, taking in the other dramatic changes.

Beyond the nave, the great stone altar had been entirely removed from the church's chancel, replaced by a centrally located, undraped communion table of plain wood. The intricately carved font, in whose shadowy depths Archer had been baptised, was nowhere to be seen. The gaudy décor maintained in Bishop Cosin's time, the rich drapes, paintings and carvings, had all been removed. Of the imposing family-commissioned sculptures formerly looming over the worshippers, only the enormous bulk of the Maddison memorial remained, presumably having proven impossible to move from its watch over the south transept. Even this was shrouded with vast coverings.

The whole of the spacious interior had, he could now see, been remodelled. Rows of benches had been installed behind and to either side of the communion table, the simple piece of everyday furniture thereby become the stark centrepiece of a wide arena, surrounded by the whole congregation.

Pearson nudged Archer on, easing the crush developing

behind them. Together, they crept forwards. Faces turned; incurious blankness replaced with keenly pointed interest. Everywhere, sleeves were tugged, voices stifled.

Boys Archer had apprenticed with, now men, sat alongside weather-beaten elders and young, dimpled wives. Several rows of pewterer and candlemaker families created a cascade of whispered excitement as he passed with the secretary, who was, by now, flushing deepest pink. To his surprise, along one whole bench to his left, he found a cluster of thin-lipped Fenwicks, established much further back in the church than their status had previously mandated. Sir John, the head of this branch of the family, was missing altogether. He wondered whether death or exile had overtaken the old man.

Among the brewers, to the right and a few rows nearer to the communion table, sat Archer's scowling uncle and wan aunt, next to the three children, including little Emily, held tight by an embarrassed-looking Katherine. The two older girls at first stared at their cousin, but a word from Weston set their eyes once more straight and their backs fully upright.

On the very front benches, Mayor Bonner and the other principal men of the corporation perched alongside their proud families. He looked for Henry Dawson, finding him one row behind, engaged in earnest conversation. Archer slowed, hopeful the alderman might look up and see him, but Pearson jerkily gestured for him to hurry on. They passed by the governor, alongside a range of his most senior staff. Heselrigg waited, broad and still, barely a flicker of emotion showing upon his blocky face.

Pearson indicated a bench three rows back, already squeezed with several junior officers. Silently and without much interest, they shuffled up to allow Archer to sit. The secretary disappeared from his side, but a moving shadow told him the whereabouts of the little man's allotted place.

The huge church was full. Archer scanned the congregation, registering the presence of each significant local family, along with a handful of absences, which notably included both the Carrs and the Liddells. Wondering if those families had suffered a similar public demotion to the Fenwicks, he allowed his gaze to extend towards the rear pews reserved for the lesser guilds. There was no sign there of the former Royalists, but his eyes were drawn again to his own kin, nestled halfway back along the nave. None among them looked back. Two benches beyond. However, Archer's attention was caught by movement at one end of the row.

A young woman, wearing a layered, hooded cape of rich green pulled down onto her shoulders to reveal a plain, grey dress, looked directly back at him. A thin, dark line of hair, combed so severely tight to the scalp as barely to show around the sides of her starched white cap, had the effect of further thinning an already straitened face. Large, shining, brown eyes held his own. Although she sat with the Armstrongs, a feltmaking family he had known passingly, he was certain he had never seen her before. She offered no smile, nor any hint of recognition, but rather continued unbrokenly to hold his gaze. It was as if she were set upon communicating something to him above the heads of the gathered people, over the yards of tombstone-paved floor.

To his irritation, Archer's attention was torn from the woman by a slow, insouciant voice from his immediate left. 'Good day to you, Ensign,' said a handsome, bearded captain of cavalry wearing the insignia of a senior aide. 'Captain-Lieutenant Matthew Draper, formerly of Norton's Horse, latterly of Sir Arthur's own Cuirassiers.'

One of Heselrigg's personally raised cavalry regiment, known as 'Lobsters' by virtue of their scaled saddle armour, Draper spoke in the lazy drawl associated with its officers. His keen eyes belied such languor, giving the impression of a lively, detached wit determined to find amusement in every situation.

After Pearson's nervous affectation and the crawling self-consciousness of his own entry into the church, it was an encounter that instantly bolstered Archer.

'Ensign Archer of Colonel Barkstead's regiment. Currently seconded to the service of the Council of State.'

'And before that, with Lilburne's mutinous rabble, come to investigate the deaths of the women.' Draper gave out a rolling laugh at the look of surprise upon Archer's face. 'Your fame goes before you. I am the governor's personal Captain-Lieutenant. Naturally, I have been made aware of your coming. I am glad to make your acquaintance and hope that I will very soon have the opportunity to be of service.'

Captain-Lieutenant Draper leaned in closer and continued more intimately, 'I hope also you are ready for some rest. These fellows are likely to speak on for some hours. That,' he openly indicated the first lecturer, already sedately approaching the steps of the lectern, 'is one Thomas Woolfall. He, I have not heard lecture until today, but he brings with him quite some notoriety.' He paused as Archer glanced towards the thin, pale lecturer and back. 'One which speaks of solemnity and fire. So, enjoy,' he concluded, with a lupine grin and a shake of his long, curling hair, before settling as far back as the bench would allow.

The fierce reputation Draper had imputed to the preacher was strongly supported by a sharp, angry set to the man's brow and the thick mane of dark hair topping his swaying black robe. The combination, as he settled and a rustle of nervous pleasure rippled through the arena, lent Woolfall the appearance of a great raven perched on a skeletal, winter-stripped tree.

He did not now disappoint.

The text for the day was taken from the Book of Revelation: "And I saw the holy city, new Jerusalem, prepared as a bride adorned for her husband. And I heard a loud voice from the throne saying, 'Behold, the dwelling place of God is with man'."

Woolfall's contemplation of the passage began softly. Archer had to lean forwards and focus keenly in order to catch all of his words as they drew upon images of the divine hope offered to man and of the love of the Lord for His people.

From this gentle opening, the lecturer patiently expanded in a display of forcefully rising oratory. Archer pressed against the hard back of his bench as the grinding voice increased both in pitch and volume, filling the farthest spaces of the church with a dire revelation of the terrible anger of God. The torrent of scripture grew and grew, like a wave which finally crashed upon the lowered heads of the congregation as an apocalyptic denunciation.

'The Devil,' Woolfall declared, 'has disported himself in the town for too long. We must prepare the way for the entry of Lord Jesus into this place, that sinners may feel the warming embrace of His love.'

He paused and turned towards the front benches directly under his pulpit. In an urgent, angry hiss, he addressed the governor and corporation officers. Their civil power, he exhorted, under the guidance of the town's godly clergy, bore the responsibility of making of Newcastle a new Jerusalem, a place for the Saints, the House of the Lord upon the earth.

With a voice by now strained and almost, it appeared, failing, but one also steeped in impatience and longing, he made clear to the new town leaders how the building of such a city fit for the just and the godly would require the hard-hearted destruction of all that had so sinfully come before.

'The late efforts,' he whispered, 'by those engaged in this hellish plot of Anti-Christ to subvert true religion in this Commonwealth and in this town, has, by the grace of God and the strength and inspiration of His soldiery, been itself subverted.'

Glaring across the bowed heads of all of Newcastle's leading families, Woolfall recovered some of his earlier vigour. 'But those malignant persons remain at large among us.' His robed arm swept across the whole church. 'They are hid and supported by the wicked and deluded people. Therefore, beware you the lures of vice, or the temptations of sin. Those who shall not are marked out as followers of Anti-Christ.'

He stopped, allowing time for his words to echo back from the old stones.

Archer raised his head to see what effect this was having. Several others were also looking to see if the denunciation was, at last, over. The woman who had stared at him earlier risked an upward glance, dropping her head as the lecturer's eyes appeared to fall directly upon her. Archer saw her tense, her already apologetic features becoming even more strained.

The preacher's baleful glare passed on to encompass, in turn, each of the girls and younger women present. The silence built, suffocating in its intensity, until each head in the congregation had shifted subtly upwards and every eye was straining towards the towering black figure. Only then, crooked finger pointed towards the rows of cowed women, did Woolfall spit out his final attack.

'See here these loathsome fashions of you women, led in vanity and weakness to powdered hair, painted faces, naked breasts and fantastical garb. This shall not be borne among the people of the Lord, or all shall perish in torment.'

Mayor Bonner and his aldermen sat upright on the front benches and, for the first time, cracks showed in the studied severity of their expressions. Smiles emerged from pursed lips as they looked over the hunched forms of the wider congregation. Their women folk kept greater discipline, remaining stern and prim, the sobriety of their appearance pointedly becoming its own silent reproof.

The woman on the Armstrong bench had shrunk even lower. She cowered, painfully aware, it seemed to Archer, of the simple lace collar of her otherwise unadorned dress. She remained unmoving even as Woolfall descended from the pulpit and the wider congregation gave a collective exhalation, with a rustling and creaking of benches old and new, as people stretched, offered a brief, complicit look to their neighbours, and prepared themselves for the second lecturer, who was already approaching.

Archer turned to Captain-Lieutenant Draper, who he found

to be regarding him with a detached air. 'That woman, there on the left, at the end of the bench towards the back,' he whispered. 'The one in the grey. Do you know her?'

Languidly, Draper looked over. 'Back there? Among the, what, the lesser trades? I should say not.' He fixed Archer with an amused look, broken only by a swift glance to make sure the new lecturer had not yet fully ascended. 'An extremely odd choice to fix your attention upon. I can introduce you to many a finer-looking woman.'

They fell silent. Archer's discomfort grew as, alongside him, the captain-lieutenant only gradually allowed his attention to shift away from the young woman and on to the beginning of the next lecture.

Sore from his back down to his legs, dazed and unsteady, Archer emerged into the slanting mid-afternoon light. His senses struggled to come to renewed terms with the outside world following the past hours of unbroken preaching.

Pearson, appearing at his side, seemed, by contrast, calmer and somehow more rested than before. 'Did I not tell you right,' he said, 'that your time would be well spent in exposure to such erudite and godly men?'

'The lectures were highly instructive. Thank you again.'

Pearson beamed back, his eyes restlessly moving among the crowd of civic and military dignity, saying its collective good-days in the triangular open space leading to Rosemary Lane.

'Will you dine now?' he asked. 'The town officials will surely be eating together. You have some hours before you, if you still intend to seek them out today.'

The man had spoken easily enough. It could be nothing more

than gentlemanly manners on his part, and clearly Pearson had been well raised.

'I shall keep my own company in The Blue Anchor,' said Archer.

The secretary, already hopping up and down as he strained towards the dispersing crowd, made the excuse that he would be required to attend upon the governor as soon as he had dined. The man sidled away, leaving Archer blessedly alone.

Craning his neck at the people disappearing down Church Steps and along Newgate Street, hoping to see the strange young woman from the Armstrong bench, Archer found instead Captain-Lieutenant Draper taking a casual leave of three other officers and loping over. As Draper drew alongside, he cast a scornful look at Pearson's retreating back, gave out a sound in between mirth and disgust, and clapped Archer hard between the shoulder blades.

'Now that your soul is cleansed, perhaps we can offer you some material sustenance. We go to dine, those fellows and I, and would invite you to join us.'

Here, out in the open, Draper cut an even more striking figure. Standing, he was nearly a full head taller than Archer. His exquisitely cut uniform, finely worked gloves, trimmed beard and artfully curled hair recalled the charismatic, infamously outlandish, Major General Harrison. Archer was further tempted by the offer of food. His stomach ached. The lectures had, as Pearson had promised, stolen well past the normal dinner hour. He even looked up at the southernmost clock face high above the church, despite knowing what it would tell him, that if he delayed, he would miss the rising tide and, with it, the chance to investigate along the quay. He offered Draper a softer version of the lie he had slipped to the little secretary.

'I should very much like to, and I am grateful, but being pressed for time, I will have to settle for simpler fare in my lodgings.' Feeling the need to back up this refusal, he added, 'I have need to be on Sandhill to attend upon the town officials hard after, you see.'

Draper took Archer's answer calmly. He signalled across to his fellow officers.

'It is a pity you are in such a hurry, for we will dine well.' The captain-lieutenant pivoted his neck to take in the departing crowd and the cluster of old buildings surrounding the church precincts. 'Well enough, given the conditions.'

Draper took a few steps away, stopped and turned. Bestowing upon Archer another warm smile, he called back. 'Do come to see me at the castle early tomorrow. I shall ensure you are expected. You will get nothing worth your while from Pearson, but I shall do what I can to help you. You see, Archer, I was there.'

Chapter 12

'I think that will be all. You will want to be on your way,' said the Dutch mate. To make the point clearer, his eyes flicked down towards the shore.

Only a minute earlier, the man had been answering happily, and at length, Archer's questions about trade, the current state of the river pilotage, and the welcome to be found in Newcastle. Just in time, Archer held back his readied challenge as the salt tang belatedly reached his nostrils.

The ordinary sailors idling in groups about the main deck began to disentangle themselves. As the tide rose, the crew of the Baltic merchantman needed no verbal instruction to begin their preparations for departure.

Offering a quiet thanks, Archer toed his way down the quivering plank and back onto the quay. Looking along its length, he could see similar signs of renewed activity on board the other ships. The snaking, mud-banked river was notoriously difficult to navigate. The current high lee was anticipated to allow plenty of draught for the most whale bottomed of ocean-going vessels, such that near to half of the traders in port, heavily loaded and low in the water as they appeared, were intent upon taking full advantage. The Newcastle merchants, knowing the tidal conditions upon which their livelihoods depended, would, he realised, have ensured that their obligations to God that day were precisely timed to match with the requirements of business.

It had proved to be a good afternoon of work. The sheer number of masts along the quay more than justified the trade figures Pearson had shared with him. It also made clear that it was not only the coal merchants who prospered.

The inland shipping which transported the coals to London and a few other fortunate southern ports lay at anchor further along the river off Jarrow, Hebburn and the scattering of settlements upriver from Tynemouth and its protective castle. A swarm of flat-bottomed keelboats would shuttle back and forth, ferrying their precious black loads downstream to feed this armada, incomparably increased in scale since Archer's exile.

If the domestic coal trade had grown, Newcastle's overseas business thrived even more. A forest of sea-going vessels crowded between bridge and Ouse Burn, emptied of wood, furs and amber from the Baltic, or herring from the Dutch Republic, and now making ready to depart laden with great quantities of coal, alongside wool, manufactured cloths and, as he had discovered that afternoon, newer exports such as finished leathers and an extraordinary volume of beer, which at least helped to explain the bustling activity at the Weston brewery.

There was no substance then to the Council's concerns about either the critical trade in coals or the wider economic health of the town.

The Newcastle merchants' Charter of Monopoly funnelled all of this business through their own warehouses and wharfs, empowering them to deny trading rights to any of the downstream towns and even to other northern rivers, most notably the nearby Wear. The monopoly was the source of the town's wealth and the enabler of what had become an extraordinary expansion.

All along the waterfront, Archer had encountered labourers, skilled dock workers, warehousemen, tradesmen and casual sellers who were, for the most part, newly come into the town. Accustomed accents from Northumberland, Durham, or the borders clashed with new voices from elsewhere in England, from Scotland and even from overseas. Newcastle was far from the close-knit, closed-in town of his youth. The least changed aspect was the identity of the families who reaped profits from these ventures.

No matter where he had been, the same names had recurred, confirming that many former Royalists, such as Riddell, Marley, and especially Carr, were commissioning as widely as ever. Of these traditionally dominant families, Cole and Liddell were the only wholesale absentees. Any slack that had left in the trade was more than taken up by the rival Puritan faction. The godly merchants, including the two Dawson brothers, had always traded well, but it was clear that their business prospered far more than before the wars.

Archer's eyes strayed beyond the Dutch ship towards the ugly outline of the battered trader *Caroline*, two berths along. The name of one other merchant had come up repeatedly, relating most of all to this vessel. The *Caroline* was commissioned to sail by a William Blackett, bringing in cargoes of flax from the Baltic.

He had not previously heard of Blackett, but by now he understood the man's trading interests and investments to be unusually wide-ranging. As well as the import of Muscovy flax, the merchant was engaged in the export of wheat, pig-iron, cloth and a range of finished commodities in the holds of several more of the ships currently preparing for departure.

The *Caroline*, it seemed, had made Blackett's fortune. Among his very first investments some years previously, she was, of the whole northern flax fleet, the only survivor from storm and piracy. The profits Blackett had reaped from his accidental monopoly had since been put to extensive use, although he was said not to be made Hostman, nor otherwise active in the corporation. Archer wondered whether Blackett held Royalist or Puritan sympathies. Did that even matter in this new, expanded world of Tyneside commerce?

He looked back at the shabby old *Caroline*, allowing himself a thin smile at Blackett's fortuitous upward journey. What he had learned regarding the condition of the trade was more than enough to satisfy the Council. That part of his work was done. The officers of the corporation would by now be back at their positions, even allowing for the late dinner occasioned by the church services. There could be no more than an hour or two left for him to examine the official Guildhall records of the witch trials.

With that, much as he recoiled from what he might possibly find, could come some clue relating to Meg.

A knot of men hunched together against the heavy curtain wall, blocking Archer's passage towards Bridge Gate.

Broad-shouldered, weather-worn and slant-eyed from lifetimes spent upon the open river, the keelmen were instantly identifiable by their tough canvas breeches, worn over high stockings and close-fitting clog shoes, most also sporting the characteristic saffron-yellow neck scarfs. Shallow boat navigation suspended until the tide turned and the big ships had vacated the stream. They further stood out for their inactivity in the wider bustle.

Archer considered approaching them to seek a different perspective upon the revived trade. Mostly, he recognised this urge for the indulgence it was. The clannish group would not relish the questions of a regimental officer, however much history the man inside the uniform had once had with them. Or at least, he thought, with their fathers, their uncles and their older brothers. Moreover, his were not the only eyes fixed upon them.

A larger group of grey-uniformed corporation watchmen clustered next to the arched gateway. Ostentatiously, they displayed the thick wooden staves and clubs with which they habitually kept order. It was a natural part of the watchmen's business to monitor the quay. Archer had already picked up signs of hold-stuffing and unregistered cargo as he had passed from ship to ship, but this band was concerned with neither the dockers nor with the ship loading. Their focus remained completely fixed upon the keelers.

The hairs on Archer's neck pricked up. Even as he tensed, the keelmen detached themselves from the wall, formed into a loosely regimented line, and eased past the cold stares of the watch to disappear through the gate and onto Sandhill. The grey uniforms closed ranks behind the men, temporarily hiding them from view.

Archer waited quietly for the line of watchmen to relax, step aside and allow him his own uneasy passage into the town. Keeping his head down under their hostile examination, he could not help a sideways look to where a big, heavy-featured civilian in patched clothes relentlessly stared at him from under a shock of dark hair.

There was something familiar about the man which could not be placed. Archer might have stopped, but at that moment a pair of watchmen moved across his view. By the time they had passed by, the huge onlooker was gone.

Emerging onto Sandhill, Archer's attention snapped to the commotion unfolding outside the Guildhall complex. The group of keelmen who had preceded him were advancing to join a crowd of their fellows. A larger number of women and children were dotted as a rag-tag fringe about their menfolk. The keelers and their families were observed, at a distance, by a ring of silent townspeople, sailors and sinewy, glassy-eyed miners.

He stepped a few paces nearer The Close, to the shelter of a boarded-up stall, taking up a position beside a trio of old pitmen. Just outside the low entrance arch to Guildhall, he could see two keelmen, separated from the rest, engaged in animated exchange with a single corporation official. Beyond them, in the shadow of the arch, stood several armed watchmen. As Archer looked on, the two keelmen broke away from the town official, setting off a low murmur of frustration and disapproval among the crowd.

'Why do they protest today?' he asked the nearest miner.

Bloodshot pale eyes narrowed to appraise him, set deep in a labour-shrunken face scarred by curling worms of coal dust under the skin. 'Who wants to knaa?' The old man let loose a disfigured grin to reveal a black, gapped mouth. 'Keel's gan owa.' He shrugged towards Guildhall. 'The masters make the loads bigger. Gets the ships filled faster. Fast as we can dig oot the coals.' He shrugged once more, words seemingly exhausted. The larger of his two white-haired companions noisily ejected a thick glob of black mucous, to the amusement of the smaller third man, before all turned their focus back to the keelers.

At the very front of the protest, one of the pair who had been negotiating with the official ascended the high mounting block which kept sentry outside the arch. Fair-haired, unusually lean and tall for a keelman, but kitted like the rest in canvas and wearing about his neck the saffron scarf, the man stilled the clamour with a gentle waft of his arm. An expectant calm settled across Sandhill.

The tall keeler's slow and strong dialect reached to the very edges of the marketplace with practiced ease. 'Brothers. Today we have lost three good friends. Three families tonight will have neither food nor shelter. Instead, they will be cast out and we, who come here to seek understanding, are met only with contempt!'

Archer trembled. A look to his right revealed the entire patrol of watchmen from the quay to have emerged through Bridge Gate. They made no move to approach the protest, but instead fanned out, forming a loose cordon along the line of the walls.

Upon the mounting block, the speaker continued, establishing a rolling, liturgical rhythm before which the weather-worn keelmen swayed along as one.

'How is justice turned to wormwood? Yet I say to you, "God will bring into judgment both the righteous and the wicked, for there will be a time for every activity, a time to judge every deed". That time, it draws near. For the Lord has given us his command: "let justice roll on like a river, righteousness like a never-failing stream".'

The crowd rumbled with anger. The fair keelman regained control with another languid gesture. In the long seconds before he spoke again, the only sound was the incessant rattling of the rigging on the masts of the Baltic ships. On the far side, towards the Kale Market, Archer saw another group of grey uniforms spread out, as if intent upon blocking off entrance to its slope and the adjacent steps.

'Shall this stand?' demanded the keelman-preacher, his voice rising, then falling into a caress. 'Shall you wait until it is your keel that goes under? Or stay your hand until it is your wife or your daughters who are cast out to sell themselves in the street? The Lord both sees and hears your sufferings, for He has said "Give ear, O my people, to my law: incline your ears to the words of my mouth". The wicked have drawn out the sword, and have bent their bow, to cast down the poor and needy. I tell you, "Their sword shall enter into their own heart, and their bows shall be broken".'

His listeners loudly voiced their approval. Some brave apprentices and a few of the younger miners moved forwards to join the central crowd. The preacher's words echoed high and clear.

'"Behold, the day of the Lord cometh, cruel both with wrath and fierce anger, to lay the land desolate: and he shall destroy the sinners thereof out of it. Your wealth is all rotting. All your gold and silver are corroding away, and the same corrosion will be your own sentence, and eat into your body".'

The shouted responses rose higher, dividing to become yet sharper and angrier, even as the crowd restlessly shifted. The third group of watchmen, spilling out from Guildhall, evidently reinforced from within the guardroom, had taken up position outside the arch.

Slowly, clubs thudding against uniform breeches or slapped against gloved hands, they began a calm advance upon the keelmen. Archer saw lines of grey uniforms close in with similar patience from the Kale Market side of Sandhill and press forwards from the positions taken up along the quay wall. The joined movement had the effect of corralling the protestors and their families as if they were held in a gradually tightening sack.

Archer registered the smallest vestige of admiration for the discipline of the watch before taking a glance towards his sword hilt. He made to step forward, only to find himself held back by the nearest miner, in a grip of vice-like strength.

'Them's not the fight for youse.'

All around, Archer could see fearful onlookers parting to allow the watchmen to pass through, immediately afterwards slipping away east along Quayside or up the nearest chares.

Singly, or in small groups, the protest began to break apart. Men emerged from the crowd to find their families among the women and children. Only the fair-haired preacher remained distinct, high upon the block. Archer saw him continue to signal for calm, right up to the moment he was hauled down by a squad of watchmen, disappearing into the general confusion. Moments later, the closing lines of grey cut off any further view.

The watchmen had deliberately left open a narrow channel heading towards the western chares. A shrieking stream of keelmen, women and children stumbled their way along its threatening uniformed perimeter onto the open space before a series of warehouses, to scurry away piecemeal up steps or into alleys. In less than ten minutes, without any apparent violence, the whole manoeuvre was complete. The crowd and the keeler families had been dispersed. Sandhill was all but empty. Even Archer's elderly companions were nowhere to be seen.

He took one last, fruitless look for the blond orator, opened up his cloak to display his badges of rank, and stepped across the deserted space towards the arch.

Chapter 13

Entering the centre of Newcastle's administrative and political life, a curt demand for the town clerk sent a suitably intimidated old servant to hurry off in search.

Archer paced about, angry with himself for showing such distemper. After the scene he had just witnessed, the sudden cool order of Guildhall only unsettled him further. Purposely, he stopped still, finding the calm he sought in looking about its familiar entrance saloon.

Here were the old firearms, halberds, cutlasses and other weapons belonging to the corporation which had excited him as a boy, on those rare occasions when Weston had brought him along hoping that the historic status of the Archer family might bring benefit. On the far wall hung some fragments of armour, Turkish, he had heard it said. To one side was a wide stone fireplace over which sat a new over-mantle, carved in a dark, exotic wood.

Archer went across to examine the piece more closely. The working was difficult to make out, since the new wood glistened in the pale light. He stepped back again and moved about in front of the carving. It depicted supplicants of some sort, two women, their heads covered, each kneeling before a bearded and crowned figure who sat enthroned between beautifully crafted fluted columns. Clearly, he thought, this was not an English King. Perhaps it was an image of Mary before God the Father? No, too Popish, if the current Town Council had commissioned this, and it certainly looked completely new.

'Ensign Archer, I see you are admiring our Solomon.' The clerk's voice was reedy, suited to his lean frame. His small eyes darted all over Archer but settled nowhere. 'A new work, and quite beautiful.'

'Solomon in judgement,' replied Archer, only now noticing the tiny carved baby and crib set in between the figures of the women and the throned King.

'Just so, sir. It is an image of the wise magistrate, that we may contemplate the very strength he must needs show. To business,' he simpered. 'My name is Edward Man. How may I help the officer who carries the Council's warrant?'

Edward Man did not like it. He kept repeating 'The mayor will not approve this; it is most irregular.' Faced with Archer's letter and the presence, moreover, of this battle-scarred man, commissioned by the Council of State, claiming to have come straight from the castle, the clerk's resistance melted away. He called out to a junior to 'fetch the witch file and some wine.'

As he turned back, the ingratiating tone came back into his voice.

'You are that James Archer, formerly of the town, who left to join with the army of the Parliament, are you not, sir?'

Archer demurred.

'You are welcome back to Newcastle. There are few who were as brave as you, if I may say. I remember you as a boy from the prayer meetings. You would not remember me, but we always knew that the Lord would ride with you.'

Archer did not remember the man, failing to place him either in Henry Dawson's house or at any of the other meetings he had secretly attended. The return of his junior, carrying the slim file, saved them both from any further exchange.

Refusing an offer of wine, Archer opened the folder of ribbon-bound cloth. Man filled a large cup and nursed it, eyes fixed upon the soldier as he began to work his way through its assortment of papers.

There was little enough there.

A formal note, related to expenses, detailed how two of the Newcastle sergeants, namely Thomas Soevel and Cuthbert Nicholson, went into Scotland to agree with a Scotch pricker to come to Newcastle '*where he should trye such who should be brought to him, and to have twentye shillings a piece for all he could condemn as Witches, and free passage thither and back again*'. This was simply marked as '*From the Magistrates*'.

The note was followed by a report to the same magistrates, dated the previous December, confirming that the Newcastle bell-man had gone through the town, ringing out and crying, "*All people that would bring in any complaint against any woman for a Witch, they should be sent for and tryed by the person appointed*". A separate hand in the margin noted the small sum given to the man in payment for this service.

Along with this was a warrant, dated March past, authorising the town sergeants to use a unit of militia, in addition to the town watchmen, to convey from the prison at Newgate '*twentye false women to be brought before the magistracies, accused of sorceries, witch-crafte and conjurations, at the word and evidens of persons divers.*' Archer paused. His stomach churned at the thought of Meg confined for even one night within the cells of the town's notorious prison. It was an act of will to reach for the final document.

Dated from the preceding August, this was a list of the executed. They had eventually been condemned, it noted, by the Jury of Burgesses at the June Assizes. Archer rapidly scanned the names in mounting fear, made himself read again, then returned for a third time.

Matthew Bulmer, Eliz. Anderson, Jane Hunter, Mary Pots, Alice Hume, Elianor Rogerson, Margaret Muffet, Margaret Maddison, Eliz. Brown, Margaret Brown, Jane Copeland, Ann Watson, Elianor

Henderson, Elizabeth Dobson and Katherine Coultor.'

Margaret Muffet, Margaret Brown and Margaret Maddison, but no Meg, Maggie or Margaret Archer, neither Weston, nor any such name.

He turned the paper over, a different hand had noted on the reverse side that *'These devil's servants never confessed any thinge, but pleeded innocence. One of them by name Margaret Brown beseeched God that some remarkable sign may be seene at the time of execution, to evidence their innocency, and as soon as ever she was turned off the ladder, her blood gushed out upon the people to the admiration of the beholders. Yet she was hunge unto death upon the Moore, along with the fourteene other.'*

The relief that his sister was not named left Archer no room to pity Matthew Bulmer, or the executed women, not even poor Margaret Brown.

Meg was alive. He would find her. Together, they would make everything right. Deane had lied, of course. Some day, he would have the opportunity to pay the man back. Some day he would be free.

As he read on, in spite of his relief at the absence of Meg's name from the death list, a knot of unease gathered and grew.

Archer had attended witch trials before, in garrison, to help keep order. Once, he had been called out in London, more frequently, across the western Fens and the Anglian counties. Normally, the women were accused, tried and executed all too rapidly. Not in this case. It had lasted months.

Then there was that discrepancy. Twenty women on the warrant to the sergeants, but only fifteen names, and those including the one man, Matthew Bulmer, were recorded as having been executed. Until now, he had believed that he had been dealing with just another example of Deane's bad faith. One or two women hung at a time, yes. In garrison in Anglia, he had heard of larger proceedings at Yarmouth and Bury. But, in addition to Bulmer, for twenty women to have been put to trial, fully fourteen of them to have hung?

'So many dead?' Archer raised his voice. 'These are the names of the fifteen executed last August. What of the six women who were found innocent?'

'Those are the only records I, or the corporation, is obliged to keep,' said Man. 'They relate to the executions. The court officials should have retained records of the trials themselves. It is not the responsibility of this office.'

The man's reply had come out too smoothly.

'Is that usual, Mister Man?'

The other man blinked back, taking another sip from his cup.

'No matter,' Archer said, 'I shall inquire at the court. But I would also benefit from your memory of these proceedings. It is an unusual set of delays, from the appearance before the local magistrates and a grand jury in March to the June Assizes. Then near to two further months from judgement to execution?'

'I couldn't say, sir. I am newly appointed to this place.'

'But you must at least remember the accusations, the trials? Why the long delay? Why no record, for that matter, of the women who were cleared?'

Man shrank back towards the window. 'I know only what is in our record. That is my responsibility. As I said, perhaps the court officials?'

Was that a hint of a smile about the clerk's mouth? *I could snap you out of your humour,* thought Archer. He was not more than three feet from where Edward Man stood, frail in outline against the light. A part of him relished the idea of stepping forwards and reaching for the man. Instead, with a shiver, he drew in his shoulders and continued in a lower tone.

'And these men, the court officials, they are?'

The half smile had gone. This time, the answer came more lightly.

'The sheriff in office last year, Samuel Rawling, is gone into Scotland with the army. Perhaps Lodge will speak with you, over at the Court?'

'And Lodge is?'

'The current sheriff, sir.'

'I may take a copy of this list? The Council will need the details.'

Man's pupils contracted. He hesitated before moving a fraction further away to look helplessly out of the window.

Archer took out his own notebook, made a summary of the documents, copying the dates and names carefully, including the annotations, then handed the papers back across the desk, where Man was already waiting, eager to re-inter them in the cloth folder.

Chapter 14

Archer took time in the outer chamber to check the list of the dead. When he was satisfied that he had made no error, he remained standing before the new mantle, peering up at Solomon upon his judgement seat. There was no mention of Meg, nothing like her name, but he was certain he knew several of the others.

Margaret Maddison, Elizabeth Anderson, the Henderson and Dobson women, each from the first rank of Newcastle families. There were other names he recognised. Elianor Rogerson, Jane Hunter, Katherine Coulter, Ann Watson. All of them young, all from respectable backgrounds.

Movement behind him made Archer stuff away his notes and hurry out into the central courtyard, pursued by a stifling press of questions. These were not the very poor, the old, the sort of outcast who usually fell victim to the witch hunt. In this at least, Deane had not misled him. It was fantastical. Surely, women of this estate could not really have hung. And who else, apart from Meg, had gone free?

On the courtyard's farther side, near to the doorway to the Town Court, stood two more watchmen. Armed with staves, dressed in their rough uniforms, arm bands bearing the aldermanic symbol of spears bundled with a staff, together they guarded three prisoners held fast in a pillory. By the state of the latter, they must have been locked in there since at least the previous day. The leading watchman, becoming aware of Archer staring at the pitiful sight, straightened up and came across.

'Can we help you, Ensign?'

'No, I seek Mister Lodge in the Court.'

'Then ye'll want to get inside and see him right away, won't you?'

Archer took the man's lead, resisting the temptation to look back before disappearing into the low doorway leading to the judicial chambers.

In spite of its great scale, the panelled court room beyond felt claustrophobically oppressive. Tiers of benches overlooked platforms set aside for judges, jury and accused. Behind the justice bench, the royal arms remained fixed upon the wall. Such weak light as bled in from the line of small, high windows rendered the scene even starker.

An older man, long-limbed and upright, entered from a hidden door behind the bench. 'The Sheriff is occupied, but I may perhaps assist you? I am Thomas Milburn, his clerk.'

Milburn took his time in looking over Archer's official accreditation. His long face wore an unchanging, subdued expression. Eventually, he handed the papers back.

'This all seems clear,' he said sedately. 'You have already, then, paid attendance upon the governor?'

'Naturally. His secretary, Pearson, received me. And I have just now come from the town clerk, Edward Man, in the Guildhall.'

Milburn's nonchalance contrasted with the fussy nervousness shown by Edward Man. For the first time, however, some inner thought disturbed his waxy surface.

'So, ensign, how can the sheriff's office help you?'

'You can inform me about the recent witch trials conducted in this court.'

'The Court is busy in these days, rooting out the sinful ways of the town. Hearings take place here or in the castle. Sometimes, when needed, even by Saint Nicholas' yard. But, yes, those followers of Satan were indicted and later tried here in this very chamber. Some were charged in January, a number in the early part of Spring and more since. Together, they came before the justices at the Summer Assizes.'

'In that case, may I see the court records relating to their trial?

Mliburn's face remained oddly still. A new strain entered his voice. 'Such records are not retained here. This is a functional place, not an archive. All of those records will be lodged in the Guildhall. Mister Man would have shown you.'

'I told you, I have just left Man. What do you mean there are no further records? There should be transcripts of the hearings before the Grand Jury, records of the main assize trials, of sentence, some record maintained of those released.'

'All I can tell you is that no such records are held here. Perhaps, you may inquire of the previous sheriff?'

The man's barely perceptible smirk showed he knew this was impossible. His face remained otherwise blank, but Archer sensed the tension inside him.

'You are an officer of the Commonwealth. Tell me, how can it be that such records are not made?'

Milburn squirmed before Archer's uniform and his reference to the government, but whatever he knew he was keeping back. The clerk smiled, crookedly. 'I have never seen such. There has been much disturbance in the town. The records have been lodged in several places. Perhaps some have been mislaid. The officers at the castle, perhaps?'

Dead ends everywhere. He was being sent around in circles. Someone, or many people, had gone to a great deal of trouble to ensure that records associated with the court proceedings were missing.

There would be no point in railing at this man, and also danger in drawing too much attention to himself. He would note the absence of official trial records and leave Deane, Skippon and the Council to make of it what they could. Officially, he felt certain, the documents would have met with some unfortunate accident. He stepped backwards.

Milburn began to breathe more easily. Without any further leave taking, Archer turned curtly and exited the courtroom.

Storming across the open courtyard, careful not to look back at the attentive watchmen or the wretches in the pillory, he arrived back on Sandhill, directly across from the wide row of remodelled houses.

Appraising them afresh, he could fully appreciate the effort behind their majestic appearance. The overhanging frontages had been taken back as far as safety allowed, furthering an impression of unity, harmony and order. Each window jamb on every house had been decorated with the same motif of bound weapons, staffs, spears or lances, symbols of the aldermanic status of the families lodged within, and a very obvious, very public, representation of the physical weapons the same magistrates, through their watchmen, had the power to bring to bear upon miscreants and sinners.

These houses of the new Jerusalem had been remade as a show of heavenly space and light, but also as a very public reminder of God's dreadful, punitive power.

Chapter 15

Archer needed time to think.

His elation that Meg was confirmed as alive competed with the tensions of the long day. Weston's anger and fear, Pearson's nervous dissembling, the plight of the keelmen and their families, the dead ends he had faced at every turn, the very names of the executed women, each weighed heavily upon him. And, while his sister might have escaped, he was not for all this even one step closer to finding her.

It combined into the habitual dull ache behind his eyes as he made his way back to the Blue Anchor. He would take food alone in his room. He would keep the fire unlit, open the window and allow in the cold air along with the stench of the quay. And he would rest.

Mrs Veitch apprehended him as soon as he stepped into the inn. 'You have a visitor,' she said with a smack of satisfaction. 'I have placed him in the back parlour.'

Heart sinking, Archer took his time in the corridor, trying to prepare for whoever might await him, before he approached the parlour door.

From inside, to his surprise, came a low crooning, the voice of an old man, singing softly. Entering, Archer saw only a straggle of white hair, the man's seat facing away from the door. But now he caught the song itself, waveringly exhaled in strong Tyneside dialect.

> 'Ride through Sandgate, up and doon
> There you'll see the gallants fighting for the croon
> And all the cull cuckolds in Sunderland toon
> With all the bonny blew caps cannot pull them doon.'

'They will hang you up if they catch you singing that, William,' said Archer, gently.

The singer stopped and rose from his chair with difficulty. It took a few seconds before a wrinkled grin broke out across the collapsed mouth. 'I dare say I'm so far gone in my heed that there's none would follow my words anyway, Master James.'

Archer warmly embraced the man. His fatigue forgotten, he called out of the door for a jug and some food, then turned back into the room, giddy to see the old servant.

'How is your family?'

A shadow passed over the sunken face, but the voice came steady and clear. 'All gone to the Lord, sir. Anna and our Beth both taken by the sweat in '47. My William was killed away at Marston Moor, with the Duke's Lambs.'

William observed Archer through slits of eyes, pained at the memory of his son, and of the doomed, locally raised, Royalist regiment, named for their undyed white coats. The telling of their courage, as, one by one, each of those garments had been stained red in a futile, solitary defiance had spread admiringly through Parliament's opposing New Model Army.

'They told me how it was,' William said. 'They stood their ground when the other regiments had broken. Stood and fought. Blasted and cut to pieces, they were. Thirty men left alive to tell the tale, out of three thousand.'

His forehead crumpled, and his voice became hoarse.

'No need to fret. My boy knew what he was into. Aye, good lads, every one of them.'

William went back to the song under his breath. Archer was surprised when the old man's voice broke above the soft humming.

'I know you weren't there, Master James. There's some in this town says in malice that you were, but others know better. We did hear tell of you seeing fighting in the south country.'

'I was not there, William. I promise you that. My fighting was among the London men and all across the south, you have that right. I had nearly forgotten what a good Newcastle voice sounds like until I found you here today. I am truly grieved for your sorrow.'

Archer looked at William more closely. He was thinner than ever. Watery eyes rested in deep, lined sockets. His skin was a sickly, clammy grey.

'You no longer work for my uncle?'

'Ah, there's need for a younger man than me in that house, Master James. I do bits elsewhere now.'

Tenderly, Archer shuffled the servant back into the high seat.

'I heard of your return,' William said. 'I knew I had to see you. I'd not thought to encounter such a grown man, or a fine officer.' He pointed to the scar. 'With plenty to show for it. Where'd you get that?'

'In Ireland. A terrible time.'

The food and drink that Archer had ordered arrived. When the round-faced girl had gone, not without lingering to ask if there was more they wanted and to take as many glances as she could at the odd pair of them, they were left in a more comfortable silence, each happy to wait for the other to speak or act first.

Archer began to pour out two cups of beer.

'Master James, no, you must not.'

'I can offer my guest a drink, can I not?'

William looked uncertainly at the dark beer until Archer had taken a first, long draught. The old man took the slightest sip, put his cup down, and sat forwards. His slack face shook.

'My master asks me to tell you, that is to tell your own master, he'll accept the offer. But he says he needs to meet you himself.'

He broke off, his eyes desperately searching for a response.

Archer's scar tingled. William had failed to produce the required word-sign to secure the meeting with the Royalist. Its absence meant that this was a trap, unless it was, in some manner, an attempted warning. But Archer had been trained, in such an event, to back away from any meeting. And to find a way of disposing of the false contact.

The flicker in Archer's right eye grew strong before William stutteringly spoke again.

'I mean the sea-winds, they're sharp from the east this time of year, and bad for the Baltic trade. I meant that, first.'

The word-sign. Or at least a recognisably mangled version of it.

Archer's hand closed over his sword hilt at the sound of boots sloping down the short corridor beyond the parlour door. The need for a response hammered away within his head as the steps receded.

'But good for herring from the Dutch,' he said, eyes still fixed upon the door. 'An easterly is very good for herring from the Dutch.'

With the counter-sign, William collapsed into a series of hoarse wheezes. Archer carefully offered him the beer cup. This time the old man made no objection, swallowing a half mouthful before sitting back, lips trembling.

Archer felt the outflow of tension mingle with the sour taste of a fear renewed as he contemplated the treason they were already committing. 'William,' he continued, reluctantly, 'tell your master I shall attend him at his convenience and that my master is grateful.'

The servant seemed neither pleased nor relieved. Rather, a greater weariness appeared to descend upon him. He remained sitting silently for some time, head down, eyes restlessly moving between the fire, the door and the floor. At last, he looked towards Archer and gave a slow nod of his white-stubbled chin.

'Master James. There's more, not to do with my master. You must get this done quick and leave town. You're in danger here, for your life.'

'My life has been in danger many times. I shall have to bear it.'

The old servant's lips moved noiselessly as his face turned in upon itself.

'What have you heard, William?'

Watery eyes looked up. 'I've heard your name spoken today more than once. People telling old stories about how you deserted the town and new ones about how you're come to spy upon their families. Some of them saying you should be bundled into the Tyne.'

'Who is behind this?'

'Them that should know better and should know you better. From the old houses, friends of your own family.'

'Do you still hear then, of my father's friends?'

'Most of those catchfarts are safe in their old positions and for Parliament now.' William's face creased even more deeply. 'They'll be for anyone who'll guarantee the trade and the keeping of their families' control over the coals.'

'Anyone I should look out for in particular?'

'They could come at you from anywhere, Master James, just take care.'

'But?' said Archer, noticing the narrowing of William's glossy eye.

'You remember Joe Marsden? Big lad, about your age, always a bit akka?'

Archer recalled an overgrown lump of a boy, daft to the point of madness as William had said, belonging to a family in service to the Carrs. Joe Marsden had been much mocked among the more privileged apprentices, talk that Archer had never liked.

'What of him?'

'He lost his father and brother in the siege. They died alongside Carr's boy Cuthbert. Old Carr keeps Joe on, but the lad's gone right radgie. He's one of them raving about you coming back, and with him it won't all be talk, so look, you'll need to gan canny.'

Archer brought to mind the tall, shock-headed onlooker who had stared so intently at him as he had passed through Bridge Gate. His distinctive, close-set eyes and wide, loose mouth placed him as Joe Marsden, grown into a brute of a man. He wondered if old Carr festered in the same kind of bitterness about his dead eldest son. It would certainly explain the vicious look he had given Archer under the castle's Black Gate that morning.

William began to rock back and forwards on the arms of the chair, struggling to rise.

'Stay, a while yet,' Archer said, looming over him. 'I beg you.' He pressed ahead, against the old man's mounting distress. 'Those same old families, Henderson, Anderson, they lost relatives in August just gone as well. On the Town Moor. I have seen the names. Do you know why?'

William's lips again moved in silence. He took another sip from his cup, setting it down with a trembling hand. 'Not only them ones,' he said. 'Others from families of means found themselves hanging alongside the Devil's whores.'

'You mean to say that they were not, all of them, truly witches?'

'I can only tell you what I saw, Master James. When they first sent out the bell-man they got back precious little of the ordinary wickedness that accuses lonely aad women. You'd expect some settling of scores, but there were only four or five taken then. What you'd expect, the sort we've all seen, odd ones, aad wives, ye knaa. Well, them women were brought to the Town Court and examined by the Scotsman, where they were all declared to be witches. The lecturers and many of the hotter sort of corporation men must have been left sore disappointed.' William had been growing in confidence, but now he gave Archer a sideways glance. 'You'll remember them well enough, Jenison and the others. All that ranting all over the place, about seeing sin everywhere and the like.'

Archer was barely able to return the old man's look.

'I remember. They always hated what they saw as the licentiousness and depravity of the town. They were convinced that they needed to root out such wickedness.'

'That's no excuse for stopping a man from singing or dancing a little, is it?'

Archer thought of the serious-faced denunciations which had been a commonplace in the meeting rooms of his youth.

'They never liked the inns. They saw drunkenness as a dreadful lure of the Devil, only enabling other sins.'

'Sin it is,' cackled William. 'It's a sin as well, is it not, to make false accusation against your fellow men and women?'

'That's a strong charge you are laying against them. I can see that they would have been outraged by such a modest response from the people, but these are good men, desiring only to do God's will.'

'Then you tell me, how such women came to hang?'

William had spoken with a force Archer had not imagined he still possessed. From the look of shock upon the old man's face, it had surprised even him. His scrawny fists clenched and unclenched. He looked anywhere but at Archer.

'I'm sorry, Master James,' he began. 'I never...'

'Do not think upon it. It gladdens me to see that you remain so hale.'

'Servants talk,' said William, newly calmed. 'So, I'm only getting this from what they say, mind. Now, there was plenty of them women in league with the Devil and few enough of them found innocent, that's for sure. But Master James, have you ever known of a witch trial without one single confession?' The old servant paled and again tried to rise. 'I'll need to get on. I've said my piece and more than I should. Gan to see my master, then leave, I beg you. Please, just listen to me. Forget them witches and get yourself out.'

'William, you have not yet mentioned Meg. Rest easy, I know that she did not hang with those other women, false as they may be or not. But she is gone from my uncle's house, and I must find her.'

'She lives. She always was strong, that one. Them of us who serve the big houses, we talk, like I said, about wor families, and Mistress Meg is said to have gone out of the town. I'm sorry Master James, truly sorry, I've heard no word as to where she is. It can't be near the town. Someone would knaa.'

'Thank you anyway. You have given me new hope and strength.'

'Ah, it's done me good to see you. But leave town tomorrow, will you? As soon as you've done with my master. Please tell me that.'

'I shall heed your warning, William, and look after myself. Do not fret. I promise to leave as soon as I can.'

Chapter 16

The four ragged stories of the cooperage leaned drunkenly above Archer, their rotting wood and flaked plaster betraying long ages of neglect. It was a place he remembered well as marking the dividing line between that public part of the town, in which business was conducted in the open, and the forsaken chares beyond, where all manner of vice could be found. Taking a final look back towards the river, he slipped into the dark fissure of Waterman's Entry.

Upon leaving The Blue Anchor, William had been unsteady, unaccustomed either to his frankness in the presence of a master or to such a volume of good ale. Archer had intended to escort him along the quay, beginning to move alongside, but the old man had brusquely sent him back. He had watched the servant stagger towards Sandgate until he reached Broad Chare and disappeared from view. When Archer had at last turned to go inside, the girl was waiting, the same solemn-eyed, pinched-faced girl who had stared so intently at him that morning. She stepped from out of the shadows into the same spot adjacent to the inn's yard gate.

His headache had at once returned. Wanting only to find a solitude to ease that tension, he had nonetheless beckoned to her to follow.

The initial ascent, straight and steep, was marked by an overpowering smell of human waste. Escaping this and following the child's detailed directions, he passed swiftly by several side alleys as well as two closed doors. Archer took the next entry on the right, built into a natural shelf in the slope and open on that side. From here, he could look down upon the roofs of the large tenements and warehouses clustered at this less heralded end of The Close.

He followed the straight passage up to and across the junction with the Long Stairs, continuing on eastwards. After only a dozen paces, Archer spun around at the intuition of an incautious step behind him. Dagger drawn and ready, he peered back along the path. For one heartbeat, he thought that he saw shining eyes in a pale face. The blade wandered, his heart leapt, and he nearly cried out for Meg. Then, the ripple in the darkness was gone. A moon that remained close to full, riding low in a clear sky, illuminated nothing more than the empty bank.

He lowered the weapon and tried to control his heaving breath. Another fiendish illusion. It was not fear that he felt. It was much worse. The visions of Meg, of the Ulster girl, of nameless others, were not only coming upon him more frequently, but also, just as now, more convincingly. He had the skills and strength to protect himself, but when was it, in these last months, that he had fallen from alertness into something weaker and much deadlier?

He must surely be unsettled by what William had told him, that was all. The old servant's suggestion that not all of the women who had died had been guilty of witchcraft was against all reason. But women of such high rank? And the new killings of which Wilkinson had spoken; were the two in some way linked?

Taking a last moment to scan the ends of the path, he inched forward until he came to an ill-fitting, slatted door. As the girl had said, this was marked, at shin-height, with three thick streaks of paint, stark against the wood. He knocked three times, then, after a pause, twice more. Seconds went by. Archer's scalp crawled. Had he mis-heard or poorly remembered the final instructions? Or perhaps she had omitted some crucial detail?

At last, slow footsteps sounded from beyond the gate. It was unbolted by a hooded man who held it half-closed and stood there, waiting.

'I have no bird in this fight,' Archer said, recalling the words carefully, 'but I have come to make a wager.'

The hood shook with a curt nod. Bolting the gate behind them again, but still without speaking, the man started down the short passage beyond, marked by a flickering light emanating from the opening at its end.

They emerged into a rough square of a yard, several paces across. The space was well lit, a series of lamps hanging above, each suspended from metal holders driven into the surrounding walls. It was warmed by three large braziers, as well as the bodies of a tightly packed crowd of men. Laughter, shouted exchanges, and excited cries filled the air. Above, a wide sailcloth had been strung, creating a canvas roof which magnified the noise, heat and light into a near-physical barrier.

Archer methodically surveyed his surroundings. Enclosed on all sides by the tenements and storage houses it served, the yard was not visible from either the neighbouring chares or the many smaller alleys interconnecting them. The makeshift roof similarly prevented any observer higher up the bank from seeing into the space. It was perfectly hidden. His only surprise was that, while he thought that he had traversed every corner of the town's back ways, this place was, to him, entirely new.

To one side, a row of tapped ale barrels sat upon trestle tables. On the other, guarded by two keelmen, an angry clacking and the raking of claws came from a row of wicker cages. In between, clusters of men gathered about sweating bet-takers. The crowd, drinking, smoking and loudly swearing, their faces reddened and blurred in the heat, milled around a low, central oval of dark brick, where the cockfighting would soon begin.

The guide tugged at Archer's cape. Entries, like that down which he had been led, opened onto each of the four sides. The man was directing him to one beyond the cockpit, leading, most likely, to the back of a house set halfway up the more respectable Castle Stairs. With a vexing sense of regret, Archer followed the hood into the blackness of this passage, pushed forward by the rising roar of the crowd as the first pair of birds made processional entry into the arena. The evening's main entertainment was imminent.

Chapter 17

Cloak pulled tightly about his neck, Archer judged the counting room to have been in use an hour or more earlier, but its coal fire was now all but smouldered out and the twin lamps set on the central worktable faltered and burned low. In the long minutes he had been waiting, the dankness had seeped all too easily in through the ill-fitting windows.

Two doors led off. The first, plain and sturdy, came from the out-house lined yard through which his guide had brought him. The other, high, ornate and brilliantly varnished, would lead, he imagined, to the other offices and public rooms of the place of business. Beyond its thick oak, he could discern no light, nor hear any voice. Had it been over-foolish to heed this summons? He had not hesitated once the girl had informed him that her message came from "she with the green cape you saw in Saint Nicholas' church today".

The panelled door clicked and opened. Through it stepped the same woman from the Armstrong bench, along with a much older companion who shared the same diminutive frame, solemn face and unusually large, brown eyes. The resemblance was only further enhanced by equally plain gowns, each cut unfashionably low upon the arms above thin cuffs of linen.

Close to, the younger of the two was even less substantial than Archer had thought. Tight cheekbones, combined with a small nose, offered her a winsome fragility. The sharpness of her jaw, however, retreating from a firm brow, took away whatever prettiness she might have had, replacing it with a strength deeper than beauty. Her dark eyes shone unsettlingly. She could not be called old, but was no longer truly young, perhaps like himself twenty-three or four. Moving forwards, she revealed an ineffectively disguised, left-sided limp.

The older woman appeared in almost every respect more robust. The nose was more prominent, the pursed lips fuller. In her, the same strong forehead seemed merely forbidding, while the eyes with which she studied Archer were a subtle shade lighter, and thereby unreadably cold. It was as if she was some wary animal assessing whether he, in turn, was predator or prey.

Upon their entry, Archer had risen. He stood before them, helpless. Momentarily, he even considered making his retreat out of the door at his back and fleeing their presence. Instead, he allowed them to sit before resuming his own place.

'I am Mistress Thompson. This is my daughter, Elizabeth,' said the elder. A dull sound reached them from somewhere at the front of the premises. Archer flashed a look towards the door, but the woman continued unhurriedly. 'It is nothing. The servants will not disturb us. Are you thinking of my husband, or perhaps of a son who would object to our meeting? There is none. This is my house, my own place of business.'

He tried to read what little he could from her gaunt face.

'You do not look like your sister,' said the daughter.

'You know my sister?'

'I have seen your sister on more than one occasion. I would not say that I knew her.'

'Meg, Margaret, you may know her as. My sister is alive?'

'I have not seen her since the last time I visited Newgate, which would be in high summer. Margaret Archer was not among the poor women who lost their lives upon the Moor. I was witness to their ending. Your sister was not among those hung.'

Archer trembled between relief and horror. The stench of his own brief imprisonment, a gut-wrenching mixture of filth and fear, temporarily overwhelmed his senses.

'Can you tell me where she is?'

'I do not know where any of them are. All now are gone.'

'Them? More than Meg?'

'Those who escaped the noose.'

'Then why have you called me here?'

Archer had not intended to shout, but his words resounded sharply off the walls. He was not sure how he had come to stand, let alone to have leaned in so close. Elizabeth paled, but met his intrusion in silence.

'If you have, finally, come back to seek your sister,' said Mistress Thompson, her voice crackling with menace, 'do not, I pray you, place any blame upon my daughter.'

For the first time in many years, a vision of his own mother, at once both vivid and indistinct, came into Archer's mind. He broke away and went over to the large window. In it he found only his hollow, enfeebled reflection.

Unbidden, Elizabeth Thompson spoke slowly and softly to the back of his uniform coat. 'We understood that an officer with a very personal interest in those who were held in Newgate was come to investigate their deaths. We understood,' she emphasised, 'that an officer was come to seek out the murderers of my sisters in Christ Abigail Walker and Sarah Turner. Were we this much mistaken, Ensign Archer?'

Archer turned back, forcing himself to look up. 'I beg your forgiveness. I want to find my sister very much. Perhaps, over much.'

'The Lord teaches us that there will never come a time too late for forgiveness, does he not?' said Elizabeth, her eyes shining with a tempered strength, like a good blade. 'Your sister had courage. She gave them nothing. Do you possess that same courage?'

Mutely, Archer sat. Mistress Thompson poured her daughter a measure of amber beer. The young woman drained the cup, cracking it down upon the table.

'You have never, I imagine, seen the inside of Newgate prison,' she said. 'I think it is beyond your very worst imaginings. Women of the streets, the distracted, and the lame held close alongside women from the very greatest houses along The Close. They were tumbled into the coldest, dampest cell that place can furnish, left there month upon month without any possibility of relief.'

'Why so long, before bringing them to trial?'

'They needed that time for the Scot to do his hellish work.'

'This Scot, he is the one called a pricker?'

Elizabeth Thompson's face took on a look of disgust. 'I shall not speak his name, but that is what he was paid to do, yes, what he called pricking. We saw the women afterwards, shaved, flesh burned, torn away, or opened up with his bodkins and needles. That word does not begin to encompass the tortures to which he and his assistants put them.'

Archer tried, and failed, not to picture Meg.

'The women had done their best to help one another,' she continued, 'your Meg foremost amongst them. But when we first saw them, they were so ragged, filthy and be-loused that there was little to tell one from the other. Elinor at first had us bind, bathe and re-clothe each of them.' Observing Archer's puzzlement, she paused momentarily. 'I run on too fast. Have you not heard, yet, of Elinor Loumsdale?'

'It is not a name I have heard of in any connection.'

The light in Elizabeth Thompson's eyes grew to a fierce blaze. 'What is it that you have been doing since you arrived in the town?'

He could not hide his shock. The woman reached out a hand towards him, as if to comfort a child. At her mother's terse whisper, it withdrew with a jerk. Mistress Thompson sat back and nodded to her daughter.

'Elinor,' said Elizabeth, 'organised a group of women to bring succour to those poor souls in Newgate. We visited them on a number of occasions, with food, salves and clothing. Elinor also brought to them something far more precious. Into that dreadful place, she brought them hope.'

She drew herself tautly upright.

'Elinor was working in all ways to secure their release. She ensured that no false witnesses could be brought. Those few whom they had forced to testify, the Lord, through Elinor, persuaded out of the darkness and into the way of truth and light. So, in search of false confession, their persecutors made use of the pricker's tortures. It was

110

Elinor who gave the Newgate women the strength to resist, to endure. She told them that it was they who possessed power over the Scot. She did not mean that the man could not hurt them. You should have seen their wounds. But she believed, and she made the women believe, that they could not be condemned without confession.'

'If Elinor Loumsdale was so persuasive, how did these women come to die?'

This time, it was Mistress Thompson who replied.

'The court determined to condemn them all on the say of the Scot alone, on the evidence of his pricking.'

'It is monstrous! There must have been more!'

'Must there? We have had enough of men telling us what must be.'

The washed-up remnants of a great roar reached them. Some peak of excitement must have been reached in the makeshift arena.

'We need to be done before their horrible sport is concluded,' said Elizabeth, 'so that you might leave under its cover. I have already wasted too much of what time we have.' With a final look towards the outer door, she hurried on. 'Of the women who helped Elinor in Newgate, five have already been killed, Sarah and Abigail included. Rebecca Weaver only last week. Several more have quit the town. Each of the murdered women was caught out alone, each found in some quiet alley.' She shivered. 'Each ripped open.'

Her breathing had become shallow, but her features remained firmly set.

'They had all been given warning. Rebecca was found barely alive, but she was able to say a few words before she died. The women are being accosted by two men and told to leave the town. One of the men is small, thin and dark. The other, quite different, is fair, very tall and broad. If the women do not heed the warning...' She faltered, leaving the thought incomplete.

Archer looked at Elizabeth more closely. 'These men Rebecca Weaver spoke of. They have come for you, haven't they?'

Elizabeth held her chin high, but for the first time he noticed her eyes dull. 'Yes, I have seen them for myself.'

'Yet you remain.'

'I will not be intimidated by them. You must find these men. You must stop them.'

Another muffled roar reached them from the cockpit yard. The women stood.

Archer scrambled for words which might meet her plea. Instead, the names of two of the executed witches, Elizabeth Anderson and Elianor Rogerson, came back to him. Both of them from good families within the wider Carr affinity. Old Carr, who had lost property and lost influence, was also closely linked with Elizabeth Dobson's family. If he were to do anything about these killers, he needed to understand more about the women held in Newgate, both those who were hung and those few who, like Meg, had escaped.

'What is it they fear so that they would kill for? What else happened inside Newgate?'

'I do not know,' replied Elizabeth. 'I pray for the wisdom to discover it.'

'Then I would speak with Elinor Loumsdale,' he continued.

'That woman was given to know how hopeless her cause had become,' said Mistress Thompson. 'She was herself threatened with the witch accusation and had to be taken out of the town and into the county. You cannot speak with her.'

'There must surely be some other who was involved with her work.'

A quick look passed between mother and daughter.

'Master Ord,' said Elizabeth.

'Ephraim,' replied her mother. 'Yes, Ephraim might know more.' She turned back to Archer. 'You and Elizabeth will meet again tomorrow, early, before your other business. You need do nothing. The same girl will come to collect you.'

'I promise you,' said Archer, as mother and daughter stood in the doorway. 'I shall uncover what is at work here.'

Elizabeth Thompson responded with a look of such compassion it might have been him upon whom the killers closed. 'Tomorrow,' she said. 'Look for the girl tomorrow.'

Chapter 18

Elizabeth and Mistress Thompson returned through the door into the main house as quietly as they had entered. Archer remained, looking blankly at its gleaming panels long after the close of the latch.

Such inertia was broken by the reappearance of the hooded guide. With him entered a piercing cold, together with another wave of crowd noise. Without a word, the man beckoned Archer back through the out-houses and into the cockpit yard. The crowd had grown and appeared more excited than ever.

'The neet's last fight,' the man hissed tightly. 'We must gan now.'

'Wait,' said Archer. The hood shrank away. 'I would stay awhile, to see this bout.'

The guide hunched forwards. He gave what was possibly a shrug. An arm, clad in a thick, greasy material, slid out from under the cloak and indicated the exit. Archer nodded, took a brief look back towards the pit, and already the man was gone.

After the dim book-keeper's room, Archer's eyes swam with the light from the many lamps and lanterns. Merchants, soldiers, working men, colliers and keelmen stood close together, fine fabric rubbing against harsh canvas, united in their excitement. The air was ripe with ale, tobacco, and the smell of the men's bodies, overtopped by a faint note of sickness.

Jostled on all sides, he worked his way towards one of the longer pit ends, allowing him a limited view of the arena's bloodstained, sanded earth. The pit master's assistants were still clearing away a mass of feathers, left from the previous contest. Of course, by this time of the year the birds would have commenced moulting, harvest being not only late for such a fight, but under normal circumstances an acknowledged rest period for the sport.

'How is it that there is such a match, out of the season?' he asked the labouring man stood next to him.

'James. James Archer. Just look at you.'

Lithe, clean-faced with naturally waved reddish hair, the man broke into the broadest of smiles. Archer responded in kind.

'Davey. Davey Wilson.'

Davey had come to Newcastle with the first Scots' army in 1640, but Davey had never gone home. It was not clear why. Some said that he had joined Leslie's force to escape a capital charge in Scotland, and that he could not return. Others, that he simply found a good niche in Newcastle for his peculiar talents and therefore had plenty for which to remain. Because Davey was a fixer. He had burrowed his way into every underworld scheme along the banks of the Tyne and could reportedly fix anything, from a shipment of wool to a cache of weaponry, to a discreet murder.

Since he was a Scot, and because he arrived with the Covenanter army, he had also fallen in with many in Newcastle's Puritan minority. Although Davey's conscience was his own business. Archer had always thought that Davey wouldn't have bothered, for his soul had King Charles enforced Catholicism itself upon both Kingdoms, so long as there was some profit in it for Davey, with a woman and a deep bottle at the end of the matter.

The two of them had become close as Archer had grown older. The fixer had taken the boy under his wing. He had revealed to James some of the hidden ways of the town. More than once, he had warned him off a particular place or person. Perhaps most of all, Davey had never once talked down to him. And the fixer, who had, Archer felt instinctively, abandoned a family of his own in Scotland, had also dearly loved Meg.

'How do you, Davey?' Archer took a glance about, but his grin remained. 'Working?'

'Aye, they try to stop the people's pleasures. You can see how that goes. My businesses thrive, a' the same.'

'You making good business here?'

'Let's no' talk about it now, James lad, eh? What about you? An officer, nae less.' He eyed the long scar. 'Wi' mair than that to show.'

Archer's mouth dropped. He looked steadily at his old friend. 'I am here to find Meg. That is all that matters to me.'

The crowd's cheering grew louder as the pit man inspected the clean-up and signalled approval to his helpers. They turned back to the cages lining the far wall.

A last few hurried to place another wager or to fill a cup with pale beer before the final bout commenced. Davey moved closer to Archer, face newly drawn.

'I'm sorry for you, James. What they've done and for it to be a Scot who did it, I'm ashamed, I am.'

'What do you mean? I know that she lives. Davey, tell me that she is alive.'

'Aye. She's safe. She's alive. Your uncle got her out.'

The import of Davey's words cut through Archer's relief. 'Weston helped her?'

Davey's eyes remained lowered. He began to move towards the side of the yard, beckoning Archer to follow him further away from the clamour.

'He brought her frae prison, had her taken out o' town. Listen, we both know your uncle's faults, but he stood by his duty. Brewer Weston's held to have paid out a pretty sum to gain Meg's release. Aye, that's what all the talk says. Your uncle had to pay to get her out.'

'I saw him only this morning. Why would he not have told me this? What else have you heard? Where is she, man?'

'I dinnae know where she is, but I do know she wasnae one of those hanged. As to your uncle, the pair of you never were the bosom friends, eh?' Davey's eyes flitted back to the pit and the heaving mass of men closed around it. He leaned in, shouting to be heard over the rising noise. 'No' now. No' here. Your Meg's alive. Hold to that. I'll dig about, find what mair I can. Day after tomorrow, I promise. Nae need to come look for me. I'll find you.'

The crowd roared at some hidden excitement. The whole courtyard shook.

'Why are they fighting these poor birds? It's not the season.'

'There's nae season nae more, wi' the cocks banned an' all. That's only the second fight's been had in the town since Candlemas. Mind, none of them we've seen tonight has gi'en any good sport. These pair won their first bouts easy.'

The volume of cheers grew yet higher alongside the increasingly anguished shouts of the odds setters, calling for last bets upon the two birds who were, even now, being borne overhead towards the arena.

'Tomorrow. Hold fast.' The fixer offered one last searching look at Archer and disappeared into the pulsing crowd.

Another roar burst from around the cockpit. Why, Archer wondered, had he ever determined to remain for such a barbaric display? He would have whipped his men, had they indulged in such an undisciplined cruelty.

The pit master called for quiet, at which the crowd, attentive to every intricate rule of the contest, quickly settled. At the opposing long ends, a pair of feeders, leather sheaths tied loosely around their forearms, readied the cocks. Each bird was suspended over the low brick wall, held a few inches above the gore of the floor. Already, stimulated by the blood-scent, both combatants were thrashing wildly about, their heads gyrating, desperate to escape their handlers and begin to fight.

Archer could only hear one bird's struggles, but he had a full view of the opposing creature. It was a huge, broad-chested monster with a plumage of russet and deepest brown. In the absence of the comb, which encumbrance all fighting cocks had removed as young birds, its dragon's face appeared oddly smooth, the unblinking eyes round and maddened. To its ankles had been fixed a pair of viciously spiked silver gaffles.

This was not a spectacle Archer wished to revisit. When he was thirteen, Weston had taken him to the last of four whole days of a Welsh Main event. Cockfighting in Newcastle had then been a major public attraction, one valued by Weston and his crowd of associates for the opportunity to drink, gamble, make business and find introductions to new, clean whores as an after-fight pursuit.

A long, drawn-out, knockout competition, a Main saw sixteen trained birds pitched one against the other to the death, each surviving cock going on to fight another round. An individual fight could last up to three hours, with the birds taking and delivering raking, lacerating blows from the hideous spurs.

His uncle had thought, presumably, that James needed this kind of toughening up. He also wanted to be able to show off to his fellows a commitment to Josiah Archer's heir. Unfortunately, young James had lasted less than ten minutes of the first bout.

The sight of the two viciously battling fowl, and in the end the exposure of a whole, torn-away eye, utterly overcame him. When he ran off into a corner to be violently sick, Weston's associates had merely laughed and raised a cup to the boy's weakness. But his uncle had remained ominously mute.

That night, the brewer had showered down such a series of blows from his hardwood stick that James had been confined to bed for three whole days, with only William permitted to tend him.

Determined not to give his uncle the satisfaction of hearing him cry out during the beating, he had stared instead at his sister. Meg had been forced to witness the punishment, kept pinned in place by Aunt Weston's trembling fingers. Her pale skin had burned. Her bright blue eyes, so like to their mother's, had filled with the tears James himself would not allow. But steadfastly, unstintingly, she had held his gaze through blow after brutal blow.

Archer squirmed at the memory as he looked around the crowd. None of Weston's old cronies appeared to be present tonight. Other than the fortunate encounter with Davey, he did not think he had been recognised by any in this company. He looked to the exit passageway. There was still time to make his way into the quiet of the alley before the birds were released.

He pushed through the last ranks of men pressing in upon the pit. The few heads remaining around the beer table and the gambling booths turned to consider the officer's early departure, but the pit master's scream for the feeders to release their struggling charges pulled all eyes back to the centre of the yard. Archer walked away from a growing cacophony.

He had barely reached the end of the exit passage before the shouts of encouragement developed a shrill edge of fear. A wave of pressure hit his back as the whole gathering reeled. Turning, he saw streams of watchmen bursting into the yard from the entries on its far side. The crowd scattered further, the watchmen fanning out in an attempt to bar the other exits.

Archer yanked open the slatted gate and ran, jinking right and taking a narrow turn leading further along the bank, soon finding himself in an outer alley he did not recognise. Formed of unbroken walls of rough stone two and more stories high. After several yards, it veered sharply to the left. Spurred on by the sound of boots hammering in pursuit, he leapt towards a planking door. It shuddered and shook, but the bolts held firm. Scrambling against loose stones, he flew the final few yards towards the next dog-leg. Taking the corner low and fast, he pushed hard off his left side, came back upright and was promptly felled as he careered at speed into the solid wall of a bald-headed watchman.

Dazed, he struggled to rise, whereupon the man gave a hoarse instruction, crudely telling him to remain where he was.

A face, dimly familiar, slender and refined compared to the bald man's blunt appearance, leant down close to his own.

'Jimmy Archer, returned to the town. What, I wonder, would bring you to this piss-hole of an alley on such a miserable evening?'

Archer's hand went straight to his sword.

'Now, Jimmy,' continued Elias Sanderson's reedy voice, 'we don't want that, do we?'

Chapter 19

They dragged him back down the alleys and into the cockpit yard. Fresh red slicks upon the packed earth provided stark evidence of the vigour with which the watch had done its work.

The crowd was gone, successfully fled or else apprehended by the raid and by now trudging warily towards the cells of the Town Court. Two watchmen guarded Archer, one of them the short but powerful bald man who had stopped him dead in the alley, the second taller, cursed by a face that was all nose and thick brows under a tangled mane of brown hair. Otherwise, only Sanderson, in his watch-captain's uniform, remained.

Archer had known Elias Sanderson as a youth. Two years older, born into a family of corn traders, Sanderson had proven to be a natural bully, casually cruel about Archer's dead parents ,and always eager to spread malicious gossip regarding Weston. Nothing, it seemed, from his sneer, had changed.

Sanderson gave a signal, and Archer's arms were wrenched back. The two men held him tight, less than a pace in front of their captain.

'I don't trust you, Jimmy.' The voice was a needling whine. 'I never did trust you. Such a shame for us both.'

The words were accompanied by a sharp punch under Archer's ribs. As he started to fall forwards, the men to either side caught him, holding him upright, face pushed against Sanderson's excited breath.

'You do not want to do this, Elias,' said Archer.

The watch-captain smiled as his arm moved back for another

strike. 'Oh, Jimmy. I think you'll find that I do.'

'Heselrigg would disagree.'

The man's arm remained drawn and ready. He let it smash forwards towards Archer's unprotected nose, but no blow landed.

'What is that supposed to mean, Jimmy?'

The other two men had fallen silent.

'I am commissioned by the Council. The governor is not going to enjoy hearing that an officer holding their warrant has been so treated.'

Sanderson kept his clenched fist less than an inch from Archer's face.

'What warrant?' he asked carefully, lowering his arm and stepping back.

Archer rolled his shoulders, glancing at the men pinning him. Sanderson inclined his head. They let Archer go but remained standing close behind. Ensuring that Sanderson could observe his every movement, Archer slowly reached into his pocket for the paper.

The watch-captain read it over rapidly.

'James Archer, working for the Council of State,' he growled. 'Who would believe such a thing could come to pass?'

Still holding the warrant, Sanderson paced about the empty yard, circling Archer.

'What I don't understand is what a man holding this warrant is doing, running away from such an illegal gathering.'

'It is my business to investigate the state of trade in the town, and any and all threats to it. Are you surprised that I should inquire in some low places? I was certainly interested to see so many men of significance gathered here this night.'

At the mention of the rank of some of those in the crowd, a shadow crept across Sanderson's face. If, as seemed to be the case, he was the man in charge of this raid, he would be concerned to establish the identities of the more notable attendees who had just been arrested. He would also, no doubt, be doubly anxious to finish up here, so as to get back to Sandhill and be able to arrange releases where it was politic, or simply profitable.

'Give me back the warrant and I shall say no more.'

Sanderson re-read the paper. 'Even if that is the case, it doesn't explain why you were so eager to run. What is it you're investigating?'

Archer smiled. 'In my business, Elias, which I am sure is in many ways no different to yours, it is better not to be seen or known. It is natural that I should not want to be detained, as I am now.'

'That's not good enough, Jimmy. If you're sneaking about my town after good men who stayed loyal, I think it's very much my business.'

'You are mistaken. I have no interest in pursuing the good men of the town. I do have a further commission concerning the witch trials. No more.'

Each of the three men cracked broad smiles, Sanderson's widest of them all. 'Ah yes,' he said, 'we had good sport over that. We enjoyed seeing the legs dancing on the Moor, didn't we, lads? Especially those belonging to the pretty young ones.'

The two watchmen barked a series of short, cuffed laughs.

Sanderson's flat, grey eyes looked directly into Archer's. 'The inquisitions were quite a spectacle as well, you know. That Scotsman, he knew just what a crowd wants. A real show, he put on, stripping those whores naked, showing us all their corrupted flesh, darting into them with his bodkins, right there in the open court.'

The others resumed their lickspittle mirth. Sanderson, grim-faced, approached closer. 'They cried out for shame and pain. Your bitch of a sister most of all.'

Archer struggled to master his urge to hit the man. Aware that he was close to losing that self-control, he tried another tack.

'If you are still concerned, I suggest that you accompany me to the castle tomorrow morning. I am due to meet there with Captain-Lieutenant Draper. He is on the governor's staff and will be glad to confirm my position and right to investigate within the town.'

Sanderson's smirk fled. Flickers of anxiety passed behind

his eyes. He hurried to return the warrant and step back, as if Archer were infectious with the sweat.

'You can go now. But mind out. I'll be sure to keep a close watch on you.'

Archer stooped to pick up his weapons-belt, which the watchmen had removed and cast aside. Carefully, with an eye upon the others, he inspected both dagger and sword, found them unharmed, and strapped the belt back about his middle. Only then did he finally turn and make to leave.

He had just reached the haven of the exit passage when Sanderson called after him. 'You were too late, Archer, coming back. Too late to save that pretty sister of yours. I saw her hanged myself, alongside the other devil spawn. She didn't look so pretty then.'

Chapter 20

After a night in which sleep was broken into shards by the image of Meg dangled upon the scaffold, eyes and tongue distended, face swollen, skin lividly discoloured, Archer awoke in a trembling sweat to a bright morning over the quay. He took in gulps of cold air, clean from the inland hills, allowing it to wash his terror away.

He reached up and touched the bruise on his left cheekbone, straining, as he did, the muscles of his stomach where the watchmen had beaten him. A part of him had known, even as he had turned back into the yard and advanced on Sanderson, how futile the gesture would be. He had not got within yards before, signalled by their captain. Both had stepped across.

Once the taller of the two had taken him full in the midriff with a thick cudgel, the shorter, bald second had immediately followed up with a heavily gloved blow to his falling face. Then, just as the first was readying a kick, Sanderson had called them off. He would be able, Archer supposed, to justify some violence, even against the warrant-carrier, but would not wish to have to explain away further injury. Instead, the man had satisfied himself with a cold repetition of his injunction, that he would be keeping close watch.

It was a lie.

Archer was certain of that.

Had he not just seen the documents?

Had William not, only the previous evening, confirmed Meg's survival? And Davey and Elizabeth Thompson had each said the same.

No, Meg had not been executed alongside those other fourteen women. She was one of the six who had escaped the noose.

Surely, it was no more than a vicious lie, born of Sanderson's humiliation.

He was sickened from all of the lies. Sanderson, Wilkinson, William, Pearson and the town officials, every one of them was hiding something. Every last one had tried to steer him in some particular direction. Their words crowded in his head, and he could make no sense of their many contradictions.

Damnation to them all!

He repeated the oath out loud. It escaped through the window and was borne away upon the dancing breeze. He cursed again, with relish. If only it could be so easy to slip the ties binding him to Skippon and to Deane, never to return.

Through his dressing, and later as he breakfasted, a little of that lightness persisted. The new morning promised the chance to unravel the knots in which he was entangled. He had high hopes of Draper, whom he would attend later. Before then, he would call upon Henry Dawson at his house on Spicer Lane, the one place in Newcastle where Archer could expect a warm and genuine welcome.

As soon as he set foot back out of the private parlour, he was flushed with an even simpler pleasure. Outside the kitchen doorway stood the pinched-faced girl. She looked up at him with her unmoving, sombre expression, ready, as Mistress Thompson had promised, to escort him to Ephraim Ord, and the prospect of a reacquaintance with Elizabeth.

Chapter 21

'Sixteen men lost in the last year. Burned alive in underground explosions. This device could have saved so many.'

Tall and thin, with unkempt, reddish-brown hair and marine blue eyes which creased with enthusiasm and glinted with curiosity, Ephraim Ord looked down imploringly at Archer.

The device before them was as large as a saddle. Ord had called it his lamp-engine. It comprised three sections. The first, a heavy leather bellows, fed into a lead water reservoir forming the base. Above this rose a bulbous glass tower, within which, surrounded by a second, inner, glass encasement, was fixed an ordinary pewter candle holder.

'When the bellows are pumped, the air the candle burns is forced up through the water. Light from the flame is magnified by the shaping of the outer glass. The ensuing foul residues cannot then escape, and become contained here,' explained Ord, indicating a jar-like protuberance on top of the glass tower. 'The second glazed layer ensures that the naked flame does not ignite the infernal vapours. But I have found no mine owner willing to employ it. Not even Mister Blackett.'

'Why do you speak of William Blackett in particular?'

'Blackett is not like the old owners, blindly groping their way into deep mining. Across all of his interests, he puts a part of his profits into experimentation. He has been a good patron. In his Wrekenton pit is installed a water engine of my design capable of keeping clear the tunnels up to eighty feet underground.'

'They are digging that deep?'

'You have been gone how long? More than six years, you said. Listen, the Hostmen's success has increased demand four or five-fold. The shallow drifts cannot supply that. It is not now uncommon, out towards Elswick or Dunston, to find newly driven shafts running to more than four hundred feet.'

'But yet he will not use your device?'

Ord sighed. 'You can see how large and heavy the engine is. Its use would require much additional digging, the tunnels they allow for being as narrow as a man is wide. That extra work costs. The bellows need to be kept in motion at all times. Even the use of a pit boy for the task is expensive. Blackett, at least, listened.'

The opening door cut off Archer's furrow of anger. Elizabeth Thompson entered, alongside the pinched-faced girl.

Earlier, escorting Archer up from Quayside to the large first floor workshop overlooking Saffron Yard, the child had not loosed her lips. Now, her face was bright and her eyes sparkled. Elizabeth looked upon her tenderly.

The engineer approached the girl, who at once fell back into her solemnity. 'Sophie, do not linger. You will see Elizabeth again soon enough. I need you to go now and fetch me that lens from Master Eriksen.'

At a gentle touch from Elizabeth, the girl relented and left.

'My only child and the help to all my work,' said Ord, more to the closing door than to Archer. 'The errand will not take long. We must be quick.'

Archer waited for Elizabeth to remove the green cape. He took it from her and laid it carefully across the least cluttered section of workbench. Only when the woman was settled on one of the engineer's high stools did he leave her side and begin to address Ord.

'Tell me what you know of Elinor Loumsdale.'

Ord's equine face lengthened further. His pale eyes clouded. 'A remarkable woman. Such determination. Such force.' He swept an arm around the chaos of the workshop. 'For all this,

I must pay for my bread.' His eyes slid towards the tall side windows overlooking Saffron Yard. 'Printing is one of my most regular sources of income. That is how I came to work with Elinor. I printed the handbills for her petitioning.'

Ord had used Loumsdale's Christ-name alone, exactly as had Elizabeth the previous evening. What kind of woman was this Elinor?

The engineer had gone over to a tall cabinet. Having searched through its many shelves, he returned with a few sheets of printed paper.

Archer looked at the heading on the upmost sheet. '*Satan's worke sette inn treyne by the magistracies of this towne*'. The second page declared '*Eliz. Dobson is innocente of all but beeying a goode and a godly woman*'. Each page contained further assertions of the innocence of one or more of the accused. He scanned all three sheets again, searching in vain for mention of Meg.

Ord hovered, palpably excited.

'Just as in London,'he said,'it is women who distribute pamphlets and newsbooks about the town. Elinor's work was left in every tavern and place of business. A portion they passed on to ordinary townswomen, goodwives and servants, so as to beset the men.'

'The corporation men,' said Elizabeth, standing, 'could not rest within their own chambers without discovering one of these papers. They could not move out of doors without encountering women pleading the prisoners' cause. Whatever their rank or position, these men all depend upon the labour of women. There was barely a cook or a laundress, nor even the youngest maid in service, who did not support the siege upon their every waking hour.'

Archer read the sheets in his hands again, paying even closer attention to the names.

He was sickened by the description of Alice Hume's arrest. The old woman had been publicly beaten in the Kale Market for begging upon the Sabbath, before being hauled off to

Newgate. Other pieces provided graphic descriptions of the sufferings of Katherine Coulter and Mary Pots. But there were also sections related to Maria Cole, April Grainger and Anna Robson, none of whom had been named upon the death list. Here were three of the five Newgate women freed along with Meg. Only two more names to find.

Archer looked over to the windows, judging the time. He was already going to have to run to fit in his call upon Dawson's house.

'Do you have more of these sheets?'

Ord shook his head. 'I should not have kept those. Why?'

'This Cole woman escaped, as did Anna Robson and April Grainger. I need to speak with them. And I need the names of the others.'

'We'll need time.'

'We have none.' Two names. Thought Archer, how difficult could it be? 'Mistress Loumsdale could not have worked alone in this. Who else can I talk to?'

Ord blinked back. 'Young Bracewell would know. He worked a rotation at the court.' He turned to Elizabeth, tongue flickering nervously across his lips. 'Bracewell would help, if it was you who asked him.'

Archer had not seen Elizabeth Thompson smile before. He flinched to see how it lightened her whole face.

'I will go to him now,' she said. 'Meet me in the main market a little after the start of the dinner hour. I will make sure that we can talk there safely.'

Chapter 22

The Dawson house lay three-quarters of the way up the steps. Full fronted and high, it was so old that its sagging upper storeys might have been trying to reach across to rest themselves upon the shoulders of the equally bowed-down building opposite.

Archer knew how it felt.

Before he drew his eyes away from the weary overhangs, he noticed the familiar bound-staves motif to have been freshly carved into a heavy beam. Of course, Henry Dawson was become an alderman, and the symbols of that authority were everywhere. It came as a relief when the door was answered.

A servant glanced at the Council papers, listened to his introduction and showed Archer into the public parlour which had, in his youth, doubled as meeting hall. He took in the pure light and simple furnishings of the familiar room. Here, more than anywhere, was where he had been imbued with a strength of faith in the cause that had sustained him through so many dark years of war.

He would slip away, after the end of formal service at Saint Nicholas, to meeting houses such as the one in Dawson's parlour. A very different sort of preacher, many of them men without formal education, training or ordination, would expound upon a sermon or a passage of scripture, drawing out its implications for the current disputes.

There were times in these meetings when he felt the spirit of the Lord fill him with a special passion, the sense that he was being chosen, fitted out to do God's work, a work that would have nothing to do with the future of rigid duty and loyalty, both to his family and to his class, which his uncle had planned.

Mixed together among men, and even women, of all ranks, the young James had kept his habitual silence, but had listened with a still intensity, enraptured by the sense of togetherness all about him. It was a glimpsed vision of a new world awaiting birth.

Archer could remember the thundering declarations in this room that Newcastle was 'a place of sin', awaiting a cleansing heavenly fire. The Puritan preachers, or at least the families who had sheltered and supported them, were in charge of the town now, backed by the force of the Commonwealth and in league with the military governor, Heselrigg. What further cleansing had they been able to put into force?

He was so deep in these thoughts that he was startled when the private door to the family rooms opened and through it entered not Henry Dawson, but a thin, soberly dressed gentlewoman in middle age. She stopped, peering at Archer through accusing, hooded eyes.

Recovering from the shock of her entrance, he offered a slow bow. 'Mistress Dawson, it is a pleasure to see you after so long.'

Henry Dawson's sister only stared at him more intently, her mouth becoming the thinnest slit in a sharp, sallow face.

'It is James Archer. I was often here when I was a boy. You were always most generous to me.'

He fell silent as the woman approached and looked closely up at him.

'The Lord shall cut off all flattering lips,' she shrieked. 'I know you for what you are, demon, and why you are come. You are here to drag me down into sin and corruption, like your sister before you.'

She threw herself bodily against him, tiny fists battering at the front of his uniform coat. Archer tried to step away but was trapped, pinned against the sturdy side table. He tried to speak, reeling against a stream of the woman's spittle, but the attack did not relent.

Henry Dawson's voice sounded from the family doorway. 'I can give you five minutes, not more. And that only because of your warrant.'

Before the alderman had stepped fully into the room, he stopped dead, looking upon the scene in surprise. 'Jennie. What is amiss that you should treat our guest so?'

The woman let go of Archer and glared back at Dawson, teeth bared, colour heightened. The tall servant who had entered the room behind the alderman moved swiftly to her side. With a gentle, practiced ease he looked down into her eyes, took her by the arm, and steered her towards the door. She went along with him readily but, just before they reached the threshold, looked back, eyes fixed upon Archer.

'None shall save you,' she hissed. 'I know that my redeemer liveth, but you shall perish and rot, and there shall be none left to mourn for your passing.'

Henry Dawson waited until after the servant and the woman had disappeared into the outer hall before he turned to his unbidden guest.

Tall, strong in body and in mind, forever with a ready smile and eyes that wrinkled with pleasure taken in every small thing, Dawson had been worshipped by the young Archer. The hair, closer cropped than ever, was now speckled with grey. The shoulders had become a little stooped. The eyes, adding to a pervading sense of burden, appeared duller, the creases around them more downturned. But Dawson's inner force persisted. The finesse formerly marking his features may have coarsened, but the alderman remained strikingly handsome.

Of course, thought Archer, he, too, had changed very much over the intervening years. The older man was peering at him, as if at a stranger.

'James Archer? I should not have known you. Lad. Look at

you.' Dawson's face lit up into an open smile and his voice lifted. 'Had I only known it was you. I am sorry, truly, for my sister. She has not been herself this past time. We pray for her restoration.'

'I am simply glad to see you again, Mister Dawson. I am greatly sorry for your sister's trials. I shall join my prayers to yours.'

His host eyed Archer uneasily, taking in the long scar and the new bruise on the other side of his face. 'I had heard that you served in the army. Is it true you were promoted by General Cromwell personally, in Ireland?'

'Yes, Mister Dawson, in Ireland.'

'It is God's labours that are being done there. We try to do His work here as well.'

'It is about that work that I would speak with you, Mister Dawson.'

'Please, sit. You will always be welcome here, James. I am sorry, for as I said I cannot tarry long, but let us see how I can help.' He gave another heartfelt smile. 'You do carry the Council's warrant, after all.'

Both men sat. Before Archer could speak, Dawson was loosing an excited flow of words, punctuated with expansive arm movements.

'Education, relief for the meretricious poor, the provision of doctors for the body and doctors for the soul. The work of the Lord we have so long desired is at last well under way in our Newcastle, James. It is a new birth for the people. Do you know what they call the town now, my boy? The Eye of the North for God's Commonwealth. So far have we come from the dark days when the town laboured under untruth and idolatry and suffered plague, starvation and all worldly torments as the mark of God's displeasure. A terrible and a just reward for its iniquity. But you will remember lad, you remember how it was? The nest of vipers who betrayed us has been expunged by a purifying fire.'

Archer itched to respond, but Dawson gushed on.

'I am right glad to see you again and to be able to share this with you. Do you remember all of the things we used to talk about, when the godly gathered in these chambers? With the help and support of the Lord, we are bringing them into very being. Say it, if we can arrange the time, and I can show you the new hospital. We have just appointed a principal master to the grammar school. Master Ritschel, he is an Oxford man, most learned, who has brought the stoutest discipline.'

At last, the alderman paused.

'I thank you,' said Archer. 'That is sweetness in my ears. But it is not, alas, what the Council has charged me to report upon.' Pained to see the pleasure flee Dawson's face, he hurried on. 'I shall be sure that all of these good and godly works are understood and appreciated in Whitehall. You have my word as a Christian.'

Dawson shot a short look towards the door before sitting back, spread wide. Now there was no hurry to his manner. 'Then, James, tell me, what else can I help you with?'

'I, that is the Council, wishes to understand more relating to the recent witch trials.'

'Go on.'

Archer hesitated, gripped by the awful sense that he had let down his old mentor in some terrible manner. 'I understand that as many as fifteen were executed upon the Moor this August past.'

'What of it?'

'Sir, I have visited the town clerk, also the Court. Things there are not as they should be. The names of those executed at Gallowgate have been retained, but that is all. The trial records, evidence and testimonies have disappeared, along with any record of six women who escaped hanging.'

Archer sheepishly cut short his gabbling, before which Dawson had visibly hesitated.

'These are difficult times,' said the alderman. 'There have been many convulsions, in the town, as in the country at large. Records can go astray.'

Dawson's regretful expression at least reassured Archer. 'I understand. It can happen. Then, one other question, if I may?'

The older man looked back at him warmly.

'The corporation, I understand, sent for and paid this Scot, this pricker. What reason, in particular, was there to take such an action?'

'Not my decision, James. This was done last year, after my time as mayor.'

'But please, I implore you to help me. You must have been a party to the decisions taken. I know not where else to turn.'

'You, of all people, know the depths of depravity into which the town had fallen. Drunkenness, wantonness, Papist idolatry and the persecution of the just. Do you wonder that we should make attempt to root out this evil in our midst?'

Archer offered only a taut shake of his head. Dawson exhaled. When the alderman looked up, his eyes were misted, his face pale, the whole piteous.

'James, it was a terrible time. Can you imagine how it felt to find that there were so many women, including those we knew and trusted, who had fallen into the most desperate sin? I can barely speak of it. The whole people walking in fear. Good families ripped apart by the corruption within. It was a most grievous punishment.'

Archer watched on, captivated and unsettled in equal measure.

'That old Newcastle we knew, that worshipped Satan, it is gone. The town is reborn. It is a beacon of hope and of light in the darkness of sin. You will have seen for yourself how there is good order in the streets? You understand the nature of the beast, that uses false images and doctrine to inveigle his wicked snares into the hearts of the people. The sufferings of the witch trials were a necessary test of our strength and of our faith. Of what we would be prepared to sacrifice to fulfil His commandments. Together, we shall move mountains to bring about the time of His glory. The Scots-man, for all his faults, was able to help us in this difficult task.'

'But Mister Dawson, I have seen the list of those killed. Surely some of those who perished were no witches, but women of good families?'

The older man appeared to wrestle between doubt, confusion,

and anger. 'The Devil desires most of all to corrupt the closest servants of the Lord. Some of the unfortunate women he seduced strayed from the very best of lives. Do you imagine that sin of such magnitude can be confronted and destroyed without the need for sacrifice? Do you think that it could easily be excised? That the fight given to the godly should be anything other than of the very hardest?'

'Many of those women came from the most godly of families.'

Dawson sprang to his feet. 'False accusations made by damned Papists! They rightly fear the wrath of the Lord and the reckoning which is fallen upon them. Some, in their wicked ignorance, laid these false charges against good and godly women. My own sister Jennie. Did you not see her? Could you not see how she is? Thanks to the grace of God, we were able to secure her release. Mark me, we have not forgotten, and they shall reap as they have sowed.'

He came to a halt, panting with emotion. Archer too had stood, stunned by the revelation that Mistress Dawson had been among the accused.

'Forgive me, boy,' said the alderman with new gentleness. 'Forgive my manner. I do not like to speak of it.'

Archer burned for shame. 'Praise the Lord's mercy in delivering your sister.'

'Her wits come and go since the ordeal. I should be grateful, I know, that she has good days when she knows herself. Even at those times, she is pursued by pain and a false guilt, believing still that the Almighty seeks to punish her. A part of her remains imprisoned with those godless devils.'

'You will know that my own sister was also suspected. Her name is not on the list of those who were executed, but it was said to me last night that she was hanged upon Gallowgate hill. Tell me that it is not so.'

'James, your Margaret did not hang. She was no witch. Who says otherwise? I shall have them sorely punished.'

Archer shook his head. 'No, I am sure it was just a mistake. Perhaps a cruel one, but all I desire is to find Meg. Is there anything you recall which might help me?'

Dawson stepped over and opened the public door. He called out of it, turning smoothly back into the room with a regretful shake of his head.

'She was not hung, and I am certain she is gone from the town. I know not where. I only wish I could help you more.'

The servant had returned and now stood in the open doorway.

'As I said,' Dawson continued, ignoring the man, 'I have pressing business to attend. May God be with you in your search for your sister.'

Dawson squeezed his hand upon Archer's upper arm, a stricken look upon his face.

'The ways of the Lord are strange to us, James, but we must keep faith, wherever they may lead us. Pray with me a minute, before you go.'

Archer barely heard the words of the psalm, even as his lips followed Dawson's slow, even recitation.

'"My soul melteth for heaviness: strengthen thou me according unto thy word. Remove me from the way of lying: and grant me thy law, graciously. I have chosen the way of truth".'

Chapter 23

Captain-Lieutenant Draper's corner room in the castle keep was surprisingly airy and open, lit by the presence of several large windows hewn through the walls. A log fire blazed in a deep hearth. Draper rose from behind a large, orderly desk, offering as he did another of his welcoming smiles.

Archer was struck anew by the man's youth. He could be no more than twenty-six or seven. During the wars, promotion had frequently come early for officers in regiments such as Heselrigg's Lobsters, deployed, as it had been, at the forefront of so many significant battles. Even allowing for this, it was exceptional to have reached the position of captain-lieutenant at such an age.

'Ensign Archer, I hope that weasel Pearson was able suitably to assist you.'

'The governor's secretary was helpful, in so far as he was able.'

Draper steered them over to the desk, sat behind it and indicated a chair for Archer.

'Tell me then, the ways the little man chose not to be forthcoming.'

Archer looked directly into the clean blue of the captain-lieutenant's eyes. 'My instructions from the Council are to report on the recent events relating to witchcraft which have afflicted this place, especially regarding any threat it may have posed to the trade in coals. Secretary Pearson was most forthcoming with information relating to the health of that trade, with an accuracy I was later able to confirm.' The two men shared a look of amusement across the desk. 'He had less to tell, about the witch accusations themselves.'

'And did he offer any justification for such reticence?'

'Pearson says he is not long come into the town and so has no personal insight to offer.'

Draper's face dulled. 'Yes. That at least is true. I would take care, as you did with your investigation into the trade, to test sorely every word Pearson says. The man has wheedled his way close into the governor's affairs in the short time he has been in post, but he looks only to his own interest. It has caused some discontent among my brother officers.'

Draper stretched out his long limbs, then half stood.

'I apologise, some refreshment?'

'Please, no, I ate well in my lodgings.'

Archer was unsure how to proceed. Draper having invited him to this meeting, he had planned to wait for the older man to take a lead. None seemed to be forthcoming. 'The Council,' he said, carefully, 'certainly requires me to report with more insight than Secretary Pearson was able to furnish. They have expressed a particular concern about the trial and dispatch of the witches.'

'I confess some surprise that the Council should be so concerned with the deaths of a few old women and slatterns.' Draper having sat back again, the fingers of his left hand beat out an impatient tattoo upon the desk's wooden surface.

'Nevertheless, those are my orders. With warrants issued alongside them requiring assistance. Shall I?'

'There's no need. I do not see that there is anything of significance to say, but I will gladly share with you all that I know.'

'Is it truly the case that the governor's administration retained no records of the proceedings? Pearson told me that this was entirely a civil affair.'

Draper appeared to ponder this before responding.

'There are no records here in the castle. I may not trust the man, but I do not think, in this at least, that Pearson has played you false.'

Archer let out a long breath, unsure now whether he wanted to ask more of the captain-lieutenant, fearful of what he might hear.

'Perhaps you can still help me. You were there, you said. How did the trials come to be? Where did the accusations come from?'

'In the ordinary way. The poorer type see the work of the Devil in every misfortune. The town magistrates invited the people to denounce witches. They even brought in a Scottish witchfinder. You know how it is up there? Hundreds after hundreds of women killed, most of them burned.' His gaze lazily followed the low cloud scudding by the window. 'It must make for a good spectacle. Quite the warning.'

Returning his attention to Archer, Draper sighed. 'I apologise. I am getting ahead of myself. The accusations were, then, what you would expect. It is unusual for the Scottish practice to have spread south. That is where the corporation comes in. This witchfinder, the one they called a pricker, had done his work in the town of Berwick, some eighty miles north from here and hard on Scotland.'

He waited for a response, but Archer remained quiet. Draper went on. 'Well, the Newcastle magistrates must have been impressed by that, because they sent two of the town sergeants off to fetch him here. When the Scot arrived with a pair of his own miserable attendants, he agreed to be hired to prove the witches' guilt and was promised payment for each one uncovered.'

'I read of this in the Guildhall. Twenty shillings for a conviction? So much would tempt one of the saints on earth to denounce the innocent.'

Draper offered only a curtailed laugh in return, even as his fingers once more began to tap out their insistent beat.

'Nevertheless, that was the sum agreed. When the man, Kincaid he was called, was established in the town, the Council sent their bell-man out through the streets, calling for all that knew any woman for a witch to speak and for the accused to be sent for and tried.'

Archer held up a hand for Draper to pause.

'What occasioned the hiring of this Kincaid in the first place? Were there accusations already abroad?'

'There are always neighbours willing to make such accusation. Not least in this town, where so many strangers are newly entered in. In truth, I do not know whether there was any special purpose behind the hiring of the Scot, or if the corporation simply took a natural advantage of his presence nearby. Does any of that really matter?'

Archer recalled all that Elizabeth Thompson had told him of the pricker's methods and considered that for the accused, possibly even for Meg, the employment of Kincaid had clearly mattered greatly. But he determined to pass Draper's comment by.

The captain-lieutenant looked away, his hand stilled. 'I do not remember many of the details, if ever I knew them. I was much engaged elsewhere at the time of the executions. Nor was I myself present at the trials, come to that. I spend much of my time about these counties on the governor's business. They went before a grand jury, of course, then before the magistrates at the Summer Assizes. That was all a formality. The Scot provided many proofs of guilt.'

Archer had seen such events before and they had stayed, uncomfortably, with him. The raising of accusations. The interrogations. The inevitable verdicts and sentences. The women, twitching out the last of their lives in agony. He could not allow it to affect him. Becoming angry with Draper would neither further his report to London nor help him find Meg. He considered asking the captain-lieutenant directly about his sister, but before he could interject, the man reached his own blunt conclusion.

'They all died, anyway. Not burned, of course, hung under good English law, up in the usual place outside the walls.'

'The corporation men of this town were not formerly such

hot prosecutors.'

'You will have to ask that of them yourself.'

The smallest hint of boredom in Draper's response unsettled Archer, but he persisted.

'I understand that there has been much change within the ranks of the corporation, to the Hostmen and the Merchant Adventurers.'

Draper looked across the desk, a new, sharp, edge catching his voice. 'This town was a hotbed of support for the man of blood. Several of the leading families supplied weapons directly to his armies, weapons which killed our comrades. Of course, there have been places lost, persons imprisoned. It should have been more. Lilburne's own brother turned his coat, and it cost two dozen good men's lives to reduce him in Tynemouth castle.'

He grinned, but without his earlier warmth. 'At least he had the grace to die there and save us the task later. I had the honour of skewering his treasonous hide myself.'

'So, place and position lost, but not by all?'

'What does this have to do with the witches?'

'I am trying to reconnoitre the ground, as any good officer would. The Council, you will understand, requires from me a full and detailed report.'

'Of course,' replied Draper, breaking out into a more rueful smile. 'I would do the same in your position. These days.' He hesitated and glanced towards the window again. 'Well, you understand, knowing who to trust.'

Archer simply inclined his head. Draper allowed his relief to show.

'Very well. Most of the merchants here are canny. They always knew that the war would be decided by money, so they kept themselves away from the closest councils of the enemy. These, naturally, remain in position. They are needed to maintain the smooth trade in coals to London and the rest of the country. The governor has discovered that the connections between the pits and the transport of the coals block up unless they are, well, unless they are properly lubricated.'

Stung when Archer failed to respond to the sardonic raising of his brows, Draper continued impatiently.

'The monopoly itself, you will find, is in many ways unchanged and with it the corporation. As to who, there are men who have always been loyal to Parliament, but there are others, such as the Carr family and the Greys. Both are still central, while Shafto is everywhere. Although how the Carrs managed to maintain their place in the town, I cannot understand. I know they have been more than generous to my lord Heselrigg. Thanks to the governor, you can reassure the Council that London's coal is safe.'

Draper's mouth twisted into a collusive leer. 'Of course, Cromwell's needs in Scotland have provided a further boost to the town's prosperity. We supply the army through Shields and Berwick, but all of the contracts come through the Sandhill. We aren't too fussy who we deal with, so long as we get a good deal. You know, boots, food, beer.'

Archer could almost taste the captain-lieutenant's mixture of disdain for the families with whom he was forced to deal, combined with his satisfaction in taking his inevitable cut for contracts and introductions.

He had emphasised his last word with a quiet relish. Did he not know, or had he forgotten, Archer's connection to Weston? Perhaps Draper recalled it all too well and the beer contract was one of his particular perks.

'The recovery of the town is no thanks at all to the keelmen,' said the captain-lieutenant, his voice uplifted. 'Now in that regard, I am happy to report, we have been able to help the corporation. A taste of military discipline has tamed more than a few. As you are interested, and for your reconnaissance, perhaps you would like to see?'

Archer followed Draper from the warmth of the office onto the damp chill of the keep's main stair. As they neared the double doors exiting onto Castle Garth, the captain-lieutenant slowed, a marked change overcoming him. He stood taller upon the last of the corner steps, pushed his shoulders fully back and glanced down the front of his uniform before coming to a rigid attention at odds with his ordinary languor.

Joining him on the tapering stone, Archer moved into a similarly respectful position, finding himself just a few feet away from the robust, sour figure of Sir Arthur Heselrigg.

The governor looked at both officers, awkwardly towards the large, bluff-faced civilian he had been escorting out, and then back to Draper and Archer with unabashed appraisal. 'Draper. You are taking all good care of the ensign here?'

It had not seemed that Draper could become any more regimental, but at this address his chin jutted out more prominently and his backbone stiffened yet further. 'Yes, Sir,' he replied in a clipped, high bark.

A ruffled collar of finely worked lace was secured about Heselrigg's neck by a thin, black, silk bow. It rustled unsettlingly as the governor turned his full attention upon Archer. There was an incongruity between the fastidiousness of his apparel and the lumpen, blotched face which overtopped it, but there was no doubting the piercing intelligence behind the man's cool, mossy brown eyes.

'Ensign Archer. Does my aide speak true? Has he been of full assistance in your quest?'

'Sir,' snapped Archer, teetering on the step.

Sir Arthur's smile was a narrow one, ill-suited to the thick lips from which it emerged. It receded quickly. 'We have heard of your work in Ireland on the day General Cromwell finally broke Drogheda. It was a fine action, and yours a part well played. I am pleased to meet you.'

Archer mumbled a few words in response, saved only by the big civilian coming to join the governor, interjecting in a quiet Newcastle accent. 'Would you introduce me, Sir Arthur?'

Heselrigg's face puffed up and reddened. 'Yes, naturally. Captain-Lieutenant Draper you know, of course. This is Ensign Archer. You should be most interested in his presence. Archer is sent here by the Council to report back upon the state of trade.'

The Newcastle man's small, pebble-grey eyes peered intently at Archer through long, thick lashes. 'William Blackett,' he said. 'For my part, I can find no complaint. You may tell the Council that the trade proceeds most satisfactorily, and that Sir Arthur here merits all of the respect which is his due. Tell them. Tell them that.' Blackett nodded sideways at Heselrigg before turning back to the open doorway.

The governor hesitated momentarily. 'Offer my regards to Barkstead, ensign. Remind him that he owes me a Spanish mare, will you?' Sir Arthur's lips curled up into another fleshy smirk, but his eyes remained cool and calculating. Then, he too detached himself, and the two men together disappeared out into Castle Garth, leaving Draper and Archer swaying together upon their narrow perch.

Using a small side stairwell cut into the bedrock, the captain-lieutenant took them down into the bowels of the keep. His easy looseness had returned, and he made no mention of the scene which had just played out at the main doorway.

It left Archer free to ponder what they had just witnessed. He already understood the extent of Blackett's significance to Newcastle's trade, but it was surprising that the governor personally should escort the merchant about the castle. If even officers such as Draper were so shamelessly taking a personal cut from the presence of the army in the town, and its need for supplies, that only confirmed Wilkinson's suggestion that Heselrigg's involvement in such corruption was greater still. How central was William Blackett to such underhand dealing?

At last, welcomed by an appalling reek of unwashed bodies, human waste and dried blood, they exited the steps into a roughly hewn corridor off which, to either side, were set cells cut into the rock, each sealed with an iron grille in place of a door.

Three soldiers came to a slouching attention at the end of the dismal passage. Archer saw at once that they had been Lilburne's men. Heselrigg's now, he assumed. They were not from his own company, but they were men that he knew, men who, from their halting reaction, knew him in turn. What, he wondered, would they make of the return of the sergeant turned agitator who had so rapidly been removed from their ranks?

Draper snapped impatiently to their corporal. 'The keelmen?'

The man stiffened. 'Just here, Sir,' came the reply in a solid Durham brogue.

The corporal led them across the guard chamber and along another corridor of cells. Following him, Archer was uncomfortably aware of the eyes of the two private soldiers upon his retreating back.

Halfway along the right-hand wall, they stopped by one of the barred gates, where the corporal gestured for Archer to look inside the cell. Chained together were three wrecks of men. Filthy, dressed only in the ragged remains of canvas breeches, they were striped with cuts and streaked with blood. Two hung motionless from their fetters. The third, lank streaks of fair hair plastered against his gaunt skull, agonisingly raised his head up on a long stalk of a neck and looked vaguely towards them with blank, sky-blue eyes.

Archer stared at the tortured man. There was no mistake. He was looking at the torn remnants of the charismatic keelmen preacher. Taking an involuntary step back, he became aware of the corporal's open smirk.

A clammy smile marred Draper's features. 'Ringleaders. Sometimes martial law can be very useful. These three have not given us much new information, but their fellows have completely quietened since we took them in yesterday.'

The captain-lieutenant stepped further down the passage. 'We have discovered another room. We shall take these savages there next. I believe that it will draw from them the names we seek.'

Draper turned the cold smile upon the corporal. Leading them down the line of cells, at the corridor's farthest end, the man unlocked another low door. This revealed an uneven stair burrowing further into the bedrock. The stench emerging from the opened doorway was different; still rancid, but deeper, older.

Pausing to light a rusted lantern, the corporal ducked through the entrance and began to descend. Draper gestured for Archer to follow. He did so numbly, his feet blindly feeling their way, all of his other senses tightly held in. It took every ounce of his strength just to keep moving on into the lower blackness and to offer no hint of his inner anguish. As he sank deeper into the seeping cold, the sight of the wreck of the keelman would not leave Archer. He felt nausea's urgent rise, pausing to steady himself against the wall. Draper's languid inquiry brought his feet swiftly back to life, and their descent continued.

A greater dread came upon him. There had been something in the captain-lieutenant's face as he had mentioned this other room which Archer had, at first, missed. A flicker of energy had passed beneath Draper's eyes, joined by the briefest pulsing of his lips. What was this place to so enervate the man?

They emerged after two dozen more steps into a cramped ante-room set apart by another iron grille from a wide, hollowed-out chamber. The walls were quarried to a height only a few inches more than Archer's. A taller man would have to stoop, as Draper now did. The effect stripped away all of his former presence and was faintly comic.

In the very centre of the wider space was embedded a stout pole. To this was attached, at approximately chest height, a horizontal length of thinner wood at the end of which was fixed a kind of harness. To the far side, a low tunnel led off.

Archer was bemused. Why would they keep an engine for drawing water or for working some other mechanism down here? He looked down at the floor of the cave chamber. It was covered in broken brick, flint, and other jagged stones. In a wide ring around the central pole these were darkened, stained black in the poor light. The realisation of the purpose of the room sickened Archer anew. This was a place of torture, designed for a man to walk and walk and all of the time cut open his own feet upon that dreadful floor, deeply stained, as it was, by the blood of the victims.

'Do you like it, Archer?' Draper's voice echoed weakly off the walls. 'No man lasts very long in here. They bring in a mule with specially protected hooves and hitch it up to that harness. The mule then draws the man behind it. I think it just the thing for our keelmen. Would you agree?'

It was all that Archer could do to keep his hands by his sides, but Draper made no move to leave.

'Funny that you were talking about the witches. The last time this was used was for Matthew Bulmer, who was their warlock. Terrible things he did, you know? Changed into a black cat. Cavorted with the devil's incubi. Held dark orgies with other witches. Confessed them all, right in here, after being drawn for twenty-four hours. Twenty-four hours. I wonder if they had to change over the poor mule?'

The captain-lieutenant paused, turning to look directly at Archer. 'At the end, they tell me, the very bones dropped out of his feet. I hope one of our filthy keelmen can keep going that long. I should like to see such a thing.'

Chapter 24

Once he got out, up away from the dungeons, once Draper had disappeared back inside the keep with a final, malicious grin, Archer pulled back his head and opened his eyes and nostrils as wide as he could. Even the tainted air of the old town, harsh with the tang of coal smoke, tasted pure and sweet compared to the foulness from which he had just escaped.

Rapidly, he began to stride along the curving street, long paces heedlessly taking him anywhere, so long as it was far from the shadow of the Black Gate.

It was the calculated cruelty, both of the torture chamber itself and of Draper's relish in exhibiting it, that most turned his stomach. What had been done to Matthew Bulmer was more than brutal. It was far worse than the torments that suspected witches or warlocks might be expected to bear to test the credibility of their confessions. More, it was almost certain that anyone subject to that appalling machine would be left incapable of telling an interrogator anything rational.

Why would Draper be at such pains to show him such a thing? For that matter, what had been the captain's intention in revealing it only after having first gained Archer's trust? Why even dangle the witch trials in front of him, only to offer up all but nothing?

He marched on, unconscious both of his surroundings and of the people who hurriedly pulled back as they saw him approach.

Twisting inside, the memory of the bloodstained cave room mingled with echoes of Draper's drawl as he went over every word they had spoken together, appalled at how easily the captain's charm had drawn him in. Most painful of all, his thoughts were regularly interrupted by flashes of searing terror for the horrors Meg may have endured.

Despite the seeping cold of the day, Archer began to feel clammy. His nostrils were flooded with the intoxicating, high tang of fresh slaughter. His thoughts and sight together seemed to blur. Feeling that he might waver or even fall, he reached out to find a steadying wall, becoming as he did so roughly jostled. Whirling around, he saw only the backs of two street children hurtling away before ducking into an alley. They were followed by a stream of invective from a bloody-aproned stall holder who flung out a final insult, spat after them and grudgingly returned, still grumbling, to his business.

Archer's headlong march had brought him as far the Flesh Market. There, surrounded by the carved up carcasses, he stood rooted as the crowds eddied around him.

Evil was surely at work in Newcastle. But everything that Archer had uncovered was of human more than diabolical doing. The terrible room under the castle was proof enough. The missing court records and the blatant cover-up only confirmed it.

Who was behind it? Why?

He scrambled in his pockets for the notes he had taken the previous day, re-reading the list of executed women, confirming the stark evidence of their very names.

Anderson, Rogerson, Henderson and Coultor. So many of the dead women sprang from significant Royalist backgrounds. Ann Watson's milliner father had cleaved to that side also. But beside them on the death list were found Elizabeth Dobson, whose family had supported Parliament from the very beginning of the troubles, and Margaret Maddison, James Maddison's own cousin, from the best known of all Newcastle's godly families.

He considered what he knew about those few accused witches who had been freed. Meg, through her connection to Weston, would count as Royalist in sympathy. So would Mistress Cole and April Grainger. But Anna Robson's family were long-established Hexhamshire sectarians. Jennie Dawson herself survived the accusation, even if she had part lost her mind for it. You could not get any closer to the heart of the Puritan interest. The two further names he lacked must hold some key.

Glancing skywards, he estimated the hour. His uncle would be in his brew house. If not, then he would be at the Exchange. Never at home. His aunt, however, would be at work in her parlour.

He would need to tread carefully, but what else did he have? Where else could he go?

The housekeeper, Agnes, had always liked James. Even now she was sympathetic, but had only news he did not want.

'I'm sorry, Master James, but Mistress Weston is gone. She left the town yesterday, took the three children and Bessie with her as well. John took them to a hired carriage on Sandhill. They were all dressed up for a long drive, with luggages for a good stay packed to follow on the cart.'

So, Weston had acted immediately to get his aunt and cousins out of Newcastle. To their manor in Durham, most likely. Was Meg hidden there as well?

'Agnes, do you know where Meg has gone to?'

The woman looked stricken.

'Oh, Master James,' she said, speaking to Archer as if he were once again a scared child. 'How can you not know?'

With the greatest difficulty, he held his composure.

'Agnes, whatever you may have heard, you should not believe any ill of her. I know that she was one of those accused as a witch, but I know it as a certainty that she did not hang with the others.'

Agnes looked scared. He hastened on.

'Your master may have helped Meg to get out before the executions, but you know how things are between him and I.'

The servant's tongue ran over her few good teeth. Archer pressed ahead.

'I know that she lives and is gone out of the town. I will find her, but I need to know more. Can you tell me what happened when she left this house? Where she went?'

The woman glanced behind her, back inside the house, then up and down the length of the chare. 'I can't say right. All that summer, that would be last year, your Meg and Mistress Weston and the other children were gone away. Afraid of the sweat in Mistress Weston's condition, they were. They all went back into Durham to wait it out. Well, sure enough, when they returned the Mistress had her new baby. The house was all a flutter with the excitement of Miss Emily, but that same night your sister was gone away. Mistress told us that she had come into her inheritance and had decided to go out of the town. We heard no more about it from them. John asked around, of course. You know how he is, and her his favourite and all. But there was no news until after Epiphany.'

She halted and looked up at him nervously.

'Be at ease, Agnes. I do not mind hearing the old names.'

The servant fidgeted on the exposed doorstep.

'We never found out more, Master James, but her leaving the town can't have lasted, for she was returned when she was arrested. Meg was living in a room of her own in the company of another gentle lady, somewhere near the Shieldfield. I don't know how ever that came to be.'

'Which lady, her name?'

'I never heard any name. There were so many folk come in from out in the county then, for fear of the moss-troopers. They've all gone back to their own lands now, since the army passed north, I mean.'

'Try, Agnes, is there anything more you can remember?'

'I can't, Master James, I'm sorry. God bless you.'

With a final, fearful look, Agnes made an excuse and re-entered the house, leaving Archer standing alone on the greasy cobbles of the chare.

The deep toll of the great lantern bell of Saint Nicholas rang out, rapidly joined by a discordant concerto of smaller peals, their resonance rippling along Peacock's Chare and only gradually dissipating into its many doorways and alleys.

The appointed hour to call upon William's master. He supposed that he had no choice.

Archer took a careful look up and down the steep steps, finding nothing out of the ordinary. There had, up to this point, been no pressing need for concern about any eyes that would have been set upon him. To visit with an alderman and then attend the castle could signify anything, or nothing. He had taken greater care in coming to the Weston house, but whoever was trailing him would surely already know of that connection. The sense of being watched had never once lifted, but now any shadow must be lost.

Ascending for a few paces, he turned into a short passage running west, directly away from his intended destination. This approach, he had planned carefully, dredging up every bit of knowledge of the back ways between the chares which he had accrued as a lad.

After a short time, the snicket ran into a yard from which branched off several further passages. He took the third of these, leading uphill and yet further west along the bank. Archer left this climb at the second entry, diverting him rapidly and directly back to an upper section of Peacock's Chare, one where he knew that he could cross swiftly over into the town's straightest and longest alley.

The extended line of sight offered by Dog Bank promised Archer an extra protection against any persistent watcher. That was why he had chosen it. Finding the path near to empty, he was able to take its first section at a light trot. Approaching the only blind corner, halfway along where four steep cross passages crookedly met, a backwards glance showed such precaution to have been well-judged.

A tall, powerful figure was sprinting down the alley towards him. Archer got the briefest glimpse of a smaller man ferreting along in its wake, by comparison a meagre shadow. Remembering Elizabeth Thompson's description of the two killers, the huge blond man and his small, dark companion, Archer chose flight.

It was too far to try to make for the comforting crowds of Broad Chare. Instinct alone pulled him up the narrower of the two rising passages. Scrambling past several small entries, this he followed as it turned left, crossed a tight, noisome nightsoil yard and ran into a steeply climbing alley. Horrified, he halted upon seeing the path before him terminate in a pair of closed wooden doors.

From behind, Archer heard a confusion of pursuit. He tried the left-hand door to find it stoutly barred. The other door proved equally unyielding. In desperation, he hammered against its planking, receiving no response.

Turning about and drawing his sword, he placed the doors firmly at his back, set up a fighting stance, and prepared to meet the two attackers.

Seconds passed, lengthening into a full minute. His brow cooled. His heart beat more steadily. He strained to hear their approach, baffled by such apparent caution. Still, nothing came up the dead-end alley.

After another tense minute of waiting, Archer began to step cautiously forward, blade held high, one slow foot over the other. He stopped again and listened, only to be met by the same impossible silence. He renewed his slow advance to the very brink of the nightsoil yard.

If they were planning to strike, it must surely be here. He had, at least, the advantage of height. It offered a clear view of nearly all of the cramped space. The alley ran through the yard's exact middle. Tall, wooden nightsoil containers had been built into each of its walls. The men had to be waiting in the near left corner, the only one he could not see.

This close, the stench was full and noxious. Archer's mouth and sinuses burned. His eyes began to weep. He loosened his grip upon the sword hilt just enough to relax his wrist and offer him a fraction more flexibility for the close-in fighting which must now come.

Archer leapt forwards, bursting around the corner, arcing the double-edged blade in a rapid downward sweep, attempting both to cover the blind spot and to surprise the nearest attacker. His sword cut through nothing more than empty air. He danced backwards, part from long training, part from shock.

It took several wild heartbeats before he could make sense of what he saw. There, slumped upon the befouled ground, was the same large man who had charged towards him along Dog Bank. In its fall, the body had broken the sides of the nightsoil barrel. The dead form lay in a stream of filth, that of the ordinary inhabitants of this part of the steep cleugh pooling with the fresher contents of the man's own viscera. Underneath, Archer appreciated the deft precision behind the deep cut which had opened him up. Whoever had done it had been strong, fast and horribly experienced. The large man had stood no chance.

He brought his own weapon about, searching for any sign of the second pursuer. He was not to be seen, and there was nowhere to hide.

Reappraising the corpse, Archer took in its plain outdoor clothing and calloused, working hands. He registered also the close set of the eyes below a shock of dark brown hair. Joe Marsden, the Carr family servant who William had called a radgie, and whose hate-filled stare had fallen upon him at Bridge Gate, lay butchered at his feet.

Backing away, Archer quickly retreated to Dog Bank. He sheathed his sword, waited until he could tuck in behind a small group of laden washerwomen returning from the bathing house, and stepped out into the safety of Broad Chare.

Chapter 25

He had half expected to see William, but the rear door to the Fenwick house was opened by a stocky, rumpled footman. Archer was ushered into the deserted kitchen. Hurried through it, he felt the heat coming from the ovens and took in the half-prepared food left upon the central table. Dinner would be served late.

Climbing the back stairs, the footman led him up four unkempt floors, each in increasing need of repair, each progressively colder. They ascended to the top-most landing, where a bored looking young man waited. Taller and leaner than Archer, hawk-eyed and showily well-dressed, he leant casually against a door frame not much than two plain, unvarnished boards wide.

Gruffly dismissing the servant, the young man peered down the stair long after the noises of descent had ceased. Only then did he speak in a deep, heavily accented voice which sat incongruously with his fashionable costume and offhand demeanour.

'Weapons. You'll need to leave them here. All of them, mind.'

Archer unbuckled his weapons-belt and placed it on the wide window ledge. He took a step back as the man began to advance upon him.

'I'll need to check you, man. You can't expect us to take you on trust?'

Performing only a perfunctory inspection, the young man rapped heavily upon the door. It was opened just enough for whoever was inside to see out and for the two to exchange whispered words. The guardian continued to block the doorway. Finally, with a flourish of his arm and a look encompassing arrogance, disdain and a sense of possession, he moved aside.

Stepping into the chamber beyond, Archer received the fleeting impression of a crowded but unexpectedly bright study. A coal fireplace set with an unlit fire was placed directly opposite. To its left was a closed door of more ordinary width and stoutness, its inner surface seamlessly continuing the surrounding shelves, each chaotically strewn with books, ledgers and folders of papers.

All of this was almost instantly obscured by a dazzling brightness. Overhead, the whole of the centre of the ceiling comprised an octagonal window, its topmost glass tapering together, so that light funnelled down into the room. After the gloom of the back stair, it disoriented Archer until his eyes adjusted and the room came back into focus.

The floor was crowded with a wide-legged desk table, three battered reading chairs and a stand supporting a half-empty wine decanter alongside two stemmed crystal glasses. In the chair pulled closest to both desk and wine sat a grey-faced, lank-haired old man, heavily encumbered by layers of woollens. Hostile eyes glared out from within deeply lined sockets.

Sir John Fenwick, William's new master, ever proud, always suspicious, and very much diminished. There was nothing frail, however, about the piqued voice which sallied across the cold, bright space.

'So, lad. It is true that you are returned. You must either be very foolish, or else foolishly over-brave.'

The well of light formed a barrier of dancing dust. Archer glanced back, seeing at once both that the young man had disappeared and that, closed, the little door fitted so neatly into the panelling of the wall as to be nearly invisible.

'Oh, that is only young Blackett. There is no need to worry about him. Edmund is a good lad. He helps me. Which I need without my sons.'

Archer registered the name, but also Fenwick's strain. The thought *Helps you, or keeps you?* flitted across his mind.

'The token. You do have the token?'

Archer twisted the scuffed ring from the middle finger of his left hand. He stepped into the light, catching, as he did, the inscribed writing on its inner side and the tiny, finely wrought, death-heads on the outer. He stopped, in part from reluctance to give the piece up and in part as a response to Sir John's evident impatience. Eventually, he placed the *memento mori* gently down upon the desk and retreated back into the shadows.

Fenwick snatched the ring up between two bony fingers, gave it a brief inspection, grunted and, to Archer's alarm, called out a loud summons.

There came a soft click as the bookcase door opened. Archer was anything but prepared for the shock of recognition as a man emerged through it.

Of middling height, he was, nonetheless, a powerful figure, strength rippling down from a bull's neck onto broad shoulders. Plainly dressed, he could have been taken, indeterminately, for a lesser merchant or some sort of scrivener, but Archer would know him anywhere. The same waved hair, strong brow and clear, penetrating eyes; the same open face, disconcertingly boyish in a man well into maturity, built to frame and support the classically aquiline nose; the whole reposed, as ever, in a quick good humour.

The Royalist commander, Colonel Edward Massie.

Archer snapped to a soldierly position of attention.

'Colonel.'

'Archer. It is a fine thing to enjoy your company once again,' replied Massie's seductively rich voice. 'And in such very different circumstances.'

For all they had spent no more than a matter of weeks together following the colonel's arrest the previous year, Archer could not entirely hide the very real pleasure he felt at seeing Edward Massie.

Fenwick watched on, a look which might equally have been

pain or a taut smile upon his face. He reached out a bony hand, holding in it the delicate *memento mori*. 'Is this good? Does it pass?'

Massie took the ring, examining it in the flooding light. 'It is mine, alright. And I am right glad to have it upon me once again.' With a swift and smooth movement, he removed a chunky signet from the little finger of his right hand, replacing it with the smaller piece.

The deaths-heads and their inscription belonged to Edward Massie. Did Deane know? Had he and Skippon planned for the colonel's presence? If so, then their design for Archer personally to act as intermediary at last made some sense. Massie's presence however had also hugely raised the stakes.

A parliamentary hero for his defence of the city of Gloucester, who upon the trial of the old king had turned against the army, been imprisoned, escaped and finally gone over to the Royalist side, Massie was the single most sought after of all of the Commonwealth's current enemies. His entry into the room meant that the extent of Archer's treason had, even in these past few minutes, increased without limit. He felt his throat constrict as if the noose were already being tightened about it.

Massie eased away from Fenwick, smiled a regretful smile and clapped Archer about the shoulders.

'Easy, Ensign Archer. You look like you've seen a ghost. If I surprise you, then I venture that it is a happy chance for us both.'

'How can you be here, Colonel? I had understood you to be in Flanders, with…'

'With Charles Stuart, do you mean to say?' Massie interjected.

'With The King, you both mean,' exclaimed Fenwick, before erupting into a rolling, wet fit of coughing.

Before the old man could take this any further, Massie turned back to Archer. 'I am named by him Major General, under instruction to bring south a force from out of Scotland.' He laughed. 'But General Cromwell's invasion and the Scots' collapse before him at Dunbar has blighted such an enterprise and left England secure. I am thereby at my leisure. For now.'

He stole a look towards Fenwick before turning back to Archer with another smile.

'There is no need for either of you to look so pale. Do you think that Scott and Bishop do not already know all of this? That the Council does not already have a hundred paid informants who have long since sent such news south?'

Fenwick's tortured breathing rattled off the walls of the study. Archer wanted to retreat from the glare of the skylight, further into the gloom, but steeled himself and waited. When, finally, the old man spoke, it was Massie he addressed.

'These are strange and dangerous times we are living through. Tell me, how does it come to pass that a gentleman, who is also so honoured by His Majesty, has maintained such close relations with a mere junior officer?'

'If that shocks you, Sir John, then know that Archer here was an uncouth sergeant when I knew him last.'

It was all Archer could do not to laugh out loud.

'He will do, Sir John,' continued Massie. 'Do not fear, he will do very well. My captors allowed the sergeant, as he was then, to converse with me during those weeks that I was held in Saint James' Palace. He is, after all, a gentleman's son.'

'I know who he is, better than you.'

'Nonetheless, he gave me good cheer. James has been educated well, and the palace had become the resting place of the royal library. We found much to explore and more to talk about. Although I dare say that the Parliament men also wanted somebody to keep a very close eye on me over those days.'

Massie's eyes twinkled. He granted Archer a conspiratorial look.

'Besides, during that time Archer here was deemed fit company for the Princess Elizabeth herself. I had it from the girl's close maid, Makin, she that was her tutor, how very much Her Grace valued our dear sergeant's company and conversation. If he is good enough for the Princess, then he is surely permitted in your private study?'

For a minute Archer drifted away, remembering the clever, thoughtful girl. He pictured her probing him with questions, glancing for approval towards Bathusa Makin. The image was dispelled as the animal howls of her grief echoed in his ears, from the day when he had escorted her to see her father the King for the very last time. He and Makin between them had needed to carry the fourteen-year-old child back out to the closed carriage, her thin body, already ailing, convulsed with sobs. Young Elizabeth Stuart was dead now in her turn, taken by the cough in the cruel dampness of Carisbroke Castle. All of that promise and intelligence forever lost.

He was jerked back to the present in time to catch Massie's last words before they were strangled by an angry gesture from their host.

'...the best means of communicating with Skippon...'

'Skippon? That devil? Skippon who did contribute more to the villainies of the sectaries and the betraying of the Parliament than Cromwell, Ireton and St John combined?' Fenwick stopped abruptly, fixing a jaundiced eye upon Archer. 'How did you come by that ring, boy?'

'My master gave it to me, to offer only into your hands, sir. That is, into the hands of the contact I was to make. He said that it would prove my identity and offer you surety.'

'Your master. That treacherous, slithering, underhand butcher.'

Massie cut in like the sweep of a sword.

'Calm yourself, Sir John. Be restful. I know Skippon. Yes, many, myself included, felt bruised by his siding with the army at Newmarket, but heed you, he will ever be consistent in his desire to see a middle way proceed.'

'What middle way? How can there be any middle way, after the murder of the King?'

Fenwick turned bloodshot eyes upon Archer.

'That pretty piece of timber that is your master went abroad to defend the army in subverting its own Parliament. When our very Sovereign was so shamefully and illegitimately placed on trial, he was sure to arrange his own absence. He is as slippery as any eel. Tell him that I shall not treat either with him or with his traitorous errand boy.'

Having risen while making his thunderous speech, Sir John now slumped forwards, his breath coming in stuttering pants. Massie guided him back into his chair and poured out a restrained measure of the tawny liquid from the decanter. The old man grasped at his glass and took the wine greedily, resting against the high back of the chair only after every drop of liquid was drained. As he recovered, Fenwick's eyes flicked between Massie, Archer and the now sparsely filled decanter.

It was Massie who broke the silence.

'The Sergeant-Major General, whatever his motivations, at least supported General Fairfax in trying to find a path other than murdering his Highness. If there is division within the traitors, he is our best and our only chance of uncovering it. Besides, the King himself approves this approach.'

Fenwick had by now recovered his former liverish colour. His voice was calm, if still insubstantial, as he met Massie's challenge.

'At least General Fairfax has had the good sense and grace to take himself back to his estate at Nun Appleton. Tell me, boy, has your Phillip Skippon similarly renounced this government of desperadoes and sectaries? Has he forgone all of the appointments and incomes the pack of criminals that you call a Council has seen fit to bestow upon him?'

Fenwick reached unsteadily for his wine glass and indicated the decanter.

Massie took it up, but stood to his full height, keeping his hand furled over its glass stopper. 'Yet, Sir John, we must keep all avenues open to the rightful return of King Charles, must we not? Do you have a better idea? Another contact in Whitehall, perhaps? Have you discussed this reluctance with the Carrs, or with any of the other families?'

Massie at last unstoppered the decanter and poured again.

Fenwick drank, put on the same half-pained grimace and drank again, before gasping a reply. 'Aye. Alright. We will proceed.'

The old man stopped to glower at Archer, some new thought crossing his mind. 'You betrayed your family, boy. You ran away from your town in the hour of its greatest peril. Why should we ever trust you now?'

It was Massie who replied. 'Because he's here. Because he's already committed enough treason for a very unpleasant and very short stay under the castle. Because I say that you can trust him, as His Majesty trusts me.'

'Ah. You? The turncoat who turned again.'

'And you, Sir John, who, like so many of your fellows, was careful to have a son in each army and to take no sides yourself. Can anyone then trust you?'

'How would you know? To see the work of generations destroyed. To have your own name, and the name of your family, your own sister, besmirched by the wildest accusation. To hear blasphemers in our pulpits and see all propriety fall away from public life. What do you know of what we, who remained, have had to endure?'

Fenwick's rant ended in a fit of coughing, Massie again filled the man's glass and helped him to drink. The fit subsided with another of Fenwick's fierce coughs.

'Tell your master not to dare play us false. Tell him that, in you, he has chosen an odd emissary. Tell him also that we agree to remain in contact. Massie vouches for you. I shall forbear to trust him.'

The tightness in Archer's chest eased just a little. Hoping that the other men could discern no hint of such relief, he risked searching their faces.

Fenwick appeared frailer than ever; his breathing become more laboured. Massie's cheeks, by contrast, shone with excitement. He reached towards Fenwick's side of the desk to retrieve a small box of a light wood, generously inlaid with small studs of polished red stone. Sir John, with surprising speed, flicked out a claw to snatch it away. Massie, his hand frozen over the now empty surface, looked sharply at the old man, who at once dropped the box back down. The major general gently picked the object up, opened it upon tiny brass hinges, and drew out from within a small metal cylinder. Gesturing for Archer to approach, this he placed carefully into his hand.

Plain, except for twin bulbous, banded decorations at top and bottom, the item, not more than three inches long and of a finger's width, proved to be surprisingly light. Its end pieces were intended to turn, presumably in order to be able to wind something tightly inside the device. A small piece of ivory coloured parchment protruding from a slit cut into one side confirmed this appraisal. The end of the parchment was made fast to the metal body by a blob of dirty orange wax, embossed with the unusual seal image of a tiny leaping dolphin. In itself, this meant nothing to Archer, but it was quite clear that his role was restricted to the transport of the secret message, not to its access.

'The seal must not be broken until this comes into your master's hands. The message it contains is ciphered, but he will have men who can unravel it. Deliver it to him in person. Not even Captain Deane is to have possession of it. Can we agree?'

Archer returned the solemnity of Massie's look, and quickly stowed the little cylinder away close to his skin.

As soon as the device was out of sight, the harsh edge disappeared from Massie's eyes and something of his former self returned. 'Our business for today is done then. James, I wish only that I could take some leisured time in your company. You will forgive me. It would not be safe to remain longer. Sir John, do you yourself have anything more to add?'

Fenwick looked pained. He glanced towards the decanter, then between each of the two younger men. 'A toast, gentlemen. Archer, I include you in that for your father and for your mother's bewitching charm, whatever her birth. Let us toast His Majesty together, that we may be sure of our true loyalties.'

Having completed this strained speech, Fenwick glowered anew at the level of wine left in the decanter. Archer thought he might abandon the toast, but the old man shrugged, indicating to Massie a cupboard near to the main door. 'In there. Find something in there.'

Massie returned with a tiny, intricately etched goblet. At a nod from Fenwick, he shared the remaining liquid carefully between the three glasses, two of them broad, the other thimble-like. Archer's heart began to beat so hard that he was sure they would both hear it.

'To The King,' began Fenwick.

'His health,' Massie responded.

The two men together raised their glasses and drank. Archer followed suit, but barely wetted his lips, all the while keeping his eyes fixed upon the forlorn decanter.

Taking a circuitous exit from the house through a succession of hidden courts before emerging into Pandon Chare, Archer stepped into the stream of people headed down towards Sandgate.

The little cylinder lay uncomfortably against his chest, as if he were bound with some heavy chain. What had they done?

Deane might have said that all was fair in such quiet work, but Archer knew that what had just occurred in Fenwick's study could easily bring on his own swift and unlamented death. Scott and Bishop's men would take delight in uncovering treachery on such a scale at the heart of Skippon's private operations. Whatever might befall Deane and his master, any discovery of this meeting would certainly prove to be Archer's own end.

More than fear, the realisation brought with it an irritation which came close to anger. What he had presumed, foolishly, to be a piece of everyday work handling paltry information was become something very much more dangerous. The peril it presented for Archer complicated and endangered his search for Meg.

It was because of Massie that he had been requested in person. For all the major general's easy charm and the intimacy of their former brief acquaintance, the man had reached out and made use of Archer as nothing more than another pawn in his self-aggrandising games. It felt raw, as if a scab had been pulled away too early.

He found himself rubbing at the finger upon which he had carried Massie's *memento mori* ring ever since Deane had handed it across to him in the little cell of an office in Whitehall. It was absurd that he might miss the trinket. Even in its absence, however, he found himself to be deeply comforted by the reminder that death, soon, would come to all.

Was he ready to meet that friend who a dozen times had swept so close to him? He hoped that he was. But not yet. He had to stay alive at least so long as to be able to find Meg.

Chapter 26

Draper never liked coming here. It was too public, too exposed.

Damn this provincial merchant. Every time there was a kind of arrogance about the manner in which Draper was summoned that both antagonised and, in truth, scared him.

It was the same this afternoon, the servant's verbal message given just when he would not have expected it; the excuses to make; the difficulties in approaching the big house unobserved only to be shown into a back room like any common street seller. And all because the man now knew that Archer had returned, the boy who spied for the Council.

It was insupportable.

He considered the room in his forced leisure. The Turkey rug hung upon a side wall. The dresser, with its tableware over-ostentatiously displayed, took up the whole of another. The map of the sea routes to Amsterdam and Danzig was well placed, occupying the greater part of one section where, in the day, it would be illuminated through the tall, east-facing window. A full decanter of golden wine sat mockingly to one side. Draper knew that it would never be unstoppered for him.

He toyed with his boot across the new straw strewn over the boards. These ridiculous people in their backwards, reeking town. He considered with distaste how he had to flatter them, with no end in sight. This man in particular, who thought that his money could buy anything and who affected such grace. Perhaps one day he would be free to show him how the world really worked. He smiled at the thought, smoothly wiping the look away as the merchant entered through the hanging drape.

They took several minutes to exchange what new information they had. Then the host sighed and looked witheringly across at Draper.

'I am sure of the town officials.' The loose skin on the man's forehead puckered as he spoke. 'You are certain there have been no mistakes, no trail he might pick up?'

'You do not need to teach me my role. It is all long taken care of against this very eventuality. Nothing remains for him to find. In any case, this Archer who they have sent. Is he really such a threat?'

The Newcastle man emerged from the shadows, revealing a subtle strength half-shrouded by weariness. 'What is there to tell? Archer is of no consequence. The plague took his parents, so he and the girl came to live under Weston's roof. As a boy, he was an over-eager pup, but useful to the Parliament cause. When the Scots came, he ran. He abandoned the town, his duty, his family, even his only sister. He is weak. He lacks guile. If you have done all that you say, then he presents no difficulty.'

Draper's emerging smile was cut short by a curt bark.

'Except for one thing. The girl. He cannot be allowed to get to the girl. Leave Archer to us. Your task now is to get to the girl before he does. Make sure that particular trail comes to an end.'

'You are sure that nobody else knows where she is?'

'That was the arrangement.'

'Then I know where to look. Leave it with me.'

As Draper turned to go, the other man caught him by the arm. It was all he could do not to reach across for his dagger, but he stayed his hand.

'He will look for her and will not cease looking. That is why they have sent him. He is not to find her. For your own sake as much as for mine. Do you fully understand me?'

Chapter 27

The food was good. Herring fillets, greased, salted, fresh from a hot skillet and served in a wide, soft roll of bread. The weak beer in the pewter jug before Archer had been brewed to be sharply refreshing, the street stall justifiably busy. The short, lank-haired man who worked incessantly at gutting and salting and cooking had even provided rudimentary table space in the form of old boxes. A pair of boys weaved in between them, taking money, delivering full platters and fresh jugs.

Perched upon a stool at the end-most of the box tables, fish oil drizzling down his chin, Archer's warning came from a shift in tone of the chatter emanating from the other men taking an early dinner. Voices were lowered. A few ceased entirely. By the time the four newcomers reached him, he was ready, left hand free, cloak pushed back.

They were well dressed enough in their shining boots, long coats and stiffened hats. The pair at the back were unknown to him, but he recognised the front two at once.

Charles Reade came from an old Catholic family aligned with the Carr affinity. The same age as Archer and of similar prospects, the two had apprenticed together with Master Sandal. It was clear from the scowl upon Reade's unmistakable, flat features this was no happy reunion. Archer's former workmate stood alongside the taller, ruddier Bell. Along with other local Catholics, the pair had joined up with Francis Anderson's Royalist regiment of Northern Horse earlier in that same summer when Archer had flown the town.

'You aren't welcome here, Archer,' said Reade.

The talk around them faltered utterly.

Archer kept his eyes low and said nothing, but moved his feet around under the stool.

The four stepped in closer. 'You should not have come back, traitor.'

This time, Archer did look up. 'I return under orders from the Commonwealth. Let me be, Charles.'

'You remember Jed Tate, don't you Archer, who apprenticed alongside us? He stayed and fought to protect his town and his family. Jed was blown up by a filthy Scots' cannon while you ran away. We don't forget.'

Archer held the man's quivering gaze.

'And you remember my brother, Henry? Henry stayed loyal to the King. He went to Ireland.' Something in Reade's voice changed. 'He went to Drogheda.'

It must have been an arranged signal, meant to trigger a combined assault. No sooner had the words left Reade's pudgy lips than the group, as one, made to lunge forwards, hands reaching to knife belts.

Colonel Anderson's regiment could not have trained them well enough. Over-eager, they had made the mistake of drawing in too close, too early.

At the first flicker of movement, Archer had brought the beer jug up into Bell's chin. The man stumbled backwards, causing Reade and one of the others to swerve aside. Even as the last of them fumbled for his dagger, Archer had risen, drawn his mortuary sword, taken one step away for room, and disarmed him with a neat, sideways sweep of its double-edged blade.

The single backwards step had also taken Archer just out of reach of their knife hands. It gave him all of the time he needed to bring his sword about and to level its point at Reade's chest. Keeping the shining blade steady, he took another half pace to the side to cover Bell.

'You were best to withdraw, gentlemen.'

From his left, the youngest of the group made a dart. Archer parried the thrust with a flick of his heavy basket hilt. The young man's knife dropped into the mud, an agonised yell confirming a break to some hand bone. Together, Reade and the fourth man made to come on, but again Archer's weapon was there before them, arcing around to slice through the front of Reade's coat.

Reade looked over to his whimpering companion, down at his own cleanly-cut coat and across at Bell's trembling lip. He and the others took one step back, then another, before all four fled across Quayside and away up the nearest steps.

Archer took some time to survey the scene. Only when satisfied that the four men had been alone, and this had not been some elaborate diversion, did he sheath the sword and turn back to the fish man's two staring boys.

'Nothing to see lads. No blood shed, no harm done.'

The scarred ensign, only a few minutes earlier so anonymous, kept the crowd's full attention as he retrieved his hat, took a regretful look at the ruined remains of his dinner, and walked calmly away.

Chapter 28

Sir John Fenwick lay slumped across the desk, an overturned goblet resting near to the upcurled fingers of his right hand.

Since he was a young child, Edmund Blackett had known that he lacked his brother William's courage. But there were many ways of making up for that. He had remained burrowed in an untended corner until the fear Massie might return had subsided entirely. He had needed also to keep reminding himself the other officer was gone. Even then, he had taken extra minutes of vacillation before emerging to creep up the stairs and wait, listening outside the study door, until the story told by the silence within became unanswerable.

Fenwick's condition was as Edmund had expected and planned. Had he not himself prepared the second decanter and filled it with the strong Malaga wine?

He had also long since carefully observed and noted all of Sir John's hiding-places. The vain search he now conducted, for all its patient system, did not therefore take long. When it was finished, he looked down upon the old man with a sneering disappointment.

No evidence. No papers left behind for him to take as proof to his handler. No notes. Not even the letter from London had been kept. His word would need to be enough. Surely, in this case, it would be more than enough?

A plot between the traitor Massie and someone important in Whitehall. The conversation had been indistinct. He may have misheard. One or other of the major generals was involved, the young officer as intermediary. It didn't matter. They would get the real names soon enough when they interrogated the man.

More importantly, what could such intelligence be worth?

With a last dismissive look at the unconscious Fenwick, Blackett left the room through the thin, secret door. He waited on the little landing, looking intently down to be sure the back stairs were clear. Alone in the darkness, Edmund allowed himself to bathe in the most pleasurable of thoughts. This knowledge was his. For once, he would do something for himself and not at the behest and direction of his brother.

How insufferable William had become. It was not as if he had even earned the fortune brought upon him by the miraculous survival of the *Caroline*. Now he would see he was not the only one who could take advantage of a piece of providence.

Edmund considered how to approach the meeting with Scott's intelligencer. How best should he ask for his reward? Would it be better to demand a sum up front? It would need to be a large sum, more than he expected. Or should he wait for the first offer to be made, scorn it whatever it was, and so push on for more?

How much would he need to realise in order to discomfit William?

News of such treason, better still news bringing the possibility of arresting one of the conspirators, must surely be worth a great deal. How much could he get Watch-Captain Sanderson to pay for the head of the traitorous scarred ensign?

Chapter 29

The fight, such as it was, had done Archer good. His mind was made clear.

The concerns of the Council were not his. Deane and Skippon could keep their plots and the likes of Heselrigg his bounty. Even Massie, although it pained him to think it, could go his own way. The return to Newcastle had given him something to replace his masters. Once he had made what report he could, he would find a way to leave them all behind. He and Meg would go away together, up into the empty hills. Perhaps out into the wilds of Wanney, or north to high Redesdale. Somewhere no one would ever find them.

Only the very current threat overshadowing Elizabeth Thompson caused him any pause. He would see that threat extinguished.

He stopped as if to turn back, making a habitual check he was not being followed. There was no hint of anything other than the everyday bustle of women and youths, but the sense of being tracked remained as real as it had since his departure from Doncaster, felt all the more claustrophobically since returning to Newcastle. It long pre-dated the unfortunate Joe Marsden. Not that the lumbering servant could ever possibly have been the practiced shadow he knew to watch over him, never seen but always present.

At least this shadow was real, flesh and blood real, and not merely one of his treacherous visions. The wound which had killed Marsden was appallingly, expertly, real. Whoever was following him, they were neither vision nor spectre. There was something near to relief in that.

Moving onto Sandhill and its busy market, he found himself returning to the two killers as described by Elizabeth, the tall, blond man and his small, dark companion. Who were the mismatched duo sent to warn off those who had helped Elinor Loumsdale, the pair who returned to butcher those who did not heed the warning?

Something women like Abigail Walker and Sarah Turner had seen or heard inside Newgate prison was important enough to these men that they would kill for it. He planned to visit the prison, but knew already the full secret must lie with the women themselves.

Meg, thank the Lord, had escaped. So had April Cole, along with the Grainger and Robson women. He needed to find them and the other two as yet unnamed survivors. This Bracewell might be able to help.

A wrinkle of concern ran across Archer's thoughts. The otherwise hesitant Ephraim Ord had been very quick to mention the court official. Possibly too quick. He would pay another visit upon the tall engineer, this time without Elizabeth's restraining presence.

Moving beyond Guildhall, towards the centre of the marketplace, Archer raised his head, eager to catch a first glimpse of the woman. His search was soon rewarded by a flash of bright green glinting through the drab browns and greys of the crowd.

Cape flowing behind her, Elizabeth appeared to be busy selecting bread from a cart manned by a boy of about twelve. Idly, she turned over the loaves. Stretching to examine the rye piled towards the rear, she flicked out a sideways glance and saw Archer.

The woman said something to the bread boy and stepped away. Turning with an exaggerated swing of her bad leg, she stumbled, saving herself before she fell into the filth of the open marketplace, in the process upturning her basket just enough for a handful of beet bulbs and a cascade of loose greens to fall out.

Archer strode forwards, knelt and began to retrieve the vegetables from the mud, Elizabeth squatting beside him. Their eyes met.

'Thank you, sir,' she said as both straightened up. Remaining a careful inch away from touching her, Archer guided them towards the sheltered side wall of the Butcher's Bank conduit. Steadily, he pumped the water while she made a fastidious show of washing the dirtied produce. Finally, they could talk.

'Would Mistress Thompson be content to see her daughter washing beets at market like some common serving girl?'

'Do you see my mother here?' Stifling an escaping laugh, she rewarded him with the same unexpected, face-softening smile she had unfurled in Ord's workroom that morning. But, this time, the smile was for him.

Under Archer's hesitation, Elizabeth recomposed herself. 'I was able to see Bracewell at the court. He has agreed to speak with you tonight. The family warehouse. Do you know it?'

'Just beyond the Long Stairs, fronting The Close?'

'Yes. There is a back entrance.'

Together, they worked on, Elizabeth laying out further instruction in a series of low hisses, Archer dogged by concern.

'This Elinor Loumsdale, who is she to have put you in such danger?'

Her deep eyes held his. 'How can I explain? It is not in her look. She is even smaller than I, and darker besides. You see, Elinor comes from the old people of the hills. I have heard her speak with Margaret Muffet in their strange tongue. It is something in her manner. There is a power in her which cannot be gainsayed. You would know, were you to meet her.'

'But the peril she has placed you in?'

Elizabeth moved closer to him. He could feel her breath upon his face.

'You have been so long away. You did not ask, last evening, about my father. He died. My uncle Thompson died. So did my cousins ,Peter and Edwin. They went to the wars and never after came back. Like my mother, the women they left behind managed all too well without them. Should we be expected to give all of that up? Believe me, there was a ready army for Elinor's work.'

'To give succour to witches?'

'To give strength to women.' She stood upright and swayed before him, taut with anger. 'Those women, they were no witches. I tell you, master officer of Parliament, they were none of them witches. Alice Hume, a blind, crippled old woman, was killed simply because she would not take the approved charity from the parish.'

Archer was so near that he could see how dry her lips were.

'Jane Hunter, who was a close friend to your sister, was told to marry John Winter, the cutler. When she would not, her father beat her, then brought Jane to Pastor Hammond. The pastor told her that God wished her to obey her father in all things and to marry the man. She refused still, so Hammond said a devil had possessed her. Do you remember that Jane was always a pretty girl? She was badly used in Newgate.'

He did remember Jane Hunter, as a lively girl with fine, hazel hair.

'I heard Mistress Fenwick say,' she continued, 'that she believed herself to have been imprisoned only because she would not sign over her property into the care of her brother. For protecting her own property, is she to be judged a witch?'

'Mistress Fenwick was accused?'

Before she could answer, Elizabeth rocked onto her weakened left side. What spare flesh there was around her face seemed to slacken and sag, turning her, temporarily, into the exact image of her mother. He caught her above the elbow as she righted herself. The contact, swiftly broken, quieted them.

'Thank you for your assistance, sir.'

Archer handed her the basket and stepped aside. Without returning his intent look, Elizabeth Thompson melted away into the busy crowd.

In vain, Archer scanned Sandhill for a last shimmer of green.

Elizabeth's outburst had shocked him every bit as much as the revelation that Sir John Fenwick's stately cousin had been amongst the accused. He wanted to make amends for his poorly judged words. He wanted to see her face, to be sure of her forgiveness. But the woman was gone.

Breaking off his search, resolving to find space to speak with her alone when they met at the warehouse, he began to set his way towards The Close. He had passed only a few paces beyond the Guildhall when a street boy sidled alongside.

'Would you come along with me, sir?'

Archer looked down upon a lad of perhaps eleven or twelve. The russet scarf tied around his upper arm marked the boy out as an officer's temporary servant. Was this a trick, or should he take it as a reassurance?

'My master says he can be of use to you, but he can't be seen with you.'

The boy was already beginning to move away, gesturing at Archer to follow. He turned back, impatience written across his face.

'He says to tell you he'll lead you to the truth.'

Something in the lad's quick eyes and the absolute certainty of his manner made up Archer's mind to follow.

They walked quickly across the edge of Sandhill and along The Close. Archer slowed their progress as they passed the front of the Thompson warehouse. Situated to the west of the dank entry to the Long Stairs, three stories of old stone topped by wide grey slate, it fitted tightly in between a pair of newer, brick, four-story fellows. Strong double doors took up the best part of the frontage, a wicket gate providing everyday entry. Some ten feet from the ground, two barred windows winked across towards the river walls. High under the eaves, a double casement jutted out below a fixed winch, allowing for heavy materials to be lifted up for the driest storage on the upper floors. From this side, at least, the place appointed for tonight's meeting appeared secure.

Leaving the warehouse behind, occupied by thoughts of the rendezvous, the boy's hissed warning took him by surprise.

'Stay with me. I'll lose him in here.'

Without another word, his guide took hold of the loose edge of Archer's cloak and tugged him into the tightest of alleyways, leading ever upwards. Breaking into a loping trot, the boy led the way around several sharp turns, sometimes steeply up, sometimes sharply downwards, squeezing them between tall, crumbling buildings and even, at one point, seeming to double back across their path.

'Stop,' ordered Archer in an undertone. 'I'll not go further with you.'

The boy looked back down the blackened walls of the alley behind Archer's shoulder before meeting his stare.

'One more turn, master, I promise, then we can stop.'

Without leaving any chance for a reply, he jinked away down another squeezed passage, barely wide enough for Archer to take head-on. A few paces in, the boy turned back to beckon urgently at his charge. Archer tried to step forwards quietly, as well as quickly enough to keep up. He held his shoulders tight as they slipped their way through the low mounds of filth and rubble which, in parts, almost entirely blocked the path. They took another left fork, followed by a foul-smelling further sharp left, where the boy at last stopped, listening.

Archer could discern nothing out of place, but it was several slow minutes before the lad relaxed his shoulders.

'We lost him a while back. I had to be sure. No bother, see, it's right along here now.'

They took yet another, turning onto the narrowest passage they had yet encountered.

'Wait. Who were we running from?'

'I don't run. I might hide. And I might get him lost, but I don't run, alright?'

The lad's thick jaw set, and his green eyes flashed, such that

Archer almost laughed.

'That, I can see. It was canny, the way you lost him. Can you describe the man?'

The boy let slip a grin. 'Not one I've seen before, so I'd say he's not from the town. Small gadgie. Less than the middle height, lean, black hair. Unusual like. Pale as I've ever seen. Dressed like a working man, but he's not. Walks all wrong. Followed us right from the start of The Close, he did. In here was the first chance I got to lose him.'

Archer's guide looked up at the sliver of sky between the top stories of the tall buildings. 'Like I said, just along here. Howay, I can't be late with youse.'

Archer followed, for now putting the chase out of his mind. They came to the end of the path, where it opened out onto a cramped, dramatically steep set of steps. Their name came back to him unbidden. Tuthill Stairs, leading up to the ramshackle decay of Tuthill Chare. He tensed as they began their climb, but the way ahead seemed clear.

Ascending for only a short while, the boy stopped and rapped upon a plain door. When, within moments, it was opened from within, the lad was gone without a backwards glance or another word. Archer looked after him wistfully before stepping across the threshold.

Chapter 29

A house servant, decrepit and bent, led the way up a narrow flight of stairs and into a large first floor room overlooking the steps. Rows of plain benches faced inwards towards a narrow aisle ending in a low platform. The walls were entirely devoid of ornament, the ceiling no more than a clean, plaster skim. Pale light bled in through high windows. A solitary man, outlined before them, turned and approached Archer in open-handed greeting.

'Welcome to you,' he said in a resonant voice.

Short and balding, tufts of prematurely greying hair emerging from the weather-worn oval of his head. At first, he appeared unprepossessing. But the sober black clothing encasing him strained against powerful shoulders overtopping a barrel of a body held so proudly as to speak of a life more than fully lived.

'My name is Paul Hobson. I am shepherd, in my way, to the Brethren of the Baptised Way who gather in this place to commune with the Lord and to contemplate the folly of men. I give thanks for your presence, Ensign Archer.'

He could not recall having met Hobson before, although the man's reputation preceded him. Wilkinson had taken pains to mention his history as a senior officer in Lilburne's regiment, become the principal pastor of Newcastle's Baptist congregation since the colonel's brief governorship. This summons presumably had to do with the murders of Sarah Turner, Abigail Walker, and the others. Archer's response was wary. 'Every person seems to know of my movements.'

'I remain Lieutenant-Colonel and deputy governor. I have my means of establishing what takes place in the town.'

'Which makes you send out a lad to intercept me off the street?'

'Young Daniel is most dependable, and the best possible means of conveying you here unseen. I apologise, but it is better if we are not known to have met.'

Archer could not keep a smile from his lips as he recalled the boy's half-hidden pride at having his skills praised. Then he remembered the cool appraisal in Heselrigg's eyes that morning at the castle.

'What is so important as to warrant such caution?'

'You seek information regarding the recent witch trials. Allow me to help you.'

'I do not lack for help. Every faction in the town tries to help me. I fear that none wishes me to uncover the truth.'

Hobson lowered his tone. 'Truth,' he said. 'Only the Almighty deals in truth and reveals it nowhere but in the hearts of His chosen. We know that the Devil walks abroad in this world, and there be many who consort with him in wickedness. What has happened in this town would shame the name of Christ. Truly, "the spirit of the world will not justify but instead will condemn Truth". I know little then of truth, but I played my own small part in these terrible events, and it is one I would share with you.'

Archer said nothing but sat at the end of one of the benches, drawing from Hobson a meltingly warm look.

'It was Pastor Woolfall who led the prosecutions,' continued the Baptist, 'along with old Jenison. Did you know this? Both were hot for a great conspiracy, talking of witches flying off to orgies with the Devil and the like. Here, already, there was much amiss, for such accusations as there were spoke of more everyday wickedness. Mistress Cole was said to have cursed three women, causing them agonies. April Grainger, for jealousy, was accused of tying a knot in a lace at the marriage ceremony of her sister, to render the groom incapable of performing his husbandly duties. These, I could have believed, had it been that any additional witness was called forth. For "What else is a woman but the enemy? She is evil of nature, an inescapable punishment, necessary in the home but ever a temptation, painted with nice colours, always a detriment, a serpent to live with". But there were no witnesses and confessions were lacking. It seemed a strange proceeding.'

Archer pictured the Town Court crowded and expectant, the atmosphere rank with the curdling smell of the defendants' fear.

'There came a point when in frustration Woolfall loudly levied against the women all manner of condemnation. He called them "Whores of Satan". The Devil, he claimed, had seduced them. The aged and barren among them, alike to the young and fertile, were said to have kissed Satan's buttocks and held intercourse with his incubi. He used scripture to justify their condemnation. "For in the hand of the Lord there is a cup, and the wine is red; but the dregs thereof, all the wicked of the earth shall wring them out and drink them".'

Having experienced the force of Woolfall's oratory, Archer could well picture the man whipping up an expectant courtroom.

'At this,' continued Hobson, 'one Elizabeth Armstrong, a woman no longer young but of good family, stood tall and looked straight back at him. 'I know you, Thomas Woolfall.' she said. '"Do not judge, so that you may not be judged".' This raised in him such a pitch of fury as I have ever seen in any man. 'See,' he said, 'how the devil speaks through her.' The woman held her ground and hurled back her own accusations. 'You can produce no witnesses against us,' she said, 'There are no confessions where there is no sin to confess.'

Elinor Loumsdale had done her persuasive work well, thought Archer.

'Mistress Armstrong, while not of my brethren, belonged to a free congregation where all might speak as the Lord moves them. Woolfall sneered at her, describing what he called her vainglorious ignorance as a sure sign of Satan's power. The woman's reply stunned the court. 'God speaks to us all,' she said. 'His Word can be heard by all'. You can well imagine the murmuring this produced around the room. It fell away only as the Scot Kincaid stepped forwards, ready to perform his pricking. He drew out a package of bodkins, wicked things with studded handles, as they were. He said he would show signs, such as marks upon the body and by the pricking for blood, to prove guilt. At that, there in the open court, his two men roughly handled the women, stripping the top clothing from every one of them.'

The colour drained from Archer. His limbs felt weak and his fingers numbed.

'One by one,' continued Hobson, 'the Scot made a public show of searching them, taking care to remove more clothing as he did. Whenever he found some protuberance or blemish, he would pronounce it the devil's teat, or a hellish wen. He exposed each woman's flesh close to her private parts, before plunging the needle into her. For every single one of them, it came out with no sign of blood and the woman was marked as a witch. None could see clearly what he really found, but the place was rank with prurience and sin.'

'But several women survived. How, if he condemned them all by these tortures?'

Archer was astonished to see the Baptist beam with pleasure.

'Calm yourself, young man. I will tell you how some few were saved. At length, a fair young woman was brought before him. The Lord in His mercy saw fit to move me. I stood and said to Kincaid, "Surely this woman is none and need not be tried". Without warning, even as she looked upon me with the hope of salvation in her eyes, the Scot pulled her skirts up over her head, revealing her legs, her thighs and presented to the lewd crowd even her nether parts for all to see. I could see her struggle for fright and shame. He ran a pin into her thigh and let her coats fall back, hiding the very flesh he had pierced. Then he put his hand up into her coats and pulled out the pin, which showed no gore. He went to set her aside as a guilty person and a child of the Devil, but I cried out for him to stop, that I saw God's Grace in the woman.'

'Describe her to me.'

'The Grace of our Lord shone out of her. Favoured, she was, with light.'

'Do you mean she had fair hair?'

Hobson seemed like a man transfixed by a vision. 'Falling like the locks of an angel.'

It was all Archer could do not to cry out again.

'She was pure,' said Hobson, 'and I, perceiving the Lord within her, caused that she be brought back. I allowed for her clothes again to be pulled up to reveal some flesh. I required Kincaid to run the pin into the same place. Neither he nor the judges could refuse me. I watched the Scotch-man closely. This time his pin made a wound which gushed out with blood. So, he cleared her and said she was no child of the Devil, and thus it was she went free.'

Heart pounding, Archer jumped to his feet.

'Do you recall her name, sir? Was it Margaret, or Meg, Weston or Archer, perhaps?'

Hobson looked irritably back at Archer. 'Her name? Yes, Anne. Annie Walker. The daughter of a boat builder. As I say, she went free.'

'Why bring me here only to feed me more lies? I know the names of the women who survived. Six out of twenty. There is no Annie Walker among them.'

'Twenty? No, sir, there were thirty put to trial in that court room, and of those only the Walker girl, Eliza Fairbairn and Chastity Browne were acquitted. Fully twenty-six women were condemned, along with that Matthew Bonner who was so broken before the trial.'

'Another lie! It is Bulmer, not Bonner. I saw the name in the Guildhall records.'

'Bulmer, they have recorded it as, but Bonner was the man's name,' retorted Hobson. 'Bonner of the family of the mayor and the water bailiffs. His three brothers remain in post, but now cowed.'

For the first time in the exchange, Archer's anger turned to hesitation.

'How can I believe a word you say?'

'I was in the court. I know the Bonner family. I had conversed with Matthew Bonner on many occasions. I say again, thirty were put to trial at the assizes. Only three of those escaped the Scot's knives.'

Archer thought Hobson might cry. The Baptist's whole face crumbled.

'It is those other poor women who burden my soul. Could I have saved more from this mockery of a trial? My single intervention raised the ire of the crowd and the contempt of my fellow officers.'

'Yet two women from your brethren have been killed since the hangings. Sarah Turner and Abigail Walker.'

Hobson paled further. Agitatedly, he began to pace about the chamber. 'They were. Now they are taken to the Lord.' He stopped and stared, saying nothing, a wildness in his grey eyes. The man's solid frame shook. Archer rose from his bench, stunned at the transformation.

'Do you not wish their murders to be avenged?'

Hobson backed away towards the tall windows. Silhouetted by a blinding halo of evening light it was as though his words emerged from out of the pure shadow.

'We have sinned, and have done wickedly, and have rebelled, even by departing from His precepts and from His judgments. Neither have we obeyed the voice of the Lord our God, to walk in his laws. What has befallen us is punishment for hearkening not unto the words of His servants the prophets.'

Hobson sank onto his knees in prayer. '"O Lord, according to all thy righteousness, I beseech thee, let thine anger and thy fury be turned away from thy city Jerusalem, thy holy mountain: because for our sins, and for the iniquities of our fathers, Jerusalem and thy people are become a reproach to all that are about us".'

He rose and sat back in one of the benches. 'The time approaches when we shall be judged,' he said in a whisper. 'It is the duty of the saints to make all preparation. In that preparation, I have failed Sarah and Abigail. I should have been stronger. They should never have been permitted to answer the call of that seditious woman Loumsdale. My own sin of weakness brought about their deaths.'

'Why, sir, did you call me here?'

Hobson's eyes filled with pleading. 'It is written, "His severe wrath shall he sharpen for a sword". It is you, Ensign, who has been revealed to me. It is you who return as the Angel of Fire, you who carry in your right hand His sharp, two-edged sword.'

Paul Hobson's wits were surely gone, but still, Archer's slow trudge back down the stair passed in a numbed haze.

The Baptist's descriptions of the trial matched all that Elizabeth Thompson had said regarding the lack of common accusations, the spirited defiance of the accused women and the torments to which they had been exposed. Archer's chest ached with the thought of his sister subject to such humiliations.

Nor had there been any subterfuge in the deputy governor's torrent of testimony that fully thirty women had been put to trial, yet only three acquitted, even if it meant that Meg, too, had been among those condemned.

Thank God Weston had been able to get her out.

The trickery deployed in Kincaid's false pricking also rang true. Was the Scotsman working alone, or had the prosecutors known all along that the women they sent to the gallows were innocent?

Hobson truly believed Archer to have returned to Newcastle as some sort of angel of vengeance. He had lured him to Tuthill Stairs to be anointed as such. Archer felt only renewed anger that, after Deane and Massie, even this unhinged preacher proved to be just another would-be master, intent upon drawing him into a deadly game not of his choosing.

Worse, nothing he had heard from the man came any nearer to helping him locate Meg or to explaining why Elinor Loumsdale's women were still being killed.

As Archer neared the exit onto the steps, another man entered. Looking up, he waited in the cramped doorway.

'Archer. An ensign now, I see. My congratulations.'

He knew the pale, clean-shaven face, but from where?

'Captain Gower. Thomas, please call me Thomas.'

Like Hobson, Gower was formerly commissioned in Lilburne's regiment. His voice seemed more suited to shouting orders than to intimacy, but Archer could find no malice in it.

Gower swept off his broad-brimmed hat while gesturing to the rest of his sombre clothing. 'Forgive my unsoldierly appearance. I am here not on military business, but to attend to the needs of our brethren.'

Archer acknowledged the captain by the removing of his own hat, but Gower responded by putting out a casual hand to stop him from passing on.

'Be at peace. I wish only to ask how you found Pastor Hobson.'

'He is well. We have parted on good terms.'

'Forgive him, please, if he belaboured certain points. You are investigating the recent unfortunate executions of the accused witches. The deaths of our sisters in Christ as well. Paul feels the loss of those poor souls deeply. He remains quite occupied by them.'

'We spoke of it.'

Gower stood taller. For the first time, Archer saw the arresting presence he could muster when he wished.

'Listen to me, that you may understand. I was there alongside

Paul on the morning the condemned women died. I saw what happened. The governor appointed the Lieutenant-Colonel to be official witness to the execution of several moss-troopers who had been disturbing the supply lines to the army in Scotland. We were dispatched up onto the Moor and took a troop to ensure that the militia kept good order during the execution of the women who were called witches. Although it was entirely a civil matter, there was some concern about how the common people would receive the deaths.

'The brigands were dispatched readily enough, but even as they stopped their twitching, the crowd of townspeople continued to gather in their hundreds. I hasten to say there was no disturbance or unseemliness as you often get at a witch-hanging, let alone one where so many local women are condemned. Instead, the ordinary people were unusually subdued. Our presence was entirely unnecessary.

'When the very first group of women, shorn and stripped to plain shifts so as to be readied for death, was led up to the gallows-beam and the ropes placed around their necks, one of them, one of the young ones among them, you understand, fixed the Lieutenant-Colonel with her gaze and held it unbroken upon him. She said not a word and ignored the silent crowd, but went on looking directly at him.

'Well, he turned his back on her, telling me to wait with the men, keep order and report back to him when all was done, before walking off alone back towards the town. It set some of the crowd and even the men whispering, but I soon put a stop to that.

'I told the men to scan the crowd for dissent or disorder, but was myself transfixed by that young woman. Would she settle now upon some other? I prayed she would not choose me. Instead, she held her gaze unwaveringly upon his retreating back and seemed neither to tremble nor blink until the step she had been made to mount was kicked away and she was sent to her death. The Lieutenant-Colonel's thoughts remain fixed upon that woman.'

'You mean he fears she cursed him?' said Archer.

'He has never spoken of it directly, but he is consumed by the fact that he did not intervene to save more of them, apart from the one in whom he saw The Spirit. He wonders, I believe, whether, had he looked for it, The Spirit might have revealed itself in more of those women. He wonders whether the young woman who died staring at him might also have been saved. He wonders, and I believe it never leaves him, whether, had he done more, she and others besides would have been set free. Still more, that Abigail and Sarah might yet live.'

A few minutes after Archer turned away up Tuthill Stairs, Thomas Gower and Paul Hobson sat talking in the upstairs room.

'You are quite well, Paul? You remain pale.'

'I am recovered. Do not think more upon it.'

'I saw Archer on the stair. You still believe we did right to bring him here?'

'I am certain of it, Thomas. Each of these women require justice, those who they hung every bit as much our own sisters. Our hands are tied, our eyes dimmed, but God has a plan for James Archer. The fire of the Lord is within him. He is the messenger of righteousness, the best hope of the saints, a redeeming angel.' He gave Gower a sideways look. 'He is still followed? You trust your men?'

'As I trust you, old comrade, but I will away now and be ready, in case I am needed.'

'God be with you, Thomas,' muttered Hobson solemnly, 'and may He watch over that young man as well.'

Chapter 31

The young secretary closed the door of Heselrigg's office behind him. He paused to allow the information he had just received to sink in.

How happy his mother would be, and how proud his father, that he was making such use of the opening they had created for him. To be asked to manage the contract shortlists, with all the personal opportunity it would entail, after just a few short months in this service, was an honour, and a chance greater than he might have dreamed. Why, then, did the initial pleasure now feel hollow, sullied?

A scrap of scripture came to him, "Hell and destruction are never full; so the eyes of man are never satisfied".

Even as he noiselessly breathed the verse, a strong arm took him around the neck, and in one sweeping motion, drew him sharply backward and up. Behind him, his document case and pens scattered across the floor. Before he could even whimper, he was spun into the adjacent corridor and left, facing the contorted face of his assailant.

'The girl. Where is she?'

Pearson blinked in an effort to stem the welling tears as Captain-Lieutenant Draper pushed him even harder against the wall. Pain ripped up his spine as his toes left the floor and he dangled before the spittle-flecked beard of the tall soldier.

Panic began to overwhelm him. He had been warned about Draper. Surely, though, the man would not dare to do him any real harm, certainly none he could not later deny. The look in the officer's eyes and the slackness about his mouth belied any such reassurance. Pearson rapidly croaked out a response.

'What girl? Put me down, please.'

Draper hunched his shoulders in order further to tighten his grip and hoist the secretary higher. The edges of poorly dressed stone caught the young man's coat as the captain-lieutenant brought his own face within an inch of Pearson's.

'You know which girl. Archer's sister, the Weston whore. Where is she stowed?'

Pearson wanted, in that instant, to turn his head, to close his eyes, to do anything to avoid Draper's wild, animal look.

'It is imperative I find that girl before Archer does. So now you shall tell me where she is hidden.'

Praise the Lord for His Mercy, thought Pearson, that Mitchell before him had been so meticulous and had never entrusted any such secret to paper.

There was no record of the destinations of those spirited out of the town before the executions. In some cases, he knew, families had been able to arrange the flight themselves. In others, for those deemed too dangerous to be given back to their kin, Mitchell alone had determined where they had been taken. Not even the governor shared that knowledge. More, he had specifically instructed it to be withheld from the women's relatives, his own officers, and the town magistrates, right up to the mayor.

Mitchell, along with the answer Draper sought, was long gone into Scotland with the army. Pearson smirked up at the taller man and slowly shook his head.

Eventually, Draper walked away in disgust, brushing the boy's sweat and the smell of his fear from his normally immaculate uniform. He believed him. That was the problem. There was no point in trying to force answers the little secretary couldn't give.

He would, after all, need to get directly after Archer. For this, he would not take any member of the garrison. He would return to the big house on the steps. There, he would be able to pick up the kind of men required for the work he had in mind.

Chapter 32

Climbing to the very top of Tuthill Chare, Archer took the left-hand road, continuing steeply uphill. Approaching the main road from the Westgate, he was forced to wait for a gap to appear in a near to unceasing procession of carts, horses and driven flocks. Here, too, was ample evidence that Newcastle thrived, whatever complaints his uncle and the old families might have. Skippon would not like to hear it, but it was clear that Heselrigg had secured both the coal trade and the town's wider prosperity, despite the turmoil occasioned by the witch hunt.

How would he make his report to Deane and the Council? He was anxious now for it to be done with.

The ministers and their godly backers would have begun, he could be certain, with a genuine intent to cleanse the town of sin. But it was also most likely they had wanted to set a warning to others, a powerful illustration of what would happen to any who questioned, let alone resisted, God's chosen path. That fitted all too well with everything he had seen of the workings of the new town government.

Perhaps it was also true, as William had suggested, that the apathy of the townsfolk, resulting in the disappointingly meagre outcome from the bell-man's first call, had persuaded someone to extend its reach, to give the hunt for witches a helping hand.

Did it really matter then, whether he was to believe Dawson, that those he called 'Papists' used the witch accusations to attack the godly, or to prefer William's story, that some in the Puritan faction had acted first, fearing the old families' resurgence?

Somehow, perhaps because of the man's evident mania, it was

only the personal story of the baptist minister, who alone had had the courage to question the pricker and expose his tricks, that he felt able to accept without reservation. Hobson did not believe all of those women to be witches. Nor, now, did Archer.

Elizabeth Thompson had gone so far as to say that none were guilty. Could he, possibly, believe even this?

A gap sufficient for his passage appeared in the flow of traffic. Get this next task done. Then he could descend to the warehouse on The Close where she would be waiting.

His brain continued to work fast, possibilities and pathways opening up in his mind. Anderson, Henderson, Coulter. Grainger, Cole, Robson. Even Mistress Fenwick and Jennie Dawson. Royalists and Puritans among the dead and the saved alike.

They had lost control of the Scottish pricker. That was not surprising, given the bounty on offer to him for each conviction. It would also explain the extraordinary numbers found guilty despite the lack of confessions or witnesses.

For fully twelve of the condemned women to have escaped the noose, however, while so many were still left to die, could mean only that there was more he did not understand.

Was it possible, following the convictions, that there had been some sort of diabolical trade or exchange for the women's lives? Did Sir Arthur Heselrigg have to make choices as to who lived and who died, to return order to the town and to keep safe London's coals? Was it to hide this that Elinor's women were still being dispatched?

The castle had to be at the heart of things. If Heselrigg was involved, then Skippon would be very pleased to know.

Archer raised his eyes and looked with dismay at the cluster of blackened stone buildings which were his next destination. Across the way, ominously dominating its crowded, raised graveyard, stood the bulky outline of Saint Andrew's Church and behind that, the weather-worn walls of Newgate Prison.

Ducking into the gaol's low entrance arch, a rusted grille barred Archer's way. From beyond the barrier emerged a shaven-headed, filthy gaoler. The guardian screwed up his recessed eyes, growled incomprehensibly, growled again and twisted his mouth into what might have been a smile. Dimly, Archer began to apprehend that the man was asking what or who he wanted. His own town's dialect, compounded by a complete lack of teeth, had completely defeated him.

He pulled out his Council warrant and offered it across, only for the paper to be shooed away without a glance. With another hideous grimace, the shaven-headed man unlocked the grille. As Archer entered, he spoke, equally impenetrably, to another gaoler who stood to escort the visitor in.

The interior of Newgate was every bit as bad as Archer had feared it would be. The second guardian led him down a long, barely lit corridor, in places green with moss, unlocking and re-locking behind them two sturdy doors along their way. Through the second of these, they entered a low room in which sat two further dishevelled gaolers, disturbed in playing at dice. Archer was conducted through a high doorway opposite. Light filtered down into the next gallery from deep shafts set in a distant roof. At its end, the guide rapped on a final door. Receiving an answering noise from within, he opened it without the need for a key and gestured for Archer to enter.

The chamber was unexpectedly bright. Windows overlooked a pleasant courtyard garden, while the room itself was established partly as office, partly as comfortable reception area. The man who rose to meet him from behind the desk had the beak-like nose and long face characteristic of many local families. He approached with apparent warmth as Archer again handed across his papers.

'Of course. Any help we can afford an officer of the Council of State, you need only ask. I am the warden here at Newgate. Josiah Starkey is my name.'

'Warden Starkey, thank you. I am come here to check some information relating to recent inmates. Specifically, I seek the record of the thirty accused witches held in the prison during the last year.'

The man hesitated. Archer pressed home his request more forcefully.

'The ledgers you keep recording prisoners in, and out, of Newgate. I need to see them. Immediately.'

The man again looked uncomfortable and made no move to help. Eventually, he stammered a reply. 'The corporation may be able to help you, Ensign Archer, or perhaps the Town Court has that information?'

Archer stood, ensuring his cloak was pushed well back to show his red uniform coat, insignia of rank and weapons-belt.

'The ledgers, Warden Starkey. The Council of State requires me to examine your current ledgers. Now!'

Starkey turned pale. He walked around the desk to an old press, returning with two large, bound volumes.

'Thank you. If you please, sit with me,' said Archer.

Yes, the first book covered the last winter, the newer volume being current, running up to the present day. Patiently, he kept turning the greasy pages, concentrating methodically upon the columns of names and dates recorded upon them. He found that, while they were sloppily written, they were at least legible and, it seemed, comprehensive. Archer took out his notebook as his search reached the previous December. He traced a finger down the names on the first page for that month, then the second, and there came to a halt.

'The pages have been removed. There is a gap here, covering,' he checked again, 'part of the December of last year and early January of this. That is when the first of the accused would have entered the prison.'

The warden looked aghast.

'Wait.' Archer looked forwards through the second book, all the way to the present week. There, back in August, was the list of the condemned, the note simply stating '*to Gallowgate*'. He flicked back and forwards in both volumes through the months in between. The turn of each thick page rasped in the tense silence. In at least two other months, May and April, pages had also been removed. He continued further on into the ledger with mounting impatience. Elsewhere, on three further, surviving, pages, one or more entries were defaced, obliterated with a dark ink.

The warden still sitting rigidly by his side, Archer returned to each volume. The aim was clear. The ledgers recorded none of the other names he had heard to be associated with the trial. No Robson, nor Grainger. Neither Mistress Fenwick nor Jennie Dawson was to be found, nor any of the women he knew to have been held in Newgate and later freed.

He looked up at Starkey, held his eyes for a long minute, then opened the second book at the May entries.

'The page has been deliberately excised. Look. You can just about see where the knife has taken it out. How do you explain this?'

Without giving the warden an opportunity to respond, he returned to the list of the condemned written into the second book. The same list, yes, the exact same names, Jane Copeland, Elizabeth Dobson and old Alice Hume alongside the others. He read it over again. No, it was not quite the same. Here was included the name of yet another woman, a Janet Martin. Other than that, only the name of Matthew Bulmer stood out. His entry had been inked over, rewritten. He could not make out the original, which had been thoroughly defaced. He left it, knowing that underneath the name would read 'Bonner'.

'Who is this Janet Martin?'

'The woman Martin was brought in from Morpeth. The men there couldn't bring themselves to do the necessary work, so it was decided to send her to us, to let the Town executioner work upon her as with the others. You will find her name in the week before, entering here.'

Archer checked. Yes, there she was, listed as '*transferd from Moor-peth*'.

'I see it. Janet Martin, from out of the town, is recorded in, and recorded out to her death. These fifteen, along with her, are retained in the records on the day of their execution, but otherwise they have simply disappeared. They never entered this place, but they left it, warden? There is also no record at all, in or out, of at least fifteen others who I know to have been held here, accused of witchcraft. All but three of those women returned to this place after being condemned at the assizes and yet your records of them have been removed. Is this the manner in which you keep Newgate?'

Starkey looked plainly terrified. His voice was now barely a whisper.

'I cannot help you officer, because I do not know the answers. I am new in this post. The former warden is gone to Scotland with the Lord General. The entries before my time I cannot vouch for. I do not know why the record is abused so.'

Again, new men in post. Men disappeared over the border. Archer wheeled around and drew his dagger in one movement. He wasn't going to use it, but Starkey wasn't to know that. Perhaps he needed the extra persuasion?

'But you knew,' Archer said, close to the man's reddening ear. 'You knew there would be trouble as soon as I asked for these books. So don't try to play innocent with me.'

'I swear, I know nothing else. The ledgers I found like that. One day, soon after the witches were taken from here, a woman came asking what had become of another of the prisoners. It was only then, I swear, when I could find no record of that inmate at all, that I realised what was amiss. It was only then I discovered the missing leaves. I was scared. I swear by the Lord.'

'You would have reported this. To whom?'

'I went straight to the sheriff,' scrambled Starkey in reply. 'He told me that my predecessor was dismissed as unreliable, and this was why I had been appointed. Then he sent me away. Immediately after, I reported these things to the office of the governor. One of the officers threatened me and told me never to speak of this again.'

Archer considered this a minute. It rang true, and the warden seemed almost relieved to be able to share his actions.

'The woman who came to inquire, did you know her?'

Starkey's head shook. The man's eyes ran with tears. His mouth trembled.

'Think, Warden Starkey.' Archer moved the shining point of his dagger closer.

'Dawson, it was Mistress Jennie Dawson.'

'She who was formerly a prisoner here, yet escaped the noose?'

Starkey now looked utterly terrified. His hands shook and his face had turned bone white. It was some time before he could speak, hoarsely. 'She was, sir. And she did.'

'And there were others who escaped sentence. Many others, warden.'

It was more an accusation than a question. Archer allowed an ominous quiet to grow as the man considered how to respond.

Eventually, apologetically, Starkey spoke. 'It was before my time. I swear by the Lord I know nothing.'

'The prisoner Mistress Dawson spoke about. Do you remember her name?'

'Robson, Anna Robson, I swear it is the truth.'

'Meg Archer. Do you know that name, too?'

The warden's words now emerged as a torrent. 'Safe! Safe! The men here still talk about it, how her uncle, your own uncle, came in person to arrange her freedom. He was the only one who did that, sir. You can imagine to what rumour it would expose him. But I swear she is saved.'

'And where is she gone?'

'I know nothing more. Please. You must believe me. I trust in Christ and am an honest man. For mercy.'

Archer stepped back towards the door, lowering the blade as he did so. He knew real fear well enough. The man was spent. Expecting that there nothing more to be gained, he chanced one final question. 'The officer who threatened you. His name?'

'Please, sir, he will-'

'Who? Who will?'

'Draper. Captain-Lieutenant Draper.'

Chapter 33

Upon quitting Newgate, rather than walk directly back to the lower town, Archer turned right and took the long route through Saint Andrew's graveyard, skirting the blast-damaged town walls, heading towards the stench from the tanneries at Darn Crook. By his feet, tiny barred windows were set into the wall, the only light, he imagined, for the cells below ground.

Had Meg stood, looking up towards the free air through one of those pathetic openings? He worked to put the image out of his head. Soon enough, they would be reunited.

Starkey's revelation about Draper came as just one more reason to quit the town. The conspiracy reached into the castle, presumably all the way to Heselrigg. He doubted the warden would do other than run and tell someone about his visit, perhaps Draper or someone else in the governor's service. After the encounter with Sanderson, followed by the descent into that hellish torture chamber, he felt as though he were already the hunted, and there seemed no more he could discover.

He took a few hesitant steps further into the graveyard. The church, squat, black and uncompromising, abutted a series of market gardens positioned just inside the westward sweep of the walls. It offered such a bleak prospect, it might itself have been the prison. The low gate beyond was the Gallowgate. It was through here the condemned took their final journey towards the scaffolds on the southerly reaches of the Town Moor, the stretch of common land separating the surrounding farms, and the villages of Fenham and Jesmond, from Newcastle itself.

Archer stared long at the gateway, relieved Meg had not taken that dreadful ride.

Released from his morbid reflection by a blast of icy rain, he began his search of the church surrounds, moving back and forward in an even sweep of the ground. Finally, on the southwesterly side, near the low wattle fence separating the graves from the gardens, he found the evidence he had been seeking. It came in the form of an area of darker earth, damper than the surrounding soil and still in places raised. Five paces by ten, it formed a smoothed-off rectangle ending a few feet from the mossy bulk of the main wall. Enough room down there, he judged, for a dozen bodies clear, up to twenty if you didn't mind throwing them in together, as he imagined had been the case. There was no marker, no sort of memorial, but he knew it for the common pit that served the women as a grave.

A chill beyond that of the wintry afternoon ran through Archer. Another squall came in. He shivered, even under his cloak. Before leaving the prison, the combination of his uniform and a few coins had ensured that its guardians confirmed both Starkey and William to have told him the truth, the surprising truth that Weston himself had come into that foul place to confirm Meg's escape. She was not left down there in the cold clay with those others, but still, they deserved what acknowledgement he could make.

Softly, he whispered a prayer which was almost lost in the gathering strength of the wind. "'The righteous perisheth, and no man layeth it to heart: and merciful men are taken away, none considering that the righteous is taken away from the evil to come".'

He walked away down the shallow slope of the graveyard. Halfway across, the final line of the same chapter of scripture came into his head. "There is no peace, sayeth my God, to the wicked".

Head kept down by harder rain, Archer strode on as fast as he could, keeping the buildings of the old Blackfriars monastery to his right. In its ruins, shapes huddled against the developing storm. His route took him down the Long Stairs. The steep descent was hemmed in by tall, old buildings. As the thin strip of sky overhead darkened and thunder pealed its way up the steps, Archer was kept largely dry and out of the worst of the wind. It left him free both to concentrate upon his footing and to try to settle his thoughts.

It was not any one thing that Elinor's women might have seen or heard. What had been cleared out of the way, one way or another, was any record, or any witness, to the twelve who had escaped the gallows, Meg among them.

Twelve! It still seemed incredible. Someone was ensuring that the very fact and memory of their accusation, imprisonment and trial were completely erased. He needed to understand those names. This agreed appointment with the Bracewell boy provided what was possibly his last chance to uncover them. Besides, if there was the least clue the young court official could give him regarding Meg's whereabouts, he must take it.

Reaching the final side entry before The Close, Archer looked searchingly down towards the river and back up to the old town. Evening had come on with the storm and the darkness was near to complete. He left the steps, satisfied he was neither followed nor observed, his eagerness to see Elizabeth Thompson perturbed only by the memory of her earlier anger upon Sandhill.

Moving carefully along the right-hand passage until he reached the rear of the Thompson warehouse, he was glad to see that on this side the only way in was through a single, anonymous door. This was set two-thirds of the way along a high wall of dressed stone, at the far end of which three small and filthy windows, each barely wide enough to take a man's shoulders at a squeeze, would allow a murky light to penetrate into the rear of the premises. He stepped forwards the last few feet, breath held. As Elizabeth had promised, the little door was unlocked. It gave easily under Archer's cautious push.

Entering, he closed the door quietly behind him, running both top and bottom bolts back into place and checking each was secure. He had emerged between two rows of crates, stacked on either side to twice his height. Above these extended a stout timbered ceiling. It became apparent that this formed the base of a wide first floor gallery running all the way around the warehouse but leaving, in its centre, a great well of open space, high above which perched a huge skylight. Approaching night, under the dark of the storm clouds, meant that the only light came from three partially shuttered, hanging lanterns, casting warm, yellow beams across the boarded floor.

The warehouse, although much in use, was scrupulously organised. The central open area was kept clear and had been swept clean. On all sides, it was hemmed in by similarly neat crate alleys. A portable winch, by which two men together would be able to move and place these boxes, was stored away to Archer's left. The visible galleries on each of the next two floors were crammed to their very edges with piles of large, fabric filled leather sacks. The very air was infested with tiny fibres, irritating Archer's throat. He stifled a dry cough.

From his position by the rear wall, he could see directly across to the closed main doors. Upon them, a heavy timber beam was in place, nestled in iron bands and blocking entry from The Close. The slim wicket gate cut into the right-hand of the doors was also shut. The twin windows he had seen from the street were secured on this side by the presence of strong wooden shutters. Good security, he thought. But there must be also at least one guard, to protect this much valuable raw cloth and finished fabric.

He crept forwards, scanning constantly. It only confirmed what Elizabeth Thompson had told him, nothing more to see than the one door built into a thin plank wall in the right-hand corner, so as to separate off a back office. There was nowhere else to search. Presumably Elizabeth, or her mother, had ensured that the guardian was presently occupied elsewhere.

Satisfied the place was empty, Archer approached the office

door. It showed a thin outline of pale light. Overhead, the rain lashed against the wide panes of the skylight and behind him the lantern light flickered. He wondered whether he should knock, having received only the instruction to come here at the set hour. Deciding not to make any unnecessary noise, Archer took the wooden handle and tested the door. It opened smoothly, allowing a rancid, animal smell of burning oil to escape.

The room beyond was even darker than the main warehouse. A tall, unusually wide lamp burned disconcertingly white upon a central table. Behind it, two shuttered windows were set high up on the far wall. The illumination was clean and harsh, but barely reached to the timber walls, or the tall cupboards placed against each of them. In the confines of the cramped room, the burning smell rose into an overpowering, visceral stench.

Was he early? Elizabeth had been characteristically clear regarding the timings. No, the green cape lay before him, draped over the table.

Archer advanced, blood draining from his face, a cold trembling descending from his shoulders. Behind the table, appallingly clear in the stark light, lay two bodies, blood pooled about them. The larger of the two, that of a pockmarked young man, remained upwards, revealing the great, frontal, slashing wound which had killed him. The other, the much smaller corpse of a woman, was face down, but Archer knew all too well the plain, grey dress, cut low on the arms, which dragged away from the stick-like limbs.

Warned by the sentiment of a movement, he turned to see a short, sallow man with hollowed cheeks and a look of misplaced amusement step forwards from the outer shadows. The man's dark eyes shifted sideways, his grey lips curling into a full smile. Archer followed the glance, whereupon a hefty fist crashed into the side of his head, sending him staggering backwards. A blond giant of a man smirked cruelly across at him. That cold sneer was the last thing Archer knew, before the little man smashed him over the back of his head, and all went black.

Chapter 34

Elias Sanderson beat the small bounds of his watch-captain's room in mounting excitement.

The knuckles on his right hand still stung where he had struck Edmund Blackett. A little blood seeped through the loose cloth he had wrapped about them. That snivelling popinjay should be happy to have been sent on his way so lightly, not to have been arrested and thrown into the common cell. The keelmen they were already holding would have had their fun. It was just as well for the boy that he had given up everything so quickly.

Sanderson might have worked another man harder, just for the pleasure. But as soon as Blackett had mentioned the New Model ensign with the long facial scar, he had stopped the interrogation, becoming impatient only to have the informer on his way.

He had known something was wrong about Archer, Council warrant notwithstanding. He had anticipated something, but nothing so far-reaching as this.

Christ's britches, but it was good.

Good enough to get him called down to Whitehall. Good enough to be presented to Scott and Bishop themselves. Perhaps, if they found him useful and amenable, he could even get to stay there. There must be need of men like him in London, away from this stinking watch house and Newcastle's narrow, provincial jealousies.

He would need to be careful.

Where and when would he arrange to lift Archer? He couldn't risk anyone else getting the credit. He would take only his most trusted men.

They would not even bring him directly back to the watch house. The castle? No, the clear danger there was that the soldiers would take over. Besides, Scott was said to be even more suspicious of the army than of the disparate groups of remaining Royalists.

There were other places they could take the ensign to first, quiet places where they would have leisure to extract all of the information he had to give, long before there would be any need to report this further.

He could use that, too. His initiative. His independence. Sanderson considered that trusting nobody was one of the things the Council's intelligence service most admired about him. Yes, he would see this through alone, and receive all the more reward for it.

His reverie was disturbed by the arrival of Ferris, the stocky, bald watchman who had remained with him when they had apprehended Archer in the cockpit yard.

'What do you mean by coming in here unannounced?'

'There's been a double murder, Sir. The killer's locked in.'

'What does it have to do with me? I'm busy.'

'You'll want to be in on this. Cowell's keeping it away from Captain Tait. The man who did it is your friend Archer.'

Sanderson stopped his pacing, brow knotted.

'Where's this from?' he asked.

'Small lad, just came in, dark, foreign like. Maybe off the ships. Says they've got him barred up with the two he's done in.'

'Who's got him barred up?'

'I divvent knaa. Down at the Thompson warehouse. Right now.'

'Does anyone else know?'

'He came to me and Cowell, and I've come straight to you.'

The smile Sanderson had been holding in finally burst forth. 'Fetch Cowell,' he said. 'Tell no-one else.'

Chapter 35

The two bodies lay beside Archer, their mingled blood staining his own hands and clothing. Bringing their limp forms into focus, he rolled onto his side, straining to rise as if he might yet be able to help Elizabeth Thompson.

A measured kick sent him sprawling. It was followed up by a furious downward blow to his neck, knocking him back into the gore. He scrambled away, crab-like, avoiding another boot, only to find himself staring up at the grey figure of Elias Sanderson, flanked by the same two watchmen who had beaten him in the cockpit yard.

'You murdering bastard.' Sanderson jerked a hand towards the bodies. 'These two, who are they to you, eh?'

Archer reached down, but his weapons-belt was gone. Sanderson held it, scabbard scraping against the floor, just out of reach.

'Missing this? A cavalry sword's a strange weapon for an infantry officer, Archer. Good enough to butcher a defenceless woman, though?'

'Look at them, man. Both those blades are clean. There were two others here. One of them tall and blond, the other black-haired, short and dark.'

'You won't lie your way out of this.' The watch-captain turned to the thick-browed watchman. 'Cowell, get out there and find some rope or something. I'll feel happier once he's properly secured.'

Cowell disappeared into the main warehouse. Archer began to stand, but Sanderson growled a warning, throwing the belt down and drawing out his own long rapier blade.

'I'll do you in a minute if you don't stay put.'

Archer's mind raced. Elizabeth Thompson had been betrayed. The two men who had ambushed him must have followed her or otherwise discovered the rendezvous.

'I don't know why you've done this,' continued Sanderson, 'but we have you. Will we see you hang as a murderer, Archer? Or shall you earn a far worse death?'

A look of triumph spread over the watch-captain's thin face. He opened his free hand to reveal Archer's council warrant, crumpled about Massie's cipher cylinder. Even from his position on the floor, Archer could see that the dolphin seal had been broken, and that the thin roll of parchment within flapped loose.

'You think yourself so superior, me just being a watch-captain and all?' continued Sanderson. 'See, I work directly for Scott. I'm the ears of the Council in this town, and I hear things. That's why they came along to tell me, after your friendly drink with Fenwick and that traitor Massie.'

So, the Blackett boy had betrayed them.

Sanderson waved the warrant and cylinder before Archer. 'What's this about? Some sort of hidden message.'

Archer lowered his head, dizzied. A vision emerged of Elizabeth, glaring at him accusingly, before her strained features merged with those of the fierce Ulster girl. He shook his head aggressively, before they could change again into the fearful face of Meg.

Sanderson regarded his prisoner, smirkingly. 'No matter. They'll have plenty men can decode this lot. But these two here, they're just our bonus, eh? Just for you and me, for old times. What are they, more of your treachery? You came here to meet with the Thompson girl and whatever that is,' he went on, indicating Bracewell's rent remains. 'You set a filthy trap. What for, Archer? Tell me, and it may go better for you.'

'You have it wrong, Sanderson. Look at those papers again. You already know I work for the Council.'

Sanderson turned to the bald watchman, laughing. 'What do you think, Ferris? Shall we believe him?'

Sanderson's tight smile dropped into a snarl. 'I know you visited the Thompson house last night. I know you've just committed treason. And now look where we are.'

His face dropped abruptly, and he looked back towards the door. 'What the hell is Cowell doing?'

Ferris shrugged.

'Go check.'

The bald man rattled the door, but it held fast. He bent over to pull at it harder. 'I can't open it.' Fear began to seep into his voice. 'It's barred.'

Keeping his guard upon Archer, Sanderson glared at the muscular watchman, then past him, to the door. Around the line of its frame, a more intense orange joined the yellow of the warehouse lantern light.

'It's on fire,' shouted Ferris. 'The whole place is on fire!'

Sanderson looked from the door back to Archer.

'You, stay.'

Stepping away, but keeping his eyes closely fixed upon his prisoner, the watch-captain heaved his body against the central table, jerking it towards one of the high windows. 'Help me, man,' he shouted to the watchmen.

Between them, they jostled and scraped the table past the two bodies and up to the back wall. At a nod from Sanderson, Ferris stepped up onto it and began to pull at the high shutter.

'It's got a lock,' the bald man cried. 'Wait, I can get it free.' He took out his dagger, beginning to use it to hack away at the wood to one side of the shutter. As he did so, a mighty crash reached them from within the main building.

'Faster, man,' yelled Sanderson. 'Get it open.'

The outside rim of the door was now glowing a deep and steady red. Tendrils of smoke had begun to creep their way into the room.

A chunk of shutter tore away. The watchman attacked the

215

wood again, on the other side, flinging another piece down onto the floor. He grunted with satisfaction, sheathed his dagger, reached up with both hands, and wrenched away shutter and window together. Dropping them to the floor and climbing up and into the gap, Ferris's head disappeared, swiftly followed by his shoulders, body and, with one last heave, the man's legs and boots.

The watch-captain kept his sword levelled upon Archer, eyes darting between his captive, the glow around the door and the blackness of the exposed window frame.

Archer watched Sanderson's restless vigil. What would the man's plan be? Would they make any effort to get him out or simply leave him here to burn? He shuffled back a few inches against the wall, moving his feet into a position where he might gain greater purchase. It was desperate, but if only he could avoid the blade on the way in, he had a slim chance of surprising the larger man, perhaps sufficiently to disarm him.

Even if he could overpower Sanderson, what then? Not allowing for the other watchmen, outside there would still, he presumed, be the blond giant and his shorter companion to consider. But he had to try something, other than to sit and wait to die.

The window frame cracked and splintered as the bald watchman's body fell inwards in a spray of blood, landing with a heavy, wet thud.

Sanderson looked dumbly at the ragged cut across Ferris's throat. It was opening enough for Archer. Propelling himself upwards from floor and wall, he twisted his body to roll under the arc of the watch-captain's swinging rapier. Archer's leading hand grasped Sanderson's wrist and wrenched the sword free. It clattered away over the boards. He tried to leap after the weapon, but the bigger man fell upon him, the weight and the force of his attack causing them both to tumble closer to the glowing door.

The heat of the inferno raging in the main warehouse scorched Archer's left side, but before he could even roll away, the watch-captain was at him again, bringing a knee crashing down into his shoulder. Sanderson followed up with a punch to the head, leaning back to prepare another savage blow.

Jackknifing his legs off the floor, Archer crashed his boots up into his assailant. Caught off balance, Sanderson wavered sufficiently for Archer to use his size against him, rolling him across and into the wall. As the watch-captain's head and shoulder smashed against its searing planks, he bellowed, dropping onto one knee.

Archer crabbed back towards the cooler centre of the room, away from the walls, away from the bodies. Standing, his head ached and swam, his eyes stung, but the escape from the fight and the heat of the walls brought the briefest of respites. They could not have long. Smoke billowed in. Even through the thick soles of his boots, he could feel the heat rising through the very boards of the floor. The fire must already be spreading through the cellars.

Sanderson stood, re-armed. His face, darkened and distorted by anger, pain and fear, became less than human. In the thickening fug, he seemed instead a demonic presence, flickering now closer, now further away.

'What have you done?' he yelled with a very corporeal voice. His words became lost in the shriek of tearing timbers. The very walls glowed. The heat closed in as if the blaze, in its malevolence, were reaching out for them.

The watch-captain lunged forwards. Archer ripped himself out of the sword's path, feeling as he did so something tear deep inside him. He staggered away, pain threatening to pull him down. A slow flow of blood trickled down his face. A heavier cloud of smoke drifted up, further shielding his opponent from view. Sensing the weakness, Sanderson threw himself sideways, crashing into Archer and sending him tumbling towards the far corner of the room. Archer's vision blurred further. As it slowly recovered, he watched his opponent shake his long head, hawk out a glob of phlegm which sizzled as it hit the hot boards, and snarl manically across at him.

A new, jarring sound reached them over the rising roar from beyond the warehouse door. On the upper floors, the bales, boxes, stairs and floorboards were beginning to screech as they tore apart in the heat. Archer jerked to his left, Sanderson following his motion a fraction of a second too late. Jumping back off his planted foot, Archer dodged past the man's guard and leapt into the very worst of the heat and the smoke. Reaching out in desperation, his gloved fingers closed against his own weapons-belt. He scrambled for the sword hilt. Archer turned about and came up onto one knee just as the watchman sprang upon him.

The wide double edge of Archer's mortuary sword met the downwards thrust of Sanderson's thinner blade and shuddered. The watchman's lighter weapon rebounded from the challenge, coming close to disarming him. In shock, he stepped back, allowing Archer to rise and prepare for another attack. The demented mask reappeared upon Sanderson's soot besmirched face.

From above came an almighty cacophony, closely followed by a debilitating blast of heat. Both men looked up to see the planking of the ceiling crumble. A stack of burning bales teetered there, threatening to tumble into the room. Archer retreated, his back closing upon the heat of the wall. He brought his spare hand up in a vain effort to shield his face. Sanderson pressed forwards the attack, his sword making a high arc to come down upon Archer's unprotected side. More boards above them gave way. Sanderson, sword still raised, lifted his eyes as the blazing cascade forced its way through the widening gap. It hung above the watchman for one dreadful instant, then fell with a precipitous, percussive crash.

Archer called out, 'Sanderson!' but the only reply was an agonised roaring as, before his horrified eyes, the flaming bales consumed the watchman. The smell of burning flesh brought bile up into his throat so that it felt as if he were scorched both inside and out. He slumped to the floor as the flame, heat and smoke reached out to claim him in their turn. Each breath became an agony. Seeking respite, he closed his eyes to find, through their orange-tinted lids, only the throbbing image of Meg's terrified face. Deeper inside, blasted by an onrushing, crushing blackness, he moved beyond all thought. With one blistered hand, he still gripped his sword hilt, the other wrapped around his weapons-belt, as if those instruments of death might alone offer him some further protection.

In the next pained gasp, Archer felt, rather than saw, the door crash open, jolting him back to something approaching life. A black-clad man, sodden cloth wrapped about his head, burst through and scanned the carnage. Reaching down, he took Archer under the arms and pulled him, hands still compulsively clutching both sword and belt, back out into the open space of the main warehouse floor.

Hazily, Archer became aware of the open wicket-gate. Through it penetrated a damp wind. The first man was joined by another, similarly veiled. Together, they dragged him across the central void, careering between falling, fiery bales. Reaching the little door, they hurried out into the storm. Laying him down across the street, both men looked back as licks of flame began to take hold of the warehouse front. The first rescuer stood, temporarily numbed, his head covering coming away to reveal the strong, stolid features of Thomas Gower. The captain pursed his lips, gave the second man a brief order, and strode away towards the assembled rabble of onlookers.

The continuing rain soothed Archer's burned skin and brought him further back from the darkness. The second rescuer was cradling his shoulders. A leather water bottle was being gently held up to his mouth. He drank, and almost immediately began to retch. The man helped him over onto one side, where he brought up a great deal of the liquid, along with a clawing irritation which lingered in mouth and throat.

Rolling back, he found the reaction to have further cleared his head. High above them, great bursts of fire danced around the shattered remnants of the great skylight. Back at ground level, he watched limply as the inside of the warehouse began to burn a fiercer red. He saw Captain Gower, firmly outlined against the hellish glow, arms pointing about, lips moving with shouts that were lost in the roar, organising and directing the men into a chain, to ferry containers of water from the nearest pump, scrambling to soak the buildings on either side of the devastated Thompson Warehouse before the conflagration could spread.

The thought of Elizabeth, left in there to burn, threatened to overwhelm Archer. He tried to move, desperate to go back, but found he could not even stand. Against his mumbled protests, the other man dragged him through the mud, further towards the river walls and away from the heat and the light.

Through the sheeting rain, over where the Long Stairs met The Close, another face stared out, bright in the glow of the fire.

'It's him, do you see him?' the second rescuer called across.

Gower turned. 'What? Who?'

'The little man, the one who told us where to find Archer, he's here.'

Archer summoned up his remaining strength to look more closely at the figure, more like to a ghost than a man, almond eyes in a flat face showing round and pale below a helmet of black hair. The spectre retreated into the darkness. Archer was left with a last, uncomfortable prick of recognition, before slumping back into unconsciousness.

Chapter 36

Edmund Blackett veered unsteadily. His head was fogged. The urgent churning in his guts was followed by a sharp pain rising up his gullet. But neither this nor the downpour running off his beaverskin hat and fine cape distracted him from the evening's terrible misfortune.

After Sanderson had pushed him out, bleeding and without reward, he had gone directly to Scarlet Lily's. There, he had sat alone and ordered one jug after another of mouth-coating Gascon wine. He had resisted the urge to take one of Lily's girls upstairs, even the new, young, dark one. He could be proud of that. She could wait, or there would be others. But now the final cups with which he had rewarded himself felt like an indulgence too far.

The pain receded. For a few seconds, even the torrent seemed to ease. The cool of the night reached in to soothe Edmund's brow. He stood up taller to allow its damp caress to reach his exposed neck. Buffeted by a new blast of rain, he put his head down again to recommence the climb as briskly as his own fragile state and the stream of water beneath his feet would allow. His heavy shoes echoed upon each landing, their every step pinching at his left foot. They were never going to wear in, and was that the beginnings of a leak towards the heel? He would make William have the cordwainer thrashed.

Edmund stopped again and swayed, looking up towards the top of the bank and the blurred outline of William's new house. William. What would he make of this?

His cheek still throbbed where Sanderson had struck him. Tears threatened to overwhelm him. Was there nothing he could do without his brother's involvement?

Taking in a deep breath, his head cleared a little further. William was the answer, of course. He would tell his brother all about Massie, about the scarred New Model officer and the London men, whoever they were. He was sure that he would recall their names more clearly in the morning. Was it Smith, Skipwith? But he would go to William now.

William always knew what to do. Hadn't he set Edmund to keep watch over Fenwick? Well, this would be a good repayment. William would be sure to know where else to go with the information. And he would know much better than Edmund how much they could expect to get for it. He had been foolish before, not to go to his brother directly, let alone ever to have trusted Sanderson. He tried to smile, but the pain was too great. William would also know how best to handle the watch-captain.

He felt much better. His stomach had newly settled. His head remained clear. Even the shoes were not, perhaps, as poorly made as he had thought. First, he needed to get out of this infernal rain.

Edmund heard someone splashing up the steps towards him. 'Who's there? Show yourself.'

A figure detached itself from the landing below. Edmund nearly stumbled backwards, but immediately relaxed. It was so small as to be no more than a boy. He had made himself afeared for nothing.

'You lad, hurry on home.'

The small figure drew level and turned upon him. He was briefly aware of a pair of burning, coal-dark eyes set in a deathly pale face running with water, the whole framed by the darkest of slicked-down hair.

The cut came out of nowhere. Before he could even feel pain, Edmund Blackett's breath was extinguished.

Chapter 37

The storm had passed. The morning light glinted upon the sluggish waters beyond the quay with a brilliance every bit as painful as Archer's burnt and bruised body.

He had awoken with boots, coat and belts off, but otherwise dressed, on top of his bed in the Blue Anchor. His first movement had sent further intense pain shooting down spine and legs, so that he thought he might need to lay there for ever. Then, the sickness came, and, despite the agony, he was up and over to retch drily out of the window. He hung half out, closing his eyes against the shattered reflection of the sun upon the river.

At first, he could not go beyond the image of Elizabeth's rent body. He kept turning away from the knowledge that it would have been all but entirely consumed by the flames. Behind his closed lids, the memory of her intense, serious face melded with those of Meg and the blue-eyed Ulster girl. Opening his eyes spread the hurt, but at least scattered the visions. He focused upon the ever-changing shards of light and worked hard not to think.

It took some minutes before he was able to bring his head and shoulders cautiously back into the room. The usual morning pitcher of freshly drawn water had been set upon the low table before the window. By some fortunate chance, he had avoided sending it tumbling over in his rush. He poured some of the icy contents into the waiting bowl and began to slosh it around his neck and face. Panting, supported on both hands, he looked down at the bloodstained rag that was his shirt. With a sinking feeling, he realised that he would, somehow, have to take the thing off over his head. Several minutes of racking struggle ensued, after which he carefully washed down his upper body, exploring as he did the new burns, bruises and cuts to be found amidst his network of old scars.

Nothing, he thought, actually broken. He was grateful for that. It could have been much worse. A vague impression came to him of Thomas Gower's face, deep red in the fire's glow. The memory of his first sight of the bloodied bodies replaced that of Gower, threatening to make the nausea reappear. Breathing long, drawn-out breaths, Archer pushed the revived image of Elizabeth to one side and slowly, deliberately, retraced the events of the previous evening.

The men who had ambushed him, somehow, they had discovered the rendezvous. Separately from the watch-captain, or in league with him in his intelligencer guise? He had no doubt the same mis-matched pair were the woman-murderers described by the Thompsons. But to then set the fire trap for Sanderson and his men along with Archer? It made no sense.

The other little man with the pale moon face. Had he really seen him, or had it been some smoke-induced vision? He remembered the child-like figure in the shadows of Doncaster's market square, and recalled the street-boy's words, 'small gadgie, pale as I've ever seen'. It had to be the same man, connected to Williams and his Levellers. Part of the quick-fire exchange between Gower and the other rescuer came back to him. It had been the pale man who told them where to find Archer. What, then, did he want? How did he fit in to the trap in the warehouse, to Sanderson, or with the mismatched pair of killers?

He could find no resolution to any of these questions. Yet, Archer realised, the tight ball in his guts easing. That was not, now, of any real significance.

The way forward was clear, but dizzying.

There would be no report made to their Council. There would be no message delivered for Massie. The cylinder and its ciphered contents would have gone with the fire. Its absence felt like a release. Archer was done with the quiet work. He was finished with them all.

The evil at work in Newcastle had reached Elizabeth Thompson. It still loomed over her mother and the others who had worked with Elinor Loumsdale, and it continued to threaten all those associated in any way with the witch trials. He thought of his cousins Mattie and Katherine, and of the infant child Emily.

Whoever they worked for, the little dark man and the blond giant were at the forefront of the danger, a danger which needed to be drawn out into the open. That was all Archer could do to keep his promise to Wilkinson and to try and save all of those others.

Above everything else, he needed to find Meg.

It all meant leaving. The single move remaining to him. To set out the one piece of bait he had and to hope it would be enough to lure the murderers after him, away from the town. He found, in that bleak realisation, a certain calm.

What was less evident was whether his body could sustain any such plan.

After another agony of dressing, Archer descended, one wretched step at a time. Mrs Veitch came flying out of the kitchen area, a look of grave concern etched upon her face.

'Oh, you are risen. Can you walk? Come, in here, sit.'

Painfully, he took the offered chair. A cup of small beer was pressed into his hand. As Mrs Veitch and the round-faced serving girl fluttered about, serving him a platter of fresh cheese and meats, talking all the while, he understood that he had been brought back by two local men.

'They told us you were caught in the terrible fire at the Thompson warehouse. Is it true you had entered the place to rescue others who were trapped inside? They had that, they said, from the captain who was ordering water and buckets and all, to save the other storage houses.'

He thought again of Elizabeth and of the Bracewell lad who had answered her call, to his own death. But the only words he could summon were commonplace enough.

'My coat and my sword,' he said. 'Did they?'

'Yes, don't fret. The weapons we hung up with their belt in the press in your room. Your coat, I'm sorry to say, was in a bad state. Nell here has been cleaning and mending it, last night and again this morning. She'll get it back for you now.'

The girl blushed at the mention of her efforts. Archer tried to reward her with a smile and a word, but he feared that both must have come out twisted, given how suddenly she left the room.

Mrs Veitch herself remained, fussing about him, pressing upon him both more food he did not want and a breezy flow of chatter he lacked the energy to stem. Under its ceaseless murmuration, he was at least able to eat a few mouthfuls. The beer further revived him. It brought also a clearer focus upon his grim purpose.

Reclaiming his coat along with his weapons from a still-flustered Nell, and the money bag from the Inn's strong box, Archer set out into the clean silence of the Sunday morning, to the one stop he now needed to make before he placed himself into the snare.

Young Blackett might have told Sanderson about the meeting with Massie, but that had nothing to do with the warehouse or the Thompsons. Ephraim Ord, however, knew about Bracewell. The previous morning, he had been too fast to mention the court official, too eager to divert attention away from the names of the other surviving witches. The man had been hiding something and now Elizabeth and the boy were both dead.

Archer's first call would be upon the tall engineer.

Chapter 38

Alone, Sophie Ord carried the heavy basket back from the markets and along Quayside.

In discomfort, Archer kept watch upon her long struggle up Manor Chare. On three separate occasions, the girl needed to stop, setting her burden down and becoming completely submerged in the flow of people. Each time, he was distressed to see how invisible she seemed to them all, but he did not close the distance between them to help.

Alone. Except for that once when she had entered Ord's workroom together with Elizabeth, bright and happy, Archer had only ever seen the girl solemn and alone. He had misjudged Sophie. The slight frame she had inherited from her father made her appear younger than she truly was, concealing also the inner strength now in evidence.

He wavered at the realisation that soon she would receive the news of Elizabeth's death, nearly losing her as she recovered the basket once more.

Dashing Archer's last fragile hope that her errand might be on behalf of some other household, Sophie left the steep curve of the chare, taking the side path leading to Heath Court. Every part of his body protesting against the exertion, he hurried to close the gap to the cut through, arriving just in time to watch the girl turn into Saffron Yard.

Accosting Ord would be very much more difficult with his daughter present. There was no help for that. He had no time to wait, and no way of knowing when or whether she might leave again. How long could it be before the killers found out that they had failed and came after him? He needed to be out of the town long before then, and there was much to be done. Starting here.

As quickly and quietly as his injuries would allow, Archer reached the near side of the yard. He was surprised to see Sophie pass beyond the open wooden steps leading to her father's rooms. Instead, she continued towards a black-painted, square door on its rear wall. This, she opened with a large key threaded upon a ribbon tied to her dress and went in. He pulled his head back into the entry just in time to avoid the girl's parting, backwards glance.

Seizing the unexpected opportunity, Archer slipped into Saffron Yard, moving quietly up the steps. At their very top, outside the door to Ord's workshop, he looked down, made uneasy by the quiet.

Two sides of the irregular space were occupied by small warehouses, little more than storage rooms, their shuttered windows blind and doors shut up. Below the full length of the workshop, along another whole side, ran an open arcade stacked high with crates and barrels. He had a clear view of the door on the final side of the yard through which Sophie had disappeared and, thank the Lord, not yet returned back out of. It was one of three similar low doorways, including what appeared to be the coal hole.

The stillness of the place became reassuring. Saffron Yard was a place for longer term storage rather than daily activity. On a Sunday morning, he could expect it to remain all but deserted. He made one last check and prepared himself for the assault.

'Who did you tell?' yelled Archer, spittle flying into the

engineer's terrified face.

Splinters of glass and scattered pieces of metal lay across the floor below Ord's dangling feet, a shatter of debris from the fragile, complex instrument he had been working upon when Archer had burst in.

Taking tighter hold of the edges of the man's leather apron, pushing him further back into the shards upon the workbench, Archer's face was drawn taut in the white killing-state. 'You betrayed her. Tell me who you went to.'

Ord's body sagged. He jerked his head from side to side, lips loose and trembling, but no words emerged.

'Did she come back, to tell you about Bracewell?'

Archer tried to drag the engineer up onto his feet, only to find him slipping limply to the floor. Being slammed hard against another workbench restored to Ord the use of his legs. It also allowed Archer to keep him steady with one hand. With the other, he reached across to pick up a heavy body hammer.

'Did she come back here?'

'No. No, no,' Ord pleaded. 'Please, no.'

'She's dead, Ord.' Archer raised the hammer, spiked head foremost. 'Elizabeth is dead. Was that as planned?'

The engineer's look of pain and confusion caused Archer to loosen his grip. Ord, however, made no attempt to break free.

'Elizabeth? Elizabeth is dead?'

'Because of you.'

'No. How? Why?'

Tears began to cloud the blue of Ord's eyes. His whole body again slackened. Archer's confusion mounted.

'I don't understand,' squeaked the engineer. 'Did she die with Blackett?'

Archer let go of the taller man altogether. The body hammer thudded against the floor a fraction before Ord fell down to join it.

'What do you mean?'

'Edmund Blackett,' panted the engineer. 'William Blackett's

brother. It's him that's dead, not Elizabeth.'

'Who says this?'

'I heard such from the yard boy not an hour since. I swear it. Burns, the stock man, said so as well. Young Blackett's throat was cut in the shadow of his own brother's house.'

Ord's eyes had creased up to slits. His breathing was shallow. Archer stepped back. The man was telling the truth.

'Talk. Tell me what you know.'

'Elizabeth cannot be dead, surely.'

'She's dead alright, alongside Bracewell. Someone betrayed her.'

'Not me. Never me.'

'But you are hiding something. I know that you are hiding something.'

Archer saw only honest fear in the other man's face. The engineer's eyes slid once towards the yard windows, before being hurriedly retracted.

'Where is the girl?'

Ord looked at him blankly.

'Your daughter. What is keeping your daughter?'

Archer was gone, out of the door and down the steps before Ord could summon up either excuse or answer. He tore across Saffron Yard, wrenching open the little door in the centre of the rear wall.

The first things he saw were Sophie's cool, appraising eyes looking back at him from the far side of the great bulk of the printing machine. Its black metal and dark wood gleaming, the tall press occupied most of the centre of the storeroom. The air in the chamber was thick with a foul metallic tang which ripped at the back of Archer's throat, some sort of ink residue left behind by the printing.

Perhaps he had been wrong. How could anyone live in such a rasping haze? He tried to peer beyond Sophie into the farthest corner, but the girl had risen to deny him clear sight.

'Girl, move.'

She held his gaze unbrokenly, a mask of fierce determination.

A noise emerged from the shadows behind her, something in between a cry and a moan. Sophie's lips briefly pursed before she threw back at him a look of such intense hatred that Archer might have stepped backwards out of the chamber had Ord not, at just that moment, reached the open doorway.

'Tell your daughter to move.'

'Sophie. Move aside. All is well.'

The girl glared back, her thin body continuing to exude defiance.

'Daughter, this man is here to help. Do as I say.'

Slowly, small step by small step, Sophie Ord moved to reveal what she had been seeking to protect. Behind her, upon a straw mattress tucked into the tight space left between the printing machine and the far wall, lay the pathetic, bird-like form of a woman.

Ord pulled the door closed behind them, shutting out all but a halo of light around its frame. Sophie continued to stare unnervingly at Archer as he edged forwards, sight gradually adjusting to the gloom. He had to move around the great printing engine before he could get a full impression of the figure on the pallet, who shrank back at his approach.

She was tiny. Not in any way child-like, but small, always fine-boned and now alarmingly thin. Her skin showed the taut, grey look of recent, drastic weight loss. Great white streaks bled through the deep blackness of her long, free hair. The darkest of brown eyes peered out from cavernous sockets.

'*Y lladwyr.*'

Her voice was as fragile and as broken as the rest of her. The strange sound echoed off the thick walls to nest in Archer's horrified ears.

'No, he is not one of them. Be easy.' Sophie stepped back across to block Archer's way. Kneeling, the girl's voice became a protective charm thrown over the frail creature. 'It's alright, I'm here. Nobody will hurt you.'

Archer looked across at the ashen engineer. 'Can Mistress Loumsdale follow what we are saying, in her condition?'

'In part. Sometimes.'

The woman raised herself up to a sitting position, head tilted to one side, eyes lingering over Archer's cape, his weapons-belt, his scar. She stilled, fixing him with a penetrative look. He sensed in it some shadow of the uncommon power she had once conveyed. The silence grew, along with the pounding in his head. The uncontrolled pull returned to the side of his right eye.

'*Ydy hi'n dod gyda chi?*'

Sophie tried to ease Elinor Loumsdale back, only for her to strain away.

'*Ydy'r ferch deg yn dod yma gyda chi?*'

Ord gasped.

'What does she say?' Archer whispered across at him.

'She asks if she is come with you.'

'Who, what does she mean?'

'She says, "Is the fair girl come here with you?"'

Archer stared at the emaciated figure.

'*Maent yn farw. Maent i gyd wedi marw.*'

Ord looked mutely across at Archer,

'Keep translating. Do it!'

'They are dead, they are all dead.'

'*Y dialydd tywyll.*'

Ord looked more stricken than ever.

Archer continued to work alongside the engineer in silence, sweeping up and clearing away the pieces of wrecked machinery. Light streamed in through the workshop windows. They had not exchanged a word since they had left the girl to her soothing of Elinor Loumsdale in the dark print room. Finally, he could no longer contain the questions that had formed and reformed as they laboured.

'How do you know the hill language?' He appraised Ephraim Ord's tall frame, reddish hair and freckled cheeks. 'You are not descended from the old people.'

'Our congregation sheltered out in the high valleys to escape Bishop Cosin's persecution. I was much employed about the lead mines at that time. The mining families speak the old tongue.'

'What was it she said, there at the end?'

Ord paused in his work but did not look up.

'Tell me.'

'In English, she said "The dark avenger". I do not know what she means. Probably nothing. Her wits are gone. You cannot take anything she says for truth.'

Archer moved across to the windows, looking down into the peace of Saffron Yard.

'I was told she had left the town, pursued by the witch accusation. How is it that she comes to rest in your print room?'

'When the campaign failed, she was taken out to safety. As we thought.'

'But.'

'But she returned to witness the executions.'

'She came here, to you?'

'Not then, no. She stayed with one or more of her women. She was already changed. When she saw those who she had tried to save hang, it affected her more. Then, when the killings continued, she lost herself altogether, not sleeping, barely eating, speaking, as you heard, only these mad snippets in the hill-tongue.'

Archer considered the risks Ord had been running, for himself and his daughter.

'How long?'

'She has been with us for some few weeks. Sarah Turner brought Elinor to us, unable to cope with her distraction.'

Ord's sharp silence made Archer look up. 'A few weeks since? Just before Sarah herself was killed?' Renewed fear crept over him. 'The Thompsons, Elizabeth and her mother, they knew that Elinor was here?'

'No, nobody knew. Sarah was clever and brave. She told us that she had told nobody, and we believed her.'

'What if she did speak, in her last moments?'

Ord sparked with a crackling anger. 'You never knew her. You never knew any of them, not even Elizabeth. She would not. She did not, or else they would have been here long since.'

'Elinor Loumsdale cannot stay. You must know it.'

Ord waited to finish clearing his section of floor. When, finally, he stood and faced Archer, the engineer's eyes had lost all of their former light. 'Elinor must leave, that is true, but to where can she go?'

'I can arrange that. Just be sure to have her ready today. You and Sophie will need to be prepared to go too.'

'I will not. It has long been a danger to keep Elinor here, but if she is not already discovered, I do not see why I would need to leave.'

'And what if the men who killed her know about your links to Elizabeth? They will come and find you.'

'I will not go. In itself, that would be to invite suspicion.'

'But your daughter.'

'Sophie can accompany Elizabeth on her way. I will not go myself.'

Archer looked on the engineer with new interest, thought about trying again to persuade the man, but decided against. There was no time and so much he needed to know.

'Twelve women escaped. You hid it before, to protect Elinor, I understand that. Tell me those names now.'

'I never knew all of them.'

'Try, Master Ord. Try.'

The engineer kept his silence. He did not even look up, but went back to his clearing, heaving up a pile of fragments before making for the scraps box at the rear of the workshop.

Near to breathless, Archer blocked his path. 'Man! Do you want other women to die? I have to stop this, I have to know, else those very women will be next. What in the name of all that is sinful do you think that Elizabeth would have you do? What would Elinor want?'

Softly, Ord pushed past and deposited his load in the waiting container. Only when he turned about, could Archer see the glistening in his eyes.

'You read about Robson, Cole and Grainger. Those women survived, as well, of course, as your own sister. Who else do you already have?'

'Along with them, old Fenwick's cousin and Jennie Dawson. You see? Fenwick, a Royalist, and Jennie Dawson, of all the Puritan families. It is the same with the women who were killed. The accused come from both sides. What happened?'

'I don't know. But I think I can remember the other names.'

'Go on.'

'There were two townswomen, Sarah Bradley and Joan Seymour, but I think you are looking for families of means. Of those, Maria Carr escaped, as did Eleanor Huntley, Elizabeth Eden and Anne Mitford. All found guilty, all escaped execution. Those are the only others, I swear. May God be merciful.'

The Carr family again. Maria Carr was the clan leader's eldest niece. So much seemed to revolve around that proud, bitter old man.

'How did these women escape the judgement?'

'Their families got them out.'

'Carr, Huntley and Mitford. All of those families formerly supported the king. Why them? Why only them?' Even as he addressed Ord, Archer was focused upon that anomaly, Elizabeth Eden whose brothers had died for Parliament. The escaped women, like the dead, came from both sides of the town's great divide.

Ord made no reply, his face showing nothing but misery.

Archer knew that he must go at once. Sunday service would begin soon.

'One final question.'

'Anything, ask.'

'You say that the families got the women out. To where? Where can I find them? It may lead me to my sister.'

'You won't find them, and they wouldn't speak of any of it if you did. Can you not see what has been done to them? Look at Elinor. Look at Mistress Dawson.'

Archer stood in the doorway, wrestling with fear and guilt. What if Meg had been similarly undone?

'The Robson family has lands in Tynedale,' said Ord. 'My brethren in the Hexham congregation tell me Anna Robson is stowed there, but they would also know if others had been hidden in the valleys of the Tyne. I should look elsewhere in the county, to the north.'

'The man, this Kincaid, where is he now? Not still in the town?'

'No, the Scot is gone. He left as soon as he had received his wages, headed out into Northumberland, intending to try more women there. They say he expected to hang hundreds.'

Archer forced out a grim smile.

'Then he would have left a trail. A trail that a man can follow.'

Upon leaving Ord and descending to Saffron Yard, Archer paused, his mind torn between the arrangements he would need to make to get Elinor Loumsdale out of the town and the first move he must now take to set in motion his desperate plan.

Looking back towards the print room door, he was surprised to find it open. Sophie Ord stood there, looking back at him in her solemn manner.

He turned away but felt the girl's unblinking stare upon his back long after he had left the yard and exited onto Heath Court, towards the noose he had prepared for himself.

Chapter 39

One steady climb up Church Steps took what felt like hours, requiring long pauses for rest, necessary to settle both body and mind. But it got Archer where he needed. Hatless since the fire, he shaded his eyes against the sun with his hand as he approached the towering portal of Saint Nicholas.

Two armed watchmen stood by the open doors, coming together to bar his path. Surely his uniform, he thought. Then again, despite Nell's efforts, the coat was in places torn and scorched. His breeches showed stains of blood and soot.

Another man, accompanied by his finely, if soberly, dressed family, neared the entrance from the farther side. He looked at Archer, one of the daughters trailing behind him stifling a giggle, then spoke to the doormen. At once, they eased aside to allow the tattered ensign to enter. Crossing the threshold, Archer offered a word of thanks to his benefactor, lamenting his lack of headgear to raise in return.

Arriving in the body of the church, working hard to remain as upright and fluent in his movements as he could, Archer saw that his surmise had been correct. Gathered together under the ancient carved roof was almost every one of the people who had been involved in the witch hunts, in Meg's disappearance, and in the town's factional fighting over the coal monopoly.

There, preparing to lead the service, was Dr. Jenison, so skeletally angular that it appeared he was already halfway to the grave. Pastor Woolfall stood further back, flanked by three younger preachers Archer did not recognise. Mayor Bonner and Henry Dawson sat together, next to the other leading men of the corporation. On the officers' benches, he saw Draper turn with a caustic smile to say something to his neighbour. Further back in the church, among a series of other displaced Royalists, a grey-looking Sir John Fenwick propped up one end of his family bench, a few rows behind old Carr, who offered Archer his own scornful, steely grey judgement. Only William Blackett, understandably, was missing.

Carefully, Archer levered himself into the end of a row near to the back. He found himself looking towards the empty Armstrong bench and was torn from renewed torment only by Jenison's unsteady ascent to the lectern.

The lecturer's main text was taken from Exodus. "'And Moses said unto the people",' he began, "Fear ye not, stand still, and see the salvation of the Lord, which he will shew to you, for the Egyptians whom ye have seen to day, ye shall see them again no more for ever. The Lord shall fight for you".' Jenison continued with his homily. What he now lacked in force and stamina was well compensated for in erudition and the guile of long experience, such that the congregation began to settle into an easy and patient attentiveness.

He made to place before the people the further consoling sentiment of Psalm 55: "But thou, O God, shalt bring them down into the pit of destruction: bloody and deceitful men shall not live out half their days.". Before Jenison could continue his exposition upon the scripture, one of the younger preachers, his white face topped with cropped brown hair, walked up the side of the church to hover by the pulpit. Jenison noticed him, bent down his head, and the man whispered something. They looked up together, directly at Archer.

'An abomination before the Lord!' thundered Jenison with unexpected force. 'Here, among the godly of this benighted town, has entered an agent of wickedness and a bringer of immorality and deceit.'

He raised a long, trembling finger. Heads turned and women gasped. 'The brother of a whore. Scion of a nest of Papists.'

Several benches further forwards, Archer saw his uncle's face turn white.

'The serpent in our midst.' Jenison's voice shook. 'Let no man converse with him. Let no woman offer him sustenance. There is no place in Heaven for such as he.'

Archer met and held the old preacher's eyes. He felt the gaze of the entire congregation, saw their enraged, impassioned faces, heard the susurration of their joined condemnation. Only Dawson appeared to be keeping his calm. Unlike his fellows, he showed no anger. He looked not at Archer but down towards the floor with an expression of sorrow.

'Who will rid us of this sinner?' shouted the old lecturer.

'Enough!'

Weston had stood. His voice, in its strength, reverberated around the crowded nave, silencing the commotion. The brewer and the preacher faced one another as seconds slipped by. Then Weston, body uncomfortably stooped, turned his back upon the lectern and walked slowly back to Archer.

'Come, James, we shall not give these gentlemen any more satisfaction this day.'

Painfully, Archer stood to go. He leant, as he rose, upon his uncle's offered arm. Side by side, in an absolute silence, all eyes upon them, they walked from the church, away from the whole community.

Outside, the two watchmen remained on guard. Curiously, they eyed uncle and nephew standing apart upon the broad paving in a drawn-out silence.

At last, as Archer made to speak, Weston's raised palm stopped him short. 'It seems, James, that I am for family before town, after all.'

'Uncle, my thanks.'

'I need no thanks from you, boy. There is already too much damage done. It had to be stopped. That is all.'

Archer wrestled with guilt, shame and anger in equal measure. 'But my sister. I know all that you have done for her.'

Weston offered in return only a look balanced between hatred and fear. 'All? What could you know of the dangers we have endured?'

'I know you to have worked to rescue her from the gallows.'

'You know nothing! Had you known your position and kept to your duty, none of this would ever have touched the family.'

Archer nearly stumbled, the blood draining away from his extremities. Weston made no move to help, but only tightened his lips.

'I told you; your sister is gone from here. It is overlong since you should have done the same. This is the result.'

'Yet Meg escaped only with your help, uncle. For mercy, tell me where she is.'

Weston's face contorted into anguish. 'I did not lie to you, boy. I do not know where she was taken.'

'Taken? By who?'

Weston, appearing yet older and more broken, looked with some longing towards Church Steps. 'Those whose help I sought were compelling on the point. It is safer that none should know where she is taken.' He was trembling now. 'Into the county, is all,' he said, and took a short step away. Archer, in return, extended a desperate hand towards him. 'I said, it was enough!' roared back the older man. 'Have you not already done enough?'

The watchmen looked on hungrily.

'Go,' said Weston. 'Never return. Leave us to what little we have left.'

The brewer turned his back and within a few paces had begun the descent towards the quay, his broad frame sinking lower with each step. Unexpectedly, he stopped, only his head and the top of his body now visible. 'Find her,' he said quietly. 'Tell her.' Weston raised his head, as if in contemplation of the great crown above the church. 'Just find her, damn you.'

Chapter 40

Archer ducked into a low, narrow entry leading between the main west road and the uphill dog leg of Pink Lane. This last task, he thought, one final chance to understand what was pitched against him. He might even yet be able to do some good, if only his calculation was correct, if only Davey were holed-up here.

The very westernmost of the chares, one even more filthy and dank than the worst down by the river, Pink Lane was named for the geese who plied their trade there. Archer wondered if they had been driven elsewhere by the current regime. They might have shifted, gone underground, but they would still find ways to work. Here, at this time, there was not a whore to be seen, although both the short span of the alley and the greater length of Pink Lane itself, when he emerged onto it, bore witness to the familiar dealings of the night in the form of filth, vomit and a couple of places where fresh blood had been spilled.

The far side of the lane abutted the town walls. Opposite ran a motley collection of three-and four-story wood and plaster buildings, many half-tumbled down. Little light would penetrate here, even in midsummer. Although the sky remained clear, the weak sun barely touched the bottom stories at all. Down the chare to the left as Archer emerged, gaps like ugly, missing teeth along a section of wall worked to evidence the Scots' bombardment. One of the tenements behind was left almost entirely in ruin.

Halfway up, as the Lane rose towards the West Gate, he stopped in front of a crooked door, badly rotting from the bottom up. Above it, positioned at an angle to jut out over the single ground floor window, hung a board. In its flaking paint and cracked surface, he could just still perceive the outline and contours of a mermaid.

Archer knocked, grateful that his gloves gave some protection but still wincing at the pain felt across shoulders, back and neck. No answer. No sense of any movement or habitation within. He knocked again, louder, and winced once more. Stepping back, he called up towards the higher floors, finding nothing but stillness and desolation. With a look up and down Pink Lane, he rested his hand firmly upon the bare wood of the door and tested it. Unbarred, it gave way a few inches. Archer let go as if stung, in the same movement silently unsheathing his sword. Silence. Ears straining, he moved in and placed his shoulder against the timber, mortuary blade ready.

The body lay in the corner of the room, having been unable, in its dissolution, to reach even the dirtied straw mattress lying against the farthest wall. Lank hair dragged about its unshaven, grey face. Fresh stains showed upon the mouth and chin. The remnants of a flagon of dark beer lolled on its side nearby.

'Glad to see you got away.' The figure did not stir. Archer bent down, shaking the nearest greasy shoulder. 'Davey. Wake up.'

Davey rolled over, retreating against the wall. Unseeing, bloodshot eyes squinted up. A foul smell of stale beer, spirits, sweat, and worse was released. Davey's hands flailed about him, finding, in their desperation, the dagger handle he had sought. Before he could fully raise it, Archer's sword had swung around and, using the flat of its blade, he had battered the weapon away. The dagger skittered to the corner of the room before spinning to a stop. The Scot yelped and crab-scuttled back even further.

'It's me, Davey. It's James.'

Nursing his bruised hand, Davey shook his head and peered forwards, sight slowly adjusting to the thin streams of light. 'What you doing, man?' he asked peevishly. 'You think I want the likes of you to break so into my ale passion?' Crumpled, he looked back up. 'How, anyway, did you know where I'd be?'

Archer relaxed and stepped back from the stench. 'It had to be one of your rat holes, Davey. Least likely to be disturbed in here on a Sunday morning. You never were much of a one for church and you did always like a Saturday at night. My only real concern was when I saw the state of the walls, in case the whole place had gone.'

Davey shook his hand violently and took a few moments to stand, but something of his normal self had already returned.

'Aye, it still does me well. Better, I'd say, as since the siege and the rise of your old friends, the Lane isn't what it was. Quieter, like, more private.'

He looked at Archer's battered face and clothing.

'Did that bastard Sanderson do that? I thought I'd have heard if there'd been trouble after the fight?'

'Sanderson's dead.'

'How? What happened?'

'Sanderson, at least one of his watchmen, but probably another besides, and two others were killed in the Thompson warehouse down by The Close. It was a damned trap.'

Davey already appeared sobered. His colour returned and his eyes bright. His mouth pursed as he tugged on some scuffed, rope-soled, canvas boots.

'Who did this, James? I can get them fixed, proper.'

'Not for you this one, Davey,' muttered Archer.

'Tell me anyway.'

'There were a pair of men that I saw. They had already butchered the two others, a young lad called Bracewell and Elizabeth Thompson.' Archer's mouth dryed anew as he said her name. 'Listen, did you know of a woman called Loumsdale?'

'Aye, everyone in the town's heard of Mistress Elinor Loumsdale.'

'The group of women she took with her into Newgate, those who went to help the accused. They are all either fled or killed. I think it to be the work of these men, and whoever is paying them.'

'There's always women being killed, but I have heard some talk o' this. Tell me about those two men you saw.'

'A huge, blond man, for one, and the other short, thin and dark. I don't mean just dark hair, but sallow, foreign.'

'That could describe half the town any night. There's so many come into it from afar.'

'These men were working to a plan, but I cannot understand one thing. I was meant to meet there with Elizabeth and the boy. Somehow, the killers found out. They let me find the two bodies. Then they ambushed me, put me out cold, and left me there.'

Davey's nostrils flared, and the veins on his neck pulsed.

'That's it, you see,' said Archer. 'Sanderson came to the warehouse with his men. Whether because the murderers themselves summoned him, to set me up for the two deaths, or because he already had an informer in Mistress Thompson's household, I do not know. The next thing is that we find ourselves to be locked in, Sanderson with one of the watchmen alongside me. Then, the whole place is set alight. I know you'll not have heard anything since last night.' He nodded towards the soiled mattress. 'But if anyone has any useful thoughts, it has to be you.'

Davey's face was become even more grey than his binge might have allowed. 'I dinnae see how I can help you. You'll need to lay low, anyway. If there's a watch-captain and two watchmen gone, they'll be all owa' it. Besides, once that other pair of fuckbeggars finds out you're still alive, won't they just come right back at you? You'll need to disappear. I know places you can hide.'

Archer forced out a taut smile. 'I believe that it is somewhat late for that, Davey. Whoever is behind this, I made sure they just saw their failure. I have come to you straight from service at Saint Nicholas.'

'Are you gan gyte?'

'Easy, Davey. No, I am not gone mad. I hope not. And I will leave the town as soon as we are done here. I go out into the county in search of Meg. Are you sure you have no hint of where she might be? I already know that more, perhaps many, of the others were freed and taken out of the town into hiding.'

Davey looked back at him through calculating eyes. 'Aye,' the Scot began. 'All those families must have paid out a good sum to get their women away. The Robsons managed it. Carr, too. Fenwick and, of course, your Mister Dawson the same. Some didnae succeed. Or maybe they left their relatives to their fate. I dinnae know.' Davey grimaced and shifted his legs. 'I do know your uncle spent more than he had in getting your Meg freed. He still owes money all owa' the town.'

'I knew he had helped Meg, but not so much as this. I am ashamed to say I may have misjudged him. Davey, are you sure he didn't remove her to the Durham estate? It is possible, is it not, that he is still trying to protect her, even from me?'

The Scot cackled, a raucous crow's call disintegrating into a hacking cough.

'I wouldnae let your uncle off so lightly. I think you know he's no angel. As to your question, no, I've no heard nothing of Durham and I reckon Agnes would have let something slip, given my charm, eh?'

Davey's face turned solemn. 'Look, James. There's more I heard. Your uncle didnae have to help Meg. He could've kept out of it.'

'What is it? What else is there?'

'She had. That is, Meg, she'd been linked wi' a man. Wi' one of those English officers. People talk, you know. Jealous, or bitter, and some bad things have been said. If you were looking to harm Weston, it would have been easy to use those sorts of rumours. Tha's where the accusations against her came from, you see?'

The Scot began to gather together a few loose items into a leather shoulder bag. Archer observed him absently, his mind moving back and forward over all that he had heard.

'The name. Which officer?'

'I never heard. Away by now, I'm sure. These men enjoy a dalliance, but you can be sure each o' them has a wife or an arrangement in the south.'

And more than ever now I need to find Meg, thought Archer.

'Listen James,' cut in Davey. 'I wouldnae go up there. Meg will be fine. I'd have heard if any strange young woman from the town, especially one so pretty and gentle, were to have been harmed. But, for you, it's no' safe.'

Safe, thought Archer, when the walls of Newcastle already felt like one big, encircling trap? There was no more he could achieve by remaining in the town, except wait for them to catch him in one of the back alleys, or down some lonely steps. It only confirmed to him the necessity of his threadbare plan.

Chapter 41

In the back parlour of the big house on the steps, Captain-Lieutenant Draper flinched under the merchant's abruptly unleashed, needle-sharp anger.

'Damn you, Draper, those were not my orders. The woman and the boy, yes, but not Archer. Not here in the town.'

Draper's pupils contracted dangerously. He took orders only from Heselrigg. That this merchant should presume to give him such took him to the very edge of endurance. The day was approaching. He would make sure of it, when he would present evidence to the governor and have the insufferable man arrested. Then, the two of them could have a quite different conversation, deep under the castle.

'The woman and the boy are dead,' he said, carefully casual. 'Archer remains alive. There is, surely, no reason for concern.'

'And the bodies of the three watchmen? You do not think they present any problem?'

'There will be nothing left but charred bone. It will look like a party of vagrants were caught up in the fire, that is all.'

'Can you, at least, be sure that Archer didn't find anything else out from that fool of a Newgate turnkey?'

'There was nothing left there to find, I made sure of that personally, as I told you. Surely, his visit to Hobson is more of a concern for us?'

'Us? I would have thought that the involvement of that loose-tongued sectarian would rather be of the greatest concern for you? The deputy governor is not, like the rest of them, willing to overlook a piece of personal deal-making.'

This time, Draper was unable to keep his irritation hidden. He drew back his lips, baring teeth at the Newcastle man, who did no more in return than to lean back into the shadows.

'Hobson will not be of any concern for much longer. Neither for the town government nor the garrison.'

The merchant took the information calmly, only infuriating Draper all the more. Of course, he had already known that Hobson would soon be discharged from service. Before he could follow up on the suspicion, the man moved on.

'And the girl?'

'Pearson genuinely knows nothing. Nobody knows where she has been stored.'

'There is no longer any choice. If you cannot find the girl, then yes, you need to silence the spy. Last night was just the wrong place, and a little too early. Take the men and find him.'

Draper was nearly out of the door when the man's vehemence drew him back.

'Not in the town. We cannot afford for it to be in the town. Find Archer and get him out of Newcastle. Ensure that he meets a regrettable accident out there on the road, the county presently being as lawless as it is.'

Chapter 42

The sound of boots traversing the shattered length of Pink Lane came through the front windows as a warning. Archer turned back to the fixer with renewed urgency.

'Davey, do me something, would you?'

'Anything, lad.'

'After last night, Mistress Thompson needs to leave the town. Do you know anybody in her household?'

Davey's brow creased above sparking eyes. 'Aye, of course.'

'Make sure they insist that she does go. And at once. Make sure they keep a watch out until she is well clear. Can you help me with that?'

'It's done. And I'll ask around about those other two, the little gadgie and the big, blond man.' Archer's silence caught Davey's fullest attention. 'There's something else.'

'Yes. You will know Ord. Ephraim Ord, the engineer.'

'Aye.'

'Go to his workshop. In Saffron Yard. He is hiding a woman there.'

Davey was very interested now.

'Never mind what sort of woman. She also needs to get out of Newcastle. It needs to be somewhere she will not be followed or found. You understand me? I know you can do that. She must be got out, as soon as you can. It must be today, she must be kept safe, and she must not come back. She may even have to be held, but she must not return.'

'One of the witches?'

'Ah, Davey, do not call them that. Meg was thought to be

one, remember.'

The light in the Scot's eyes faded.

'No, this isn't one of those poor women, but she is important, and I entrust her to you. Can you get her out to safety for me?'

'Aye, and I know just the people. You cannae fetch her yoursel'?'

'No, but Ord will expect you.'

In an hour he would be gone, headed out on the road north. Whoever was behind the pair of oddly matched murderers, whoever came with them, after him, he would be ready. Whoever it was in league with Heselrigg and his cover-up, Blackett, Fenwick or old Carr, Archer was as certain as he could be that they could not afford to let him go. He had to believe that they would follow him out into Northumberland. However slight, he might retain some sort of chance out there in the open. He eased himself back, pain shooting across his torso. 'One final question.'

'Ask away.'

'What is the relation between William Blackett and Sir John Fenwick?'

The fixer leaned back, stretching his shoulders against the wall. 'Well, James, you've gone right to the heart of things, now, haven't you? The thing here is, Sir John is ruined. The land's almost all gone, the pits and the staithes alike. All he's left is the big house out at Wallington left to rot, and that town house o' his. You know his eldest boy was killed fighting for the King? The youngest one suffered great wounds serving in the New Model wi' Lambert. He's no' yet returned. They most like thought a brother on each side would gi' them safety, but that's no' worked out. It's said that old Fenwick spends all his days drinking through the wine cellar, with the house all crumbling around him. Before his creditors come to take the casks away as well, I suppose.'

Seeing Archer remain wholly serious, Davey soberly went on.

'It was Blackett who took most of the businesses over frae Fenwick. He's big into the trade now, works alongside Riddell and Carr. He paid far less than the concerns are worth, I hear, but it's only that ready money keeping Sir John going.'

That was what was needling Archer. Fenwick had always retained a reputation for caution. He'd been careful not to get involved with any faction before the wars, and having a son in each camp would have been his way of insuring himself against every outcome. Why, then, would such a man take the risk of associating so openly with the exiled Royalists? 'If he has not had the lands sequestered, how is it then, that his fortunes have failed so badly?'

'Perhaps he needed those boys o' his more than we know. He's no man of affairs. His town servants all cheat him. It would be the same way on his estates and mines. Whatever, it was a deep hole Blackett got him out of. Edmund Blackett, the youngest brother, is set to watch owa' the old man. I've heard it can all be bought back, at the same rate, if only Fenwick's fortunes change. If I was William Blackett, I'd want to be sure to scupper that chance.'

'*Was* set to watch over Fenwick,' corrected Archer. 'Was, not is. Edmund Blackett was killed last night. I would wager that it was young Blackett who betrayed me to Sanderson.'

'He always was a clipey little weasel.'

Archer smiled at Davey's description of young Blackett as a tale-telling sneak. 'Yes, I'll not be mourning him, but I would very much like to know how he came to meet his end.'

Archer walked off towards the door, pursued by Davey's anguished cry.

'Will you no stay? The hills are full of brigands and if you go by the coast roads, you'll as like get raided by some pirate band. Some of those have even burned and stolen as near as Heaton village. It's one thing Cromwell going up there with an army, but for you to go alone? Please, James, dinnae do it.'

It was good to have the warning, but it wasn't going to stop him.

'Get Mistress Thompson out of the town. Get the other woman who Ord is hiding out as well. Do those things for me. And stay safe yourself. I will be back some time and I shall know where to find you.'

Chapter 43

The first thing Agnes saw was the great hummingbird bowl.

The master's most prized possession, set apart, unlike the other treasures never once considered for sale, was now no more than a mass of blue and white shards. She was shocked to witness the dull, earthen colour of the ordinary clay hidden beneath its fine glaze.

The rest of the room had been similarly despoiled. It was as if the three men had been intent upon a complete destruction. Each of the woven wall hangings was cut clean through. An entire cabinet of Mistress Weston's glassware and amber lay overturned, its contents, broken, spilling out towards the central matting from the great wound in its front. A quick look told her that none of the others had been spared.

Having waited upon the landing throughout the raid, quiet in her sobs, the housekeeper had scurried into the day room as soon as the men had tramped back down the stair.

There was nothing she could have done. Once the street door was open, they had burst in, the huge blond man taking hold and looking down upon her with his pale eyes, so cold that she knew he might snap her neck at any moment. The little dark one had then put his reeking mouth so close to hers and let out such a strange, sibilant hiss that it was all she could do not to fall completely away. At a word from the tall, bearded leader, however, the men had left her, following him upstairs to find Weston, making no effort to mask the noise of their advance.

Creeping after them, Agnes had stood for long minutes

listening to the sounds of violence, punctuated with the leader's angry questions, delivered in a south country drawl. When they had marched back past her without a glance, upon entering Weston's study, she now found herself utterly unprepared for the destruction within, focusing upon the shattered bowl before slowly, unwillingly, allowing her gaze to move beyond the splintered porcelain towards the window side of the desk and the unmoving body of her master.

Agnes' hands shook as she bent down towards Weston. Her breath came short, her neck flushed, but she made no sound. Gently, she peeled back the top ruffs of his bloodied shirt. She numbed with relief as the man shuddered under her touch. He looked up at her through one swollen eye and she had to rest both of her hands upon the blunt slab of his head to stop him from twisting his neck and opening up the wound. He relaxed his efforts and allowed the woman to smooth the hair away from his pale forehead, surprising her by opening his mouth into what was unmistakably a silent smile.

'Master, rest, please rest. Let me stem that blood, then I'll go for John.'

This time, the old brewer managed a few, gargled words. 'Nothing, Agnes. I told them nothing about the boy.'

Once more, the excruciating smile emerged from the side of his pallid, torn face.

Chapter 44

Archer passed out of the town early that afternoon, taking the road past Newgate. Saying in his mind a final respect to the bodies lain in the fresh pit behind the prison, he pushed the horse up the Gallowgate hill and towards the high Town Moor.

He eased her on, passing the miners at work in the Spital Tongues pit. To one side, a high spoil was raised, adding to the desolate feel of the wind-blown expanse. He could see here the magnitude of change since his youth. The numbers of pit men, strong, lean and solemn-faced under their blackened skin, had markedly increased. As Ord had claimed, the surface coal had been quarried out. A straight path led under the ground, several miners, each carrying a rough pick and an open candle, disappearing into its inner blackness. Archer remembered the engineer's lamp engine, designed to protect these men from underground explosions. He offered up a prayer for their safety.

To the other side of the road, a strange trackway had been constructed. A lattice of wooden rails and braces ran away down the hill towards the distant river and its staithes, where the newly mined coal would be loaded into waiting keels. Several stubby, small-wheeled wagons stood at its head, waiting to be filled and hauled along the fixed lines of track. Two strong ponies grazed nearby. If such wagon-ways were to be laid up and down the banks of the river, he realised, then it would greatly expand the measures of coal the Hostmen could exploit and vastly increase the whole scale of the trade.

The damned trade, which lay at the heart of it all.

The winning of the war had become just one more betrayal. The old families had seeped their way back in. The families who were raised up - and that from the second, rather than any lower, rank - were far more determined to retain their own power and status than to look for a world where a man might prosper because of his abilities rather than his birth. None of them would help the keelers or the miners, nor make meaningful change to the short and brutal lives of the poor. Even under this Commonwealth, life in the town would go on much as it had.

He turned the horse about and trotted away. Away from the town with its miasma of coal dust, smoke and sickness. Away from Weston and Dawson. Away from Fenwick, Carr, Heselrigg and Hobson. Away from any remaining hope of home.

Climbing higher up onto the open moor, Archer peered towards the soft lines of hills disappearing to the north, repeating to himself his plan, over and over, as if speaking it aloud might make the gamble more possible, more real.

He would survive this. He would find Meg and he would take her away. He would no longer continue his bare existence in the shadows cast by the wars. No more of Skippon's service. No debt to Massie. No masters of any kind. He would escape from all of their intrigues. He had skilled hands and a steady head. That was more than enough to be able to keep them both, somewhere hidden out there in those gentle highlands.

Feeling the sword resting heavily on his thigh, he knew that whatever happened, so long as he found Meg, he would also be able to keep them safe. Together, they would be free from it all. Then, perhaps, he could begin to make the necessary amends.

His war, at last, was nearly done.

He took one last look back from under the wide-brimmed hat he had been able to purchase at one of the stalls at the top of Castle Stairs. Did he really think that whoever was behind the witch accusations and the murders would come out of the town and after him? Had that, too, just been so many fine but empty words?

He felt sorrow for Wilkinson and the other grieving families. He hoped that Mistress Thompson had already escaped, that Davey had kept his word and in some small manner helped to hurry her on the way. Davey was good for that. Archer did not doubt that the fixer had also reached Ephraim Ord and would get the poor Loumsdale woman out to safety.

What else was there that Archer could do now, other than to take this gamble?

He spurred on his horse and rode swiftly across the moor, leaving behind the sulphurous coal-reek which hung stiflingly over Newcastle and its whole valley.

Chapter 45

Oars muffled, no light shown. The boatmen worked together to pull their skiff out into the turning tide. After a short tussle with the choppy cross-waters before they entered the central stream, they settled together into a smooth rhythm, propelling it upriver with a speed which both surprised and dismayed the two men looking on from the Skinnerburn shore.

Ephraim Ord leaned forwards, his eyes fixed upon Sophie's receding face, pale and fragile in the darkness. Elinor Loumsdale was no more than an ill-defined shadow behind her, hunched low in the tight bows of the craft.

'You sure it's right to send your daughter with her?' asked Davey. 'She could have remained. The Ridleys will no' misplace or misuse the woman.'

This softly spoken argument had been running unbroken between the men for some hours now, but it had been the girl Sophie who had proved quite unrelenting. Ord peered after her as the outline of the little boat melted away into the night. In her courage, he found steel enough for his reply.

'That woman needs Sophie. Let it be.' He looked across at the little Scot. 'You swear that my daughter will be safe?'

'Safer there than here, if you stick to your plan.' Davey returned the man's look. 'I can still get you a place to stay. Keep you hidden. I could ha' kept you both well hidden, without that poor woman.'

So, Davey already understood the identity of the distracted creature who Sophie was accompanying up the broad Tyne and on into high Allendale.

'There is no purpose in that. I told Archer. For what would they come? None knew of Elinor's presence. If I were to disappear, surely then they will begin to suspect. Sophie would never more be safe.'

They stood together, looking up the silent river until the boat had completely disappeared into the thicker blackness which was the eastern edge of King's Meadow. Even then, Ord would have waited, holding his ground until Davey broke into the engineer's grief.

'Safe is what she'll be out there. Here, on this bank, we'll no' be if we linger.'

With reluctance, Ord detached himself and followed a few steps behind the fixer on the return path towards Newcastle. They kept low and close in when, after some minutes of cautious scrambling, they reached the western end of its high quay wall.

Ord turned to look back along the silver-streaked midnight blue of the rising river. 'Are you sure,' he began, to be cut off by Davey's urgent hand movement.

Before them, the first berths of the quay sat quiet and still. The fixer took long minutes before gesturing for them to move on. Ahead, they could already see that despite the curfew, the little postern gate in the shelter of the chapel of Saint Thomas remained open.

They slipped through and into the town along the side of Sandhill, keeping tight in under the walls. Ord saw no sight of whichever guard had facilitated their passage, and was glad of it.

His concern for Sophie pressed tightly about his temples. She had taken the news of Elizabeth's death calmly. All too quickly, she had moved on to insisting that she would be needed to accompany Elinor on her journey west. In that regard, as ever, the girl had been right. They would never have been able to get Elinor to move, had the two of them not gone together. Even then, it had been a fraught journey across the town, Davey escorting them through grim vennels Ord did not know and which he would never normally have entered upon the brightest midday, let alone allowed his daughter to traverse in darkness. But now, Sophie was alone out there in the night, accompanied only by the strangers she must rely on, the helplessly distracted Elinor, and the burgeoning reality of Elizabeth Thompson's murder.

The fixer stopped again, belatedly gesturing his companion forwards. Ord put his fears aside to creep up to Davey's shoulder, following the Scot's gaze across the deserted width of Quayside, only to recoil at the dreadful scene unfolding in the open yard of the Blue Anchor.

'Get her off me.'

Out of uniform, enjoying his anonymity, Captain-Lieutenant Draper tightened his grip upon the young ostler, holding the long, thin-bladed knife before the man's bulging eyes. Across the yard, he grinned to see the inn woman smash a long-handled broom firmly down upon Proctor's hunched shoulders. He allowed the woman one more hefty swipe, and for Proctor to cry out again, before raising his voice.

'Stop, woman!'

His man, Proctor, the woman, the Swede, and the small dark man with the strange name who seemed never to leave his side, all looked up together. She lowered her makeshift weapon and took a stumbling step nearer, watching Draper's blade slip down to threaten the ostler's heavy neck. Beyond all of them, the ugly features of Dodd, the fourth man Draper had mobilised from among Dawson's servants, watched on, one of the struggling stable boys locked firmly under each arm.

God's hot blood, the place was a midden. What could have moved Archer to take lodging here?

'Bring her.'

The Swede wrenched the brush out of Mrs Veitch's hands, at the same time turning her about and scooping her up. She clawed at him, writhing in fury as he strode the few paces across the yard. In return, the giant simply tightened his grip upon her all the more painfully.

The captain-lieutenant smiled. The blond man might have disobeyed orders at the warehouse when the ugly, big-nosed watchman had unexpectedly emerged from the back room, but he at least understood the finality killing offered as a solution. The immediacy of his response to Draper's command also held within it a gratifying suggestion that he would prove to be more malleable in the future.

And still, Draper could not understand this squeamishness about finishing Archer off in the merchant's precious Newcastle.

Dumped at the captain-lieutenant's feet, Mrs Veitch glared up at him. Having got nothing from the brewer, he knew exactly what to do to ensure they did not now leave the inn empty-handed.

'Where is he?'

The woman's scornful look did not alter.

Draper tugged back the ostler's hair. 'Tell me woman, what has become of the young ensign, the one with the scar.' The blade rasped down the unshaven top of the man's exposed neck, drawing with it a thin trickle of blood.

'Gone,' gasped Mrs Veitch. 'He took a post horse and is gone.'

Draper responded with a hideous grin. 'When?'

'This afternoon. During the dinner hour.'

Draper cursed crudely. With such a head start, they would need to work all the harder to pick up Archer's trail.

Mrs Veitch watched in horror as the tall man lifted the point of the knife away from Jeremiah's neck only to turn it about and bring it back level with the ostler's eyes.

He fixed her with a calm stare. 'Tell me exactly where he is headed, as you value this man's life.'

'Also, boiled water and clean cloths,' demanded Ord through clenched teeth.

Mrs Veitch, using a clipped, high tone quite unlike her ordinary voice, repeated the command towards the serving girl who remained teetering a few tentative steps into the yard.

Ord clutched at the ostler's head, using all of his strength to prevent the man from thrashing about and causing even more damage and loss of blood from the jagged hole where his right eye had been. The two stable lads put all of their weight down upon the man's legs. A stout master scrivener, who alone among the inn's guests had summoned up the courage to descend into the yard once Draper and his four companions had departed, hugged the ostler's shivering body as still as he could.

'I had to tell him,' stuttered Mrs Veitch. 'He said he would spare Jeremiah. What else could I do?'

Ord softly shook his head back at the woman. 'Easy, Jeremiah, easy. Here she comes. All will be well.'

Nell had emerged into the yard carrying the long, flat-headed griddle-iron Ord had demanded she fetch from the kitchen. The end of the utensil showed brightest orange, deepening to blood red. Good, thought Ord. The girl had listened well. He found reassuring purpose behind the tears upon her reddened cheeks.

Davey, entering from his watch upon Quayside, came alongside the engineer, saw his intent, offered him a sidewards look, melding respect with pity, and took over the holding of Jeremiah's head.

Gently, Ord took the iron from Nell. He had seen this done, more than once, in the mines. God grant him the strength to do it well, while the iron retained its clean, searing heat. With a steady hand, he brought its glowing end down towards the running wound.

Chapter 46

Despair came frequently to Archer, as he quartered the county over the next days. He was certain that Meg was gone into Northumberland, but it was a big, empty expanse stretching out before him between Tyne and Tweed.

Armed with the names of the other women who had escaped execution, his plan was to head gradually north in wide sweeps, seeking out news of strangers come into the country, or even, as he had said to Ord, to pick up Kincaid's trail. And to hope that he could find some clue, before the killers caught up with him.

Mile after mile, village after village, his enquiries had fallen upon barren ground.

Towards Morpeth, he had encountered soldiers manning checkpoints. He got through well enough despite the lack of warrant, but this was now Cromwell's territory, from here north all the way into Scotland, ruled as a military enclave. Heselrigg and Cromwell were said to be close. How long before an apprehension order followed him out from Newcastle, initiated by the governor or by one of the families with influence over him?

Riding down the wooded hill into the small market town brought to mind Janet Martin. What, he wondered, had been her mistake? With a jolt, he realised the manner of his thinking. Surely, there must have been some real witches among those women.

He pictured again bodies swaying in the Ulster drizzle. He could no longer accept that the Irish were brute savages, or that there was a hidden army of Papists biding its time to kill all true believers. Did he really any more believe that the Devil came to tempt women in their sensual weakness?

The women's names, both those who had successfully fled, and those who had been executed upon the Town Moor, mocked him continually. He was certain now that some appalling auction of death had taken place, a trading of accusations and a buying of reprieves, but he was no closer to knowing who, from among Newcastle's seething factions, had directed such a business.

Blackett, perhaps, depending on how far that family's corruption went. Carr had the clearest reasons, following his son's death in defence of the town and his niece's involvement in the trials. Archer's violent encounters with Reade and Joe Marsden only raised further suspicions about the old man. Whoever was involved, the calculating presence of Heselrigg seemed to be at the very centre of it, acting through corrupt officers like Draper.

Finally, as the afternoon light began to soften on the fifth day, he rode the long uphill towards the garrisoned castle of Alnwick. Soldiers were camped directly outside, their tented rows filthy, pitched in straggling lines upon sodden ground. There was no evidence here of New Model discipline. Archer knew that the most broken and least reliable of troops would be assigned to this kind of thankless garrison duty, left simply to forage for food and terrorise the local population, their presence solely intended to keep any moss-troopers wary.

Heavily weary from the healing of his bruises following four consecutive nights of watchful half-sleep in hidden bivouacs, he knew that he needed warm food and a proper bed. Whatever the risk, the army camp was the only vaguely secure means to that end. Nervous, but resigned, he walked his mount into the middle of the encampment.

Halting near to the horse lines, he looked down at the young groom who had come across to take the reins. The lad's eyes opened wide as he saw, beneath the officer's trappings, former sergeant Archer. Archer did not remember the boy's name but did recall the face. Quickly, he glanced around, recognising more than a few others. Lilburne's foot. Or at least a remnant of it. This was a piece of providence all of his own.

'Peace, lad. Is Corporal Swann with the company, still in charge of looking after the officer's horses?'

'Yes, Sir. He's inside now.'

Taking Archer's mount, the groom led the beast away towards a long run of canvas-topped stabling. Archer watched them go, taking the time to register the activity within the camp as well as the location of its main paths and guard stations. He noted with interest the presence of a distinctly separate group of cavalry troopers, lounged around a low-banked fire before a cluster of covered baggage wagons. Finally, he broke away towards the thatched shelter the boy had indicated as Swann's.

Inside, the lean-to was larger and more comfortable than Archer had expected, warmed by a small coal brazier. Swann, fair-haired and long-faced, alike to one of the horses he loved so much, sat before it on an upturned chest. As Archer entered, he rose, hand moving to the salute. He half stopped; half tried to finish. 'James, er, Sir.'

'Easy, Samuel. I cannot tell you how good it is to see you. James, please, just James.'

'And I you. How is it you are come here? We heard you were left from Barkstead's and gone into Ireland. An officer now. Are you posted back to us?'

'Alas, no, for more of your company would do me good. But I would welcome a share of that warmth and a little conversation.'

Swann pulled over another box and shuffled his own across. They spoke for a few minutes of other soldiers they knew, and of the ongoing campaign in Scotland.

'You've come from the town, you say?' Swann jerked a long thumb towards the open front of the shelter. 'Did you see those troopers out there with the wagons? They're Heselrigg's own men, ridden down today from Norham. All of his campaign loot travels through that way. It's his own manor, see, where he can control everything coming across the border, official or not, like.'

The corporal stopped. He raised one brow.

'You were never much one for talking, but this is something new even for you. What rides upon you so?'

What, here, was there to lose? Swann, a Tynedale man who was as close to friendship as Archer had allowed, was, just, perhaps, safe.

'You were in Newcastle, with the regiment, at the time of the witch trials?'

Swann sat up, puffed out his chest in mock pride.

'Saw the bell-man calling around the town myself, just after the Scotsman, Kincaid, arrived. What a bastard.'

'It is Kincaid that I seek. There are some questions that remain to be answered.'

'That's no surprise. Him and his fellows left sharp after Lieutenant-Colonel Hobson caught them out. It's been given out they stole horses and fled, but that isn't true. He collected his monies from Guildhall on the day after the trial and I heard he stayed one more night to say his goodbyes to some of the grand men of the town. Nicholson, the sheriff's man, said he'd been summoned into Northumberland to try more women. There were no more accused in Newcastle after that.'

'When was this?'

'After the main sessions trials, like I said. The Hawthorn was in blossom, I remember that. Maybe mid-June.'

Archer slumped. It didn't matter anymore. The man would be long gone.

'Can you remember where in Northumberland they said he was headed?'

'Nicholson gave the name of no particular place.'

Another lost scent. Archer felt a chill of despair rise within him.

'Cheer up. You always were a morose bastard.' Swann laughed and spat into the coals. With a grin, which at first Archer did not comprehend, he continued. 'It doesn't matter. Wherever he's been, we heard from the local men here that he came back this way last month. He was apprehended by the justice, Ogle.'

Archer no longer felt the damp, his weariness or his stiffness. Nor did he any more notice the seductive warmth of the brazier. Swann's revelation swept through him like a fire of its own. He only half listened, as the corporal continued.

'Did you not hear the story about Ogle? Cromwell overnighted with the justice a few months since, on the way up into Scotland. Now Captain Ogle is held to be some character, and is of an age to be certain of his views and strong in their defence. The General maybe got more hospitality than he was bargaining for, staying in the house of a loyal officer of the Parliament. You see the two of them had some sort of disagreement, a real hot argument. It's even been settled, so they say, on the pasture outside the very next morning, using fists. And then didn't the old man go and put the General flat on his back?'

Swann laughed heartily at the thought of the altercation, and of the injury to General Cromwell's famous pride, but Archer hardly noticed.

'Where does this Ogle reside? I must get to him, as soon as I may.'

At this, Swann smiled even more broadly.

'You can get there before dark, if you'll ride on. Captain Ogle lives just a few miles up the road at Eglingham Hall.'

Archer was already up and halfway out of the makeshift shelter. 'Save me a sleeping place, would you, Samuel? I have more work to do tonight.'

Chapter 47

Captain Henry Ogle Esq., former officer of horse in Poyntz's parliamentarian Army of the Northern Association and master of Eglingham Hall, proved to be a weather-marked, round-faced man a few years older than Weston.

More concerned at first to get his uninvited guest in front of a good fire, to feed him, to put a warming glass of sack in his hand and to see to the stabling of his horse, Archer could easily see how irreplaceable, in such a tight-knit local area, a man like Ogle would be. He would inspire confidence and trust in the lowliest farm hand as much as in his fellow gentlemen. This part of the county would not be able to function without him. Hence, his retention as the local justice, whatever the quarrel had been with Cromwell.

His guest settled, common courtesies observed. Now Ogle was ready to talk.

'Yes, I took the Scotsman,' he began gruffly. 'Lucky he was it was I who apprehended him. There's scarce a gentleman in these parts would not rather see him dead, with perhaps a degree of suffering thrown in, for that which he occasioned in Berwick.'

'I heard that he saw women hang up there as well.'

'Aye. Twenty women of the town. There's always plenty who will hold up a grievance against their neighbours. The man stayed on after his pay to see the work complete when the women were hung up overlooking the river on Gallows Knowe. That was just before he was called down to Newcastle.'

'Where had he been before you took him?'

'He had come across from Rothbury, having tried his luck over by Hexham and then along the valley of the North Tyne. They are sensible men in that part of the country and would not give him the pay he wanted. Presumably, he thought to head to Berwick again, or perhaps to try the other county towns. He was alone when he got here. He told us that the fellows who usually accompanied him were gone back by themselves into Scotland. I suppose he would not have expected the warrant from Heselrigg, let alone for it to have reached here before him. My men intercepted him over by Whittingham.'

'Heselrigg sent out a warrant to arrest the man?'

'Last month. Not long after the women in Newcastle were hung. There was, it seems, an equal lot of bad feeling left in that town. The man Kincaid stirs up trouble everywhere and is known to be false. Some of my men said the only reason he was still seeking commissions in Northumberland was that he was sore afraid to return to Scotland, where several lords and justices were similarly set to apprehend him.'

And someone in Newcastle had concluded that the witch pricker might also need to be silenced, thought Archer. He must talk with the man as soon as possible.

'He is still then in your custody?'

Ogle's face appeared to swell; its already ruddy colour deepened. 'He is gone, escaped across the border. Ruffians attacked my men and forced them to let him out. He has powerful and dangerous friends. I should have run him through there and then when we caught him, but I suppose a Justice must stand for justice, eh?'

'Scots sent to rescue him? It makes no sense if they are seeking him there.'

'The strange thing is, my men report that the gang had a mixture of accents, and none of them Scots. Some, for certain, were from Newcastle, the others, they think, were foreign.'

'Is there any intelligence regarding Kincaid's whereabouts now?'

'We traced him as far as the border. It seems that he crossed over the Tweed upriver, using the ford at Norham. I would venture he has gone to ground.'

They talked for a while longer. Archer continued to warm to his host, while Ogle evidently relished the company of the young officer. But he held no more information that would help find either the pricker, or Meg.

'You will stay, Ensign Archer? The evening is drawing in. We can find you a clean bed and a good break of fast in the morning.'

He was very tempted. He felt safe in this house and with this man. But what right had he to feel safe and to take his ease when Meg was still out there, alone? When he had not caught up with the one man who could fully explain what had happened to all of those others? Or even when Elizabeth Thompson's murderers remained at large?

'I thank you, but I am due tonight at the encampment outside Alnwick. It is not far.'

'No, not above four miles, and the ground stays dry. My man can take you over there if you will, but I would rather that you stayed.'

'No, thank you. I noted the way when I rode in earlier. Please save your man.'

Chapter 48

Swann would have kept a good fire going and Archer would find the comfortable bed he craved, but he welcomed the prospect of the slow journey back to Alnwick.

While the evening was clear, the moon was waning, and the light made for caution. The horse was tired, so he continued to walk beside it, reins in hand, while his mind agitatedly turned inwards.

Who in Newcastle had arranged the pricker's escape?

Just about every group in the town had used the witch hunt for their own ends. They must have understood the pricker's art to be a fraud. It seemed likely that the Scot, in turn, knew the accusations to be false. He had probably even taken extra money from all sides to stick fast to his lies regarding the women's guilt. There was a long list of possible candidates who would want him out of the way.

When Ogle had detained Kincaid, Heselrigg might have expected that the man would be summarily dispatched, but then it made no sense for the governor to have had a hand in the Scot's escape. Some other party, such as Carr or Blackett, must have tried to intervene, seeking to ensure that Kincaid could never return to testify in Newcastle.

Why not just have him killed?

Beneath all of that, something else needled at Archer. Something said casually by Ogle in the comfort of the warm study went along with a name recently heard, but he could not make the connection.

He paused and patted the mare's flank. Her breath showed

clearly in the cold air. Following it as it dissipated, for a moment he imagined he saw movement in the shadows of the path before them. Looking again, the spectral figure of a woman appeared to stand in the distance, reaching towards him. In his confusion and fear, he at once knew it to be one of his deceitful visions, but could not distinguish whether it was of Meg, Elizabeth, or the hate-filled Ulster girl.

Archer flushed hot, stepping from the shelter of the horse's side, snatching his eyes away from the apparition, seeking the comforting, truncated orb of moon. In so doing, he failed, at first, to apprehend the ambush that was closing in.

He sensed the night to have become too quiet. His nostrils caught a tang of old tobacco. Returning his eyes to the path, the ghostly figure was now a denser, moving set of shadows which separated and grew. The warmth he had felt was brutally replaced with a familiar battle cold. Finally, his vision fully cleared.

The way was barred by three armed men. Turning towards a sound from behind, he found two more, nearer still and moving rapidly towards him, one with sword readied, the other levelling a hand gun.

Ducking, and at the same time rolling his body sharply to the left, Archer felt the shot sail past his head.

Upon the pistol's explosive orange flash, the mare had reared. She turned about, careering back down the track towards Eglingham Hall, forcing the gunman and his companion to dive apart. It gave Archer the respite he needed to set himself.

He drew his own weapon and waited, constantly on the move, turning between each encroaching assailant. Four of them, kept at bay for now by his sword point, began to pace around Archer in a slowly closing ring. He recognised one as the blond giant from the warehouse. A glance beyond the tightening cordon confirmed the fifth man, the gunman, to be the giant's hollow-faced, dark accomplice.

'We have waited awhile for you on this cold night, Ensign

Archer,' an amused voice drawled. 'Snooping about. It is long time we brought your snooping to an end.'

Moving around, then back, again and again, to face each of the group in turn gave him enough of a look at the speaker. Captain-Lieutenant Draper, sword drawn, out of uniform and in company with what looked more like servants than soldiers.

The blond giant lunged forwards. Archer side-stepped and parried gently. Gently enough to be able to twist away from Draper's secondary thrust. He brought his sword around in a great, reversed sweep, clattering the blade aside and stabbed back, forcing them to retreat to their loose cordon.

He could see how much Draper was enjoying the sport, this patient toying with Archer. The tall captain-lieutenant flashed eyes across at the others. Communicating what? If they determined to come at him all together, then he was done for, and they knew it.

The small dark man, almost lost in shadow, called out for a gap into which to fire. Two of the others backed off a little in response. He yelled a final warning and began to raise the weapon. Archer awaited a retort that never came. Instead, the man emitted a sound like a wet slap. His body slumped forwards, cut down from behind by a pale and insubstantial figure who retreated into the gloom.

Archer sensed the attackers' hesitation. Draper looked beyond Archer, yelling 'take him!' The two farthest men turned away to seek the new opponent.

Dancing quickly about, left now with only a pair of attackers, Archer could see that the confidence had drained from both. Their eyes flicked between his sword point, his face, and whatever struggle was unfolding behind him. Advancing, forcing both to retreat, Archer tested and tapped at each of their weapons before dropping his own sword to the right, inviting, as he did, the anticipated lunge from the huge man. Using the reverse edge of his blade, he deflected the thrust into the path of Draper's sword, allowing Archer space to withdraw his own weapon and counter, cutting deeply and drawing a great stream of blood from the giant's side. The big man dropped his weapon, went down and rolled over, clutching at the wound.

Now, Archer could take on Draper one to one. There was nothing left of the man's earlier swagger. The captain-lieutenant tried to pull back but was not quick enough. Archer's mortuary sword swept upward to his left armpit, sinking in two inches deep. Already unbalanced in his retreat, Draper stumbled. Archer brought his basket hilt with full force down upon his opponent's sword wrist. The weapon fell away, and Draper jerked backward, a growing terror about his face. Bringing the point of his sword close to the man's neck, Archer called upon him to yield.

'Yes,' Draper stammered, 'let me live. I bear you no grievance.'

To one side, the blond man began to whimper as more blood gushed from his rent body. He began to shake violently. It seemed as if he would cry out, then all movement ceased, and he lay still.

Archer held his sword steady.

'You. It was you that killed those women. Elinor Loumsdale's women. Who told you about them? The Blackett boy? Was it you that killed him as well?' Draper's mouth unwound and Archer knew that his effort had missed.

'We obeyed orders, that is all. We were ordered to silence the women. I know nothing about the boy.'

Archer moved the point of his blade a little nearer to the captain's long neck.

'Hold!'

'You were ordered to silence me.'

'That was a mistake. It was the Swede's fault. When the watchman came out, he panicked,' cried Draper, a high note of fear entering his voice. 'I swear it.'

'But you killed Elizabeth Thompson and the other women.' The captain-lieutenant's right eye narrowed. Archer was close to the truth now. He could sense it. 'On whose command? Was it Heselrigg's?'

A small smile returned to Draper's face, accompanied by the tightest shaking of his head. Archer kept the sword levelled.

'If you have no personal interest, then who paid you?' Archer's eyes remained fixed upon his captive. 'Who commissioned you in this? Carr then, one of the other Royalists, or young Blackett's brother?'

Draper kept on smiling, as if it were he who had Archer under his guard.

'Damn you. They had the most to lose.'

Draper still gave no reply.

Captain Ogle and a servant appeared alongside them, both with bloodied swords. Offering a brief nod to the justice, Archer saw the immobile bodies of two men lying flat in the mud of the track. Two more of Ogle's servants stood guard over a wounded third.

'Just after you left, news was given to my man of strangers come off the road but keeping hidden,' said Ogle, breathlessly. 'We gathered weapons and, thank God, appear to have arrived in time.'

Ogle looked at Draper's shirt and jerkin, sodden with gore. Pacing across to examine the giant body of the other man, who Draper had called the Swede, he stiffened.

'You know this man?'

'I have seen him in the course of my business. One of those,' he indicated the other bodies, 'is a local man, a domestic servant in Newcastle. This other,' he continued, looking down at the fallen blond giant, 'is a foreign man I know more recently to have been in service with the same household. Why, Ensign Archer, does Henry Dawson want you killed?'

Archer fractionally dropped the tip of his sword. Draper sprang at him, a dagger appearing in his hand. Archer twisted out of its path, bringing the mortuary blade around to drive it deep into Draper's open belly. A long, soft gurgle emerged from the captain-lieutenant's throat before he slumped forward against the steel, quite dead.

'A fine move, Archer. You have learned your craft well.'

Henry Ogle looked across to his servants, still holding the final assassin at sword point. He gave a brief nod, and the man was run through.

'Breaking the peace on the property of a Justice and drawing weapons against a gentleman and an officer? An open and shut proceeding.'

Chapter 49

Ogle had insisted that Archer return with him to Eglingham Hall. Only when his guest was again settled did he turn to discussion of the fight, desiring to know of Draper's position, and more about Archer's own connections with alderman Henry Dawson.

Archer was, at first, unable to answer any of these questions coherently.

That it was Heselrigg's own Captain-Lieutenant, Draper, who should have left Newcastle to stalk him was surprising enough; the officer's presence in civilian apparel and commanding a group of domestic servants, stranger yet.

That Henry Dawson, of all men, might have a hand in the ambush remained beyond his imagining. All rational thought broke down whenever he approached the idea.

Ogle now became the Justice. He led Archer on with careful questions, each gentle, searching and ever more closely framed.

So, it was there, before the firelight in the early hours of the morning, as they talked on, that Archer remembered the connection he had been missing, remembered one small detail first fed to him by Wilkinson what now seemed so long ago. A detail he had overlooked completely, even when mentioned earlier that evening by Swann and again, later, by Ogle himself.

It was then also that he had taken the decision to tell the Justice the whole truth.

The fire burned low as he revealed what he had uncovered about the Newcastle witches. He detailed the deliberate obfuscations and missing evidence. He revealed all he had learned relating to Heselrigg's corruption, the power struggles between the town's merchant factions, the venality and intrigue behind the whole affair.

Archer talked of Elizabeth Thompson. He unfolded the discovery of her body and the attack upon him in the warehouse. He detailed his encounter there with Dawson's oddly matched servants, those who, along with Draper, had ambushed him and whose dead bodies were, even now, being disposed of by Ogle's men. He spoke of Elinor Loumsdale's doomed, heroic efforts, and of the terrible price she had paid for them. He confessed to his host the pain and confusion, rendering him incapable of understanding where Henry Dawson might fit into these events. He repeated his need to catch up with the Scot, now able to explain that Kincaid would be the only man alive able to provide full and final answers.

Haltingly, but sparing nothing, he spoke to the Justice of Meg. And, finally, he asked about the remote village of Norham.

Captain Ogle, having been content with probing, listening and drawing out, grew first restless, then openly angered as Archer's testimony unfolded. Cursing, he called out to order a further wine jug. When it came, he waited, simmering, until the servant was long gone. Only then did he begin to speak, letting forth a roaring flow of pent-up frustration, sorrow and regret. As he did so, the rock-like old justice, hewn, it seemed, from the same hard whinstone underpinning Northumberland itself, softened and unfolded, becoming, before Archer's eyes, more like an ordinary man. More damaged. More fragile. More helpless.

'Curse them, Archer. Curse them for their arrogance and their damned cocksureness. It is vanity and it is pride. For that, mark me, they will lose everything they ever stood up and fought for. We shall all, because of that, lose more besides.'

He stood and paced about the room, his passion building as he spoke on.

'Look, you, I know my own people. They want stability and order, fair justice and fair wages. To be allowed to live in security and with some, shall we say, jollity. I abhor the greed of the town as much as any man. We must needs remember the causes for which we undertook a war with our own Sovereign, no?'

Was it some sort of courage or just tiredness which made Archer reply that such remembrance had deserted him over these past years? It prompted Ogle to sit down opposite with a kindly sigh.

'Then permit me help you to recall. These are terrible things you have recounted. That does not mean they are done by evil men. I can see the good in many of their intentions. Heselrigg is heavily involved with the relief of the suffering of the poor and had made several educational endowments. Did you know that? Even here, it is our local sectarians who are most active in the practical relief of the people's sufferings. Their efforts shame many of the county gentry, myself not being excluded. We needed, and I believe that we still shall need, such examples of God's love and justice flourishing upon this earth.'

Ogle gave a wry inward smile. His eyes left Archer's and lost their focus.

'But this certainty of their own superiority, of their own sainthood? The calling, they claim, for the elect to separate their earthly lives from those of that majority, who they believe already to be lost? The willingness this breeds among them to condemn almost all of their fellow men? It is an abomination. What you describe as taking place in the town speaks of the contempt born from their self-regard. Any man charged with a measure of responsibility for people will tell you that this can come to no good.'

He looked once more up at Archer, seemingly caught between anger and sorrow.

'This is their tragedy. They are so blinded by their desire to make the world anew, by a vision of a perfect world that may never be, that they believe any who stand in their way can only be in league with the Evil One. They are made blind to the evils they themselves spread. Such condescension may be borne with dull resentment for a time, but then? I say this not because of any quarrel I have had of late, nor anything endured in the late troubles, but with sorrow. Those grievances the people presently store up will be fulfilled, some day, in their welcoming back the young Charles Stuart. Few then shall weep for the demise of your Henry Dawson. I fear that day not for myself, but because all that we have gained through the strife of these times is bound to be swept away in such a reversal.'

Archer winced, not for the sentiment, but for his old habits of caution. The master of Eglingham, who had brawled with Lord General Cromwell, clearly felt safe enough in his own house not to hold back his opinions.

'Are you really not concerned about that day, which I pray God never to arrive, for yourself, nor for your family and estate?'

'I am unsure what more I should have to be concerned about. I was justice here under the late king, have retained that position for the Commonwealth. I hope to live to see my sons return and take on the same mantle. I am commissioner in the north and will seek to do the will of the Council, but with an eye to the hearts of the people for whom I bear responsibility. In my own country here? No, there is nothing for me to fear.'

Chapter 50

Early the next morning, Ogle had sent over to Chatton to fetch his neighbour, Captain Lewis. Lewis had ridden with Brandling's troop and had come to know the dealings of Tweedale and its tributary valleys as well as any outsider.

When Archer set forth again, the men had ensured he was well provisioned, both in victuals and advice. Avoiding the roads and keeping to the more hidden ways of the drovers' tracks and stream-cut paths they had outlined, he had cause to be glad of both.

Now, in his overnight encampment, huddled in a thick saddle blanket before a low-burning fire of rowan wood, Archer was tired but could not sleep.

He remained unable to make sense of Ogle's revelation about his attackers' connections to Henry Dawson, or fully to understand Draper's leadership of the killing squad. It did not matter. He felt sorrow for Wilkinson. He carefully kept all thoughts of Elizabeth Thompson at bay. He was aware of some inner pang of regret for his betrayal of Massie. It was a twinge of guilt that did not extend to Skippon or Deane. But there was no longer room within him for anything more than Meg.

More than ever, he was fully determined. He would walk away from them all.

Tomorrow, he would drop down from the hills and reach the hidden border village. There, he would, at last, find Meg. Together, they would go away. They would be free.

The man who emerged from the surrounding darkness was small, but powerfully lithe. He was also a master of his craft, for he had crept close like some eerie, fey visitation and was crouching right beside Archer before there was any intimation of his presence. He might have cut a dozen throats before once being noticed.

As he squatted down and bent towards the heat of the flames, the stranger seemed at the same time more ominously powerful, but also less ordinarily real, than any man Archer had ever previously met. Glossy dark hair, chopped roughly to the collar, framed a round face so flat that it was almost devoid of features. The coal-dark, almond-slanted eyes were similarly withdrawn and unreadable. His skin was so pale that it appeared to glow unnaturally in the dancing firelight.

There was also something comfortingly familiar about him. Archer knew at once that he was face to face with the unseen watcher who had tracked him since Doncaster. It was an insubstantial presence felt behind him along the road; a shadow disappearing into the side of a chare; a pair of black eyes set in the palest face, watching Gower and Archer outside the burning Thompson warehouse; a ghost armed with a knife who, the previous evening, had saved his life at Eglingham.

It made it no less of a shock when the pale watcher spoke.

'It pleases me to see that you live yet.'

Whatever sound Archer had expected to emerge from the stranger's lips, it was not a Tyneside dialect from Shields. The voice was calm, lifting to the end, the whole easy and rolling, like all the accents of the sea-coast.

Reappraising the dark eyes, the strange hair, the unusual pallor of the skin, Archer presumed the man to come from one of those unique communities, long established in the township at the mouth of the river by renegades, ship-jumpers and escaped slaves, or of those simply tired of the unchanging vagaries of sea.

This man's eyes settled on nothing. There was a wild danger coiled deep within them. Archer once again sensed that withheld strength and creeping otherworldliness. 'I was fortunate to have friends nearby,' he said. 'Yourself included, it would seem. It was you, who killed the man with the firearm. You who had warned Ogle.'

The man gave no response.

'You also? Who killed young Blackett?'

At first, the watcher seemed intent upon ignoring what Archer had said. His eyes burned with the reflection from the fire as he leaned in even closer. Then, near to imperceptibly, his lips again moved. 'He betrayed trust. Would you rather his tongue was yet loose?'

Having offered this brief comment, the watcher lapsed into his former silence.

Archer fed in more wood, taking his time as the wild sounds of the night closed in. Collecting his thoughts, he tried again. 'Why are you watching me?'

'Watching over you,' the man corrected. 'To keep you safe.'

'What is it you want?' demanded Archer. 'You might have killed me many times over upon the road. You had occasion in the town. Or again here, tonight.'

'That is not my charge. Your safe person is my charge.'

Archer was left in no doubt that the man would efficiently, coolly, and without any thought, dispatch him, were those orders to change. 'Who charges you so?'

'Major General Massie wishes you safe. Williams wishes you safe. I am pleased to perform that work.'

Archer sat further upright in his surprise. Williams and his Levellers working together with young Charles Stuart's general. How was it possible? 'Williams' time is done. As it is over for all those they call Levellers. That was buried along with Rainsborough.'

'Nothing is finished.' The pale watcher calmly and unsettlingly appraised Archer.

'The cause is lost. There is left only Cromwell. Look what he did at Dunbar. Without Cromwell there will be nothing but more blood.'

'Is it the Lord General who will be the "repairer of the breach, the restorer of paths to dwell in"?'

As the watcher recited Isaiah's vision of a saviour come to reshape land and people, Archer looked up. Strong, sharp teeth showed white in the darkness. Coal-black eyes glistened with animal brilliance in the flickering glow.

'You believed once,' said the acid voice, piercing Archer with each word. 'And yet you choose to stand by while the army and their slaves in the rump of a Parliament enter into a tyranny greater than any imposed by the late King.'

The man was testing him, probing for something. But Archer had no way to know which answer might prove acceptable and which would end with a dagger in his guts.

'Williams said the Sergeant Archer he knew had died at Colchester.'

In the night's chill, Archer blazed with heat. 'I do not understand.'

The pale man looked back into the dying fire. 'Tell me about Lucas House.'

In the July heat, the putrefaction of the uncleared dead would have been near to unbearable, had it not become to them so familiar a presence.

When he had approached the Lucas estate, overlooking Colchester's ancient walls, Archer had known already what was wrong. The main house had been ransacked earlier in the fighting, leaving no new spoils for the pikemen who, over the previous days, had suffered such severe losses in its storming. So now, the soldiers were taking out their disappointment on the adjoining family crypt.

Captain Denison leaned forwards, speaking quietly so that the rest of his men might not overhear. 'Leave them, Sergeant. That lying bastard Lucas defies us behind those walls and these men have toiled greatly to prise his levies from this place. Do you forget what happened to Cox?'

Archer cocked his head to one side as he looked back at the officer. Captain Cox and most of his men had been killed in the first days of the New Model's encirclement of Colchester, caught by gunnery in the open. Denison had succeeded to lead Cox's company. He was known both to feel the loss of his friend keenly, and to have developed a new ruthlessness in his approach to the siege works. It rankled all the more that the captain should try to make use of the memory of their dead comrades to restrain him now.

'Enough,' continued Denison. 'Let us set to our own tasks. Can the gatehouse be used to site a new battery, or no? That is your only work here.' The officer dropped his voice another notch. 'Remember your duty.'

But Archer had already dismounted. Their escort looked on in barely hidden amusement as, without the slightest acknowledgement that the captain had spoken, he strode away towards the blank doorway of the vault.

His thoughts, such as they were as he crossed the ravaged ground on the approach to the sepulchre, were a confused morass of guilt, fear and frustration. That morning, they merged into the clammy, sucking anger which had remained such a close companion to Archer in the months and years since.

Sinking into the ruined stonework, he became dizzied, confused as much by the feelings driving him on as by the shutting off of the bright morning light.

At the bottom of the single flight of steps, Archer stopped to allow his eyes to adjust to the gloom. Gradually, the large burial chamber and its wretched contents came into clearer focus. Most of the Lucas family tombs lining the walls or squatting in the middle of the floor had been crudely opened. Their stone lids, along with the lead and wooden coffins from within, lay upturned and broken, the whole chamber bestrewn with the fragments. The fragile remains these had contained were similarly scattered throughout the debris. In amongst this, several strong pikemen stood about looking incuriously at the new arrival.

A red-faced corporal stepped forwards. From his right hand, suspended by long strands of still-fair hair, hung a grey skull, not yet fully de-fleshed. The corporal and two of the other soldiers had woven lengths of the same hair into their hat bands.

'Is this what we fight for?' asked Archer. 'That you might so dishonour the bodies of these women?'

Their weathered, grit-eyed faces stared back as his words rang off the low ceiling and enclosing walls. The bull-necked corporal took another step closer, allowing the skull to fall. The noise it made as it hit the cold flags of the floor, a crack hidden in a thud, provoked an urgent, nauseous spasm.

'What do you care about these Papist whores?'

Archer sprang forwards with such speed and force as to take the man completely by surprise. The roars of the private soldiers, moving forwards to help their comrade, must have alerted Denison and the men of Archer's regiment above, for several of them hurtled down the stairs to pull him back from the melee, dragging him out of that dark crypt and up into the light.

'There were many hard things done in the wars,' said the strange Shields man. 'Of all we have seen, why those very bones?'

Archer's fear and anger had gone. He contemplated the dying fire for a while, its weak light recasting the pale face of the watcher into a rigid death mask.

'The hair,' he said. 'I think it was the strands of hair. It may have been that of Lucas' mother, more likely his young wife. The last had not long been buried. I saw, in the eyes of those men, the pleasure they were taking in the desecration.'

He looked across at the small man and felt the same anger overtake him.

'We spoke of justice and freedom and equality. But what we really meant was vengeance and power. We brought nothing but envy and destruction. Do not look to me to serve you or your plots or your lost causes. I am done with them all.'

'You did not enlist for Ireland then, James Archer. But only much later. Not until after the killing of the King.'

Archer did not respond. The fire was almost spent. The cold of the night closed in upon their silence, until Archer could forbear no longer.

'I would at least know the name of my deliverer.'

'A name. Does that really matter?' The watcher smiled, but there was no joy in it. His black eyes creased at the corners as they flicked back onto Archer's. 'James Archer can know me as Mishael.'

Archer straightened abruptly. One of Daniel's incorruptible Jewish brethren from Scripture. What could the watcher mean by it?

There was an extra lustre deep in Mishael's dark pupils as he stood and stretched, but no emotion showed on his moon-like face. He moved away, and seemed to become even less substantial than before, so that his voice seemed to emerge of its own accord from the deepest shadows.

'There are no more searchers behind you. The officer you killed, be assured he was the only one.'

Mishael took one silent step back into the darkness, then another, until Archer could no longer be sure whether the fading shadow was the final sight of the pale watcher, or simply his own fancy.

Pulling his cloak closer about him, Archer bent towards the

last embers of the fire. Why had he even asked for a name? There would be no need for it, no future rendezvous to keep. He thought again upon the day to come and smiled, thinking how near he finally was to Meg.

He reached out with his left hand, intending to feed in one last piece of fuel. As his fingers felt for the small pile of dead wood, they brushed something light and dry. Turning, he saw, perched upon the sticks, a single branch of rosemary.

For faithfulness.

Chapter 51

Away to the left, the gently rolling forms of the Cheviot hills were bathed in a golden mid-morning light, the clouds above them picked out in soft orange and pink. On Archer's other side, the land was well wooded all the way down to the silver ribbon of the Tweed. The trees burned with valiant colour and, as he eased the tired horse on, burst with clusters of birdsong. His head was clear, and the flicker gone from his right side.

It was as if he had entered a dream.

The track twisted around until before him loomed the bulk of Norham Castle, perched on its rise above the ford it defended. Abandoned since the union of the crowns nearly fifty years earlier, it stood half ruined. The high keep had lost its topmost floor. The great outer wall had been heavily raided for stone. A few soldiers lolled about the exposed outer bailey, Cromwell's men, here, as everywhere. They gave him barely a glance as he skirted the fortification and eased his mount down the path to the village.

Low, grey, stone cottages ran along either side of a single, long street, their tiny windows deep-set into thick walls, the better to ride out the frigid local winter which would come again all too soon.

She was so close now. His heart beat fast in anticipation.

It was on Lewis's advice that Archer rode past the castle and down the hill. On his word too that he walked the horse along the deserted street and headed directly for the patchwork of land at its end, where a group of scarecrow-like women scrabbled amongst the sparse growth.

One look at Archer, encompassing his sword, uniform, scarred face and the ice in his eyes, sufficed. Following the women's direction, he tethered the mare before he approached the church. One red-faced, older woman in particular stared at him unceasingly throughout the encounter. He felt her eyes hard upon him and was careful not to glance back as he entered the surrounding burial ground. Pausing to look up at the elaborate, double-towered front, Archer soon moved on, threading his way north through the grave markers. As the women had said, on that farther side a long, straight path, driven between enclosed fields of barley stubble, led down towards the river.

In the right-hand field, he had plenty of time to observe the lines of young children, supervised by a pair of older girls, searching across the ground, filling any useful remnants of the harvest into huge woven sacks, carried upon thick straps braced across their shoulders.

A similar picture of purposeful activity greeted him at the path's end, where it met the north bank of the river. Here, a group of bare-headed older women worked beating and rinsing clothes at a shallow incline of flat boulders. A cluster of boys and girls milled around on the bank behind them, bringing filled baskets of clothes and linens down a second path from the village to be washed, or loading clean, wet laundry back into the empty carriers for the return. As in so many of the villages and hamlets he had entered over the past weeks, no men were to be seen. The old had died in the hard winters, the young never yet returned from the wars.

A little to his left, three-quarters of the way across the river towards the Scottish bank, a sturdy coble sat anchored, steady in a gentle stream. Archer stepped cautiously nearer. From the boat's stern, four strong nets had been paid out. A pair of formidable looking young women strained to hold these in place while, nearer to his bank, their far ends were set in position. The shorter of the two, coarse sandy hair pulled back from a round, ruddy face, was shouting out in a dialect he could barely follow, instructing four further women who stood in the pebbled shallows, facing out over the water towards the boat. Their skirts tucked high into wide leather belts, each of the four stretched out an end of net, crouching in the freezing water to peg it down whenever the lead woman in the boat was satisfied. Archer watched on admiringly as, together, the six women skilfully handled the netting, working in unison to keep the heavy sides taut, positioning and re-positioning their fraying edges as, together, they took full account of the vagaries of tide and stream, and worked to complete the fish trap.

The lead woman gave out a last, deep-throated shout, called a softer instruction to her boat companion, and in a minute both women together had made the four nets secure at the coble end. Their task complete, they looked up and saw Archer, each making to shield their eyes against the lowering sun. In response, three of the four landward women stood fully up to look back towards the bank. Five weather-worn faces were now turned towards him. Five pairs of eyes looked suspiciously back. He took in five sets of muscular forearms and worn, blistered hands, and could feel the heat of their hostility. Only the last woman, squatting thigh-deep in the stream, still testing the long pins which secured the last of her edges, seemed oblivious to his presence. Finally, she too raised herself from her work, a mass of damp, blonde curls tumbling down her graceful back. Archer took another step forward.

Her first instinct was to offer him a smile of welcome. Before this was complete, it had already fallen from her face. He waited, mouth hanging heedlessly open, left facing a young and beautiful woman; an open-faced woman with soft, blue eyes and a mass of curling hair; a woman who was so closely alike to his sister; but a woman who was not Meg.

'My name is Jane Copeland, and I am a dead woman.'

They had walked some way upstream, away from her forbidding work companions. Now, where the Tweed ran wide and slow between the steep banks of the dene and the stone channel set to regulate the ford, they sat apart on two flat boulders. The lines of birch trees on either bank still carried a proud canopy of leaves, and the late sun warmed their backs.

Close to, Jane Copeland's brow was a fraction higher than Meg's. Her delicate chin was subtly more prominent. Physical labour, much of it performed outdoors, had toned and hardened her body and had scoured her exposed skin. Her eyes shone, not with that excitable brilliance with which his sister had illuminated a room, but with a wilder spark that provoked within him a cold shiver, despite the warmth of the day. Even so, she and Meg were so alike that it felt to Archer as though his sister were very near.

'I will tell you, but for her sake,' Jane began wearily. 'Your sister and I cleaved together in Newgate. It was natural. We were alike in more ways than appearance. We knew one another from our lives before, of course, and each of us had been accused and arrested on account of your uncle.'

Seeing his surprise, she paused and looked out across the stream, gathering herself.

'They used us to attack him,' Jane explained in her clear, tutored voice. 'I know he is not a great man of the town. It is rather that, through his sufferings, they hoped, I think, to gain some measure of control over other, grander families. Meg's arrest was means to hurt him as his kin. Mine, because it was well known that Master Weston had become fond of me.'

Archer was newly aware of how young the woman was, for

all her hardened state. Shyly, he tried to discern the beauty she must, until recently, have been.

'My husband, Richard, was the son and the only heir of Mister Anthony Seymour, your uncle's partner, in ownership of the brewery. I came across to him not long after you yourself left. I was but fifteen and foolish, believing myself to be in love. It was only a matter of a few weeks until Richard took a commission from Sir John Marley and marched away south with the Lambs. Like so many others, he died at Marston Moor.'

Archer was near to numb. He felt only a throbbing in his head and imagined that the babble of the Tweed before them was the flow of the blood in his veins.

'Once my Richard was gone, the old man soon died. I think of a broken heart as much as of the sweat. Weston looked after me. What family I had were all taken by the same sickness, you see. Also, I was with Richard's child. It would have been easy enough to tell the world that the position was being maintained for the new heir. Your uncle housed me and cared for me. He did that even after the child came far too soon and so was lost.'

For the first time, she showed a hint of emotion, hesitating for several seconds before she could go on.

'I came, too, to care for him, although God has cursed me for it. But I think that in some small way he did love me. Such impious sin was soon punished. The watchmen came and took me to Newgate, into the same cell where, some weeks later, they brought your sister.

'Even in those first days, Meg seemed half gone from this world. She worked harder than any to help the other women. She took on more than was her lot of the common chores by which we kept the cell bearable. But in herself she cared nothing for the squalid conditions, not when the Scots man humiliated us, nor even when she was searched, and pricked, and bled. She seemed beyond all normal feeling. Some of the other women, who should have known better, declared that she was, in truth, a witch, but I could understand how much she was suffering. You see, we both knew what it was to lose a child.'

Jane retreated from the sunlight, so that the top half of her was shaded and he could not see her reaction to his own drawn, bloodless face.

'She had been used just as I was. In Meg's case, she was led on by one of the officers of the garrison. You should know,' she said urgently, 'that your uncle stood by your sister when he might have disowned her. Part of this she herself told me, in our long months in the prison. Part, I learned only from the old woman with whom I am lodged here, when she asked after "the other one". When your Meg, our Meg, became with child, Weston paid the governor, whose people had her brought here. The old woman is skilled in birthing. Your uncle had it said about the town that she was gone into the country, to his Durham house, along with his own wife and children, in order to escape the sickness. It gave a public reason for her to stay away for the period of her growing, to the birth. All that while she was hidden here, in Norham.'

'Then Weston did know where she was.'

'I do not think so. Any more than he knows where I am. The governor protects his secrets well. This whole village is too useful to him for bringing goods in and out of Scotland. He would take great precautions against any in Newcastle, knowing of his dealings here.'

'But my uncle, he would not receive Meg after her return.'

'In that you are mistaken!'

He was taken aback by her vehemence, glimpsing in her the passion which, incredible though it still seemed to him, his uncle must once have inspired.

'I know this for truth from him and from her both,' she ran on. 'He always intended for her to return under his roof, reputation intact. It was she who refused to stay. She left the house on the same day she was brought back into Newcastle. I myself saw her when she arrived along with your aunt and cousins. Silent and wretched she was. She could bring herself to raise her eyes to no person, not even Bessie, who loved her best. She left the child, to be raised in your uncle's household, and set out on her own, into the town. Perhaps Weston passed her funds, or paid her rent, or otherwise helped. She told me later that she had made her own way and wanted nothing else. That was what the officer had left her with. I believe that she loved him, and that he had sorely disappointed her.'

She told Archer the man's name. It came as no surprise, but a feeling of terrible weakness nevertheless opened up inside him. Here was the true measure of his desertion, and of his failure as a brother. It sickened him to realise that, when first they had met in Newcastle, when Draper had deployed his charm, he had, for that while, been deceived in it. From the beginning, the captain-lieutenant had been toying with him, taking a cruel pleasure in the twisted game he was playing, as he must also have done with Meg. Sweat formed on Archer's brow. His throat tightened. His leg began to shake, and he swayed in his position on the rock. In alarm, Jane leant towards him.

'That man will deceive no more,' he said, righting himself and stopping her short. 'He died at my own hands, not two nights since.'

The woman's features wavered, then recomposed. 'Then there is some justice left in the world.'

The endless, meaningless chatter of the river filled the silence. Minutes went by and the sun sank lower.

'How did you come to be here?' he asked, breaking the calm, before addressing the question he dreaded. 'What happened, after the trial? What happened to my sister?'

She sat back again and spoke out of deepening shadow. 'At the end of the trial, I did not hear the verdicts. I kept Meg close in my arms. For my own part, I remained unmoved. I held on to your sister and observed the other women as though I were watching some tableau. The pretty girl, the one the officer had made Kincaid prick again, stood already to one side. She, who was one of the first, and one of the very few, to be set free, looked more stricken than those who were condemned. Some shed tears, one or two even emitted keening moans. Most were quieter, comforting one another in their resignation. I heard a proud voice whisper a psalm to her companions. I can recall it now. "My flesh and my heart faileth me; but God is the strength of my heart, and my portion forever". A few looked plaintively at their families, who stood, silent and broken, at the rear of the crowd.'

Her cheeks darkened as she told him more of that last day in the claustrophobia of the court. Archer listened on, without interruption, but at every turn he saw again only Draper's wide-open, lifeless gaze and found in it nothing but recrimination and regret.

'Not all were so accepting. A clutch of the grandest merchant women, among them Jennie Dawson and Mistress Fenwick, made their way over to the rail nearest to the judge's bench and stood there glaring at the hastily departing magistrates and towards those of their own families who remained. The man they called our warlock, Bonner, remained slumped as he had throughout the trial. Such was his piteous state that I doubt he knew anything of the proceedings. It was, as I prayed for him, a mercy.'

Her inner fire abated, and she spoke on more slowly.

'Before, I think, we had begun our slow trudge back to Newgate. The first deals were being struck. If a family had enough influence and money, they could get the woman spirited from Newgate and out of the town. That is, if those who had engineered their kin's fall were satisfied that the family had learned whatever lesson they imagined required such a schooling.'

Jane looked older now, tired and worn, as if telling the story were dragging her back to the Newgate cells.

'Master Weston nearly destroyed his business and all of his sources of credit to release us both, already having entirely given up his ambitions in the corporation. He had submitted to humiliatingly low contracts from the garrison officers for his beer and is made to supply the army at a loss. He will never, I think, be able to clear his debts.'

She paused and Archer looked up, finding that he was hoping that the woman had finished. Rather, she seemed to be gathering herself up for a further effort. Even as he willed her to resume her telling, so too he hoped that she might instead rise and return to the village.

'Even then, the men who hated him, those who hated all of the old families, wanted his suffering to be greater still. After he had paid them and the senior officers of the corporation, all they had asked, they told him that he must, finally, choose only one of us to save, for if one were to live then the other would yet hang.'

With difficulty Archer attended her final words, as the worm of an idea began to lodge itself deep within him.

'Your uncle chose Meg. He chose to let her live and, in so doing, condemned me to die. I do not blame him. Or her. He had to choose this way. He came to the prison in person to tell me. He could barely speak the words as he tried to explain himself. It was I who had to comfort him. The other families always sent their fixers, or sometimes their own servants. But your uncle, he braved all public ridicule and gossip and entered into that place himself. I shall never forget the look in his eyes, the look that he could not keep hidden from me when he came through the cell door. I knew then that for me there would be no reprieve.'

She could not any more look up at Archer and her voice was more strained than ever. 'He had chosen Meg, as the Devil forced him to, but Meg, you see, chose me. She took my place, so that Meg Archer was led out of Newgate and taken into the county by Heselrigg's men. All record of her in the proceedings was lost. Her name, in connection to the accusations, completely disappeared. Jane Copeland remained in Newgate, from where she was taken onto the moor and to the gallows.'

All that Archer could see was the image of his sister on that terrible, final journey. Jane Copeland misunderstood his continued silence.

'I am sorry for it. I wish I had never allowed her to. I would rather have died along with her. She would not let me be. She said that she deserved it and that perhaps she was a witch and needed to suffer. And I am afraid that at that time I still very much wanted to live.'

'It was Heselrigg who demanded that Weston choose between you?'

'No.' she replied, cutting him off in his desperation with the hard edge of her certainty. 'The governor did more, much more than you can know, to help. He furnished Weston with a new military contract to keep his business going, even as your uncle used that as a lifeline to raise all of the other funds he could.'

'But Heselrigg knew,' he repeated, hotly, 'and the officers all knew ,too. And half of Newcastle knew that the women were innocent.'

Jane looked closely at him. The steadiness within her calmed him. 'He knew, but he tried to help as many families as he could, as he thought in the end that he had helped your uncle. It was not the governor, but instead alderman Dawson who would not let it go. It was he who was determined that a certain number of the women must die. He also who insisted that poor Weston must choose which one of us would perish. I believe that Dawson knew that he could not treat the very greatest families in the same way. Perhaps, instead, he thought that your uncle's enforced choosing would be a kind of example to them.'

Archer, anger turned to despair, was left with answers he did not want. The men who had contrived to kill his sister crowded his scrambled mind. The sadistic Scot, with his venal trickery. Woolfall, who had abused Meg so vilely. Jenison too, stoking the fear and hatred. Draper, whose contemptuous rejection meant that she had, finally, given up desire for life itself. Dawson, his own Henry Dawson, who had condemned her far more surely than any of these. And Archer himself, as guilty as each of them.

His senses gradually returned to the peaceful riverbank and to the silent woman who, he realised anew, had herself lost so much.

'My sister's child. Lives it still?'

'I cannot help you there, sir.'

'No matter. Do not worry about it,' he said kindly, picturing the infant girl, the new cousin growing up in the Weston nursery.

'What will you do now, Jane Copeland? Where will you go? You cannot remain here. You must live. You owe that to Meg.'

She raised up her head, as if following a scent blown down the stream.

'Live? Yes, that I must,' she said, her voice changed now, shifting deeper and seeming in some way much older. Her strained face lost even more colour. 'I know I do not deserve it. When I saw you by the salmon station, my first thought was of relief, that you had been sent here to quite another purpose. But I should have known that way to have been barred to me.'

'You must not remain. They will come for you. I cannot allow you to stay in such a place of danger.'

'I must take that chance. The women here accept me. The old woman who keeps me will need my help as winter returns. And where else would I have to go? All of my family are gone, and I cannot very well return to Newcastle. Did you not tell me just now that that man is dead? Does anyone else know where I am?'

They walked side by side further west, to where the river foamed out of the twisting dene. He noticed that she did not look back. At the point where the looped path back to the village began to rise steeply towards a line of trees, she turned towards him and smiled.

'You must not fear for me. It is the Lord who has worked this, through your sister. He must keep some purpose for me, or else I should not have lived.'

He looked out at the swirling, white dance of the river. Could she be right? He did not wish to believe it, but he knew that nothing more could be said to move her.

'What of you now, James Archer?'

Archer could make no reply. Instead, he stood and stared into the perpetual movement of the eddying waters.

Spring Gardens, Whitehall, London
2nd August 1653

The stench from the Thames, festering in the summer heat, lay with oppressive heaviness over the walls and gates of Whitehall.

Archer felt only that taut expectation which shields a man from ordinary sensation in the pulse beats before such desperate work as he was to do tonight. The unexpected nature of this final opportunity meant that its bite was all the keener.

He felt for the hilt of the dagger, finding it cool and smooth under his fingertips. Long and thin, it would kill and barely leave a mark. Since returning to the hard embrace of Skippon's quiet work, he had been trained for this; to cut a man open in an instant, to do it silently, to have the blood spurt outwards so that an assassin might walk away without any trace.

It was above nine years since he had last seen Meg. Was this all he was left with? This training? This silent killing? This coldness, deep within?

He thought, as he so often did, of Jane Copeland. It was above a year now, since brigands had raided and razed Norham. Whether they were Scots or English, no-one had been able to establish. Not that such a detail mattered. As soon as Archer had heard, he had sent to Davey, to Hobson and Ogle, and to Wilkinson in Leith, but neither they, nor the many contacts they had approached, had been able to uncover any scrap of news of the woman.

His right eye flickered more harshly than ever. Softly, he drew out the slender blade.

With a single upward glance towards the exposed stars, Archer moved along the blind back walls of the buildings on the Whitehall side, halting a few steps before the pointed archway from which the man would soon emerge, unsteady after his late supper.

After these three long years, it was nearly done.

He had forsaken a quick vengeance. One rapid murder would only put the others on their guard. So, he had evaded the patrols on his way back across the county, had disappeared completely from the north, and had waited.

He had kept contact with Davey. He had corresponded with Mistress Thompson and Ephraim Ord. Through them, he understood that the killings in Newcastle had stopped. With much greater difficulty, he had brought Wilkinson into the patient plan.

The Scot, Kincaid, stayed with him. He could never quite un-see the empty eye sockets, the slackly hanging jaw, the elongated limbs of the emaciated corpse hanging in its gibbet cage. The man's fellow countrymen had reached the pricker first, exacting their own justice for the women he had falsely condemned across the Lowlands.

Woolfall had been easy, tracked by Davey and waylaid by Archer on the road west of Throckley as the afternoon turned to evening. He had pleaded for life and cried in the face of his God. Perhaps he feared that he was not, after all, of the elect?

Jenison had nearly escaped, the old man being all but ready to meet his God alone and unaided. Alerted by Ord, Archer had needed to give him no more than a nudge along that straitened path of judgement.

That Mistress Thompson should then, so soon after, learn of Dawson's coming to Whitehall was its own special providence.

It had always been Dawson's plan, one eagerly adopted by the ministers. It was Dawson who had escalated the accusations, using them to intimidate rival families. Dawson had controlled who, in the end, would die, and it was Dawson who had forced Weston into the dreadful choice between his niece and his young lover. Dawson, too, who had ordered the silencing of

Elinor Loumsdale's women.

So, this was for Meg and for Jane, for Elizabeth Thompson, for Abigail Walker, Sarah Turner, and Rebecca Weaver. For all of the other women, and for Matthew Bonner, whose own family had chosen to abandon him.

He heard the alderman coming long before he saw him exit the passage and turn right towards the broken fountain, unaware that there was anyone waiting in the deeper shadows. He was alone, as Wilkinson had promised, and right on time.

The deep sound of the great bell drifted across from Palace Gate. Archer padded silently forwards towards Henry Dawson's broad, sloping back.

Author's Note

This is a work of fiction, wrapped about a kernel of historical truth.

The Northumberland and Durham witch hunt of 1649-50, prosecuted with the help of Scottish pricker John Kincaid, killed at least thirty-six people.

The assizes in Newcastle tried thirty women, along with one man, that Matthew Bulmer or Bonner who was called their warlock. The scale of the proceeding makes it by some distance the largest recorded witch trial in England. The twenty women hung to death overlooking the Tweed, at Gallows Knowe in Berwick, meanwhile represent the greatest loss of life in a single English witch prosecution. No documentary evidence survives to provide any detail of the Berwick proceedings, but the fragmentary historical record relating to the Newcastle trials hints at uniquely troubling circumstances.

Much of what we know of events in Newcastle comes from near-contemporary critics of the Hostmen and their coal monopoly, published in 1655 in Ralph Gardner's pamphlet *'England's grievances discovered, in relation to the coal trade'*. The document forms part of a wider attempt on the part of merchants from Durham and the Tyneside towns downriver of Newcastle to have the town's coal monopoly overturned, presenting a case that the Hostman's Company and the Newcastle corporation were both corrupt and ineffective. Inevitably, therefore, it presents a heavily biased perspective.

The efforts made by Gardner and his patrons to paint a

damning picture of the town authorities provide, however, a unique platform for the voices of the accused. The pamphlet details Margaret Brown's fierce assertion of innocence upon the scaffold, alongside an account of Lieutenant-Colonel Hobson's intervention to rescue a young woman by exposing Kincaid's pricking as a sham. Gardiner further draws upon Elinor Loumsdale and her extraordinary all-female campaign to free the women, which is itself confirmed by a surviving court record threatening to prosecute Elinor for suborning a witch trial witness. The sufferings of the Newcastle witches become presented to us with unusual, if horrifyingly painful, directness.

Above all else, we have the names of the dead.

The anomalies contained within the death list demand their own explanation. It is unknown, elsewhere, for so many accused women to be drawn from important families. It is intriguing to realise that these families sat upon both sides of the town's political divide. There are two further salient features about the combined records. A conviction rate of twenty-seven out of thirty is extraordinarily high for an English witch proceeding. Historian Malcolm Gaskill's work estimates that a normal acquittal rate would be three in four. Once condemned in an English witch trial of this period, execution almost always followed. For twelve out of twenty-seven women in the Newcastle trials to have escaped, being hung upon the Town Moor is entirely without precedent.

It is simply not possible to know, from such limited and partial source materials, exactly what happened or why. Such is the process of history.

The fictional version of events presented here provides one possible explanation, one supported by all of the surviving evidence. Such is the process of fiction.

But fiction this is. The truth, whatever it may be, was buried along with the women underneath Saint Andrew's churchyard. If you can, visit their grave site near the ruins of Newgate prison in the shadow of Newcastle's blackened and broken town wall.

Many of the small cross alleys and passages where the action unfolds are gone, but the principal steps and chares survive. Tuthill Stairs or The Long Stairs can still be followed down to The Close and its proud row of remodelled merchant houses, while more of the old chares newly thrive along the length of Newcastle's rejuvenated Quayside. All sign of Mistress Thompson's house is gone, but the Castle Stairs can still be climbed towards the Black Gate, which continues to glower menacingly in the shadow of the high Victorian railway arches cleaving the castle in two. The cathedral church of Saint Nicholas, with its expensive, ornate memorials to many of the families portrayed in this book, is only steps away from the tightly atmospheric confines of Pink Lane, in which it still feels as if Davey might at any moment emerge from some anonymous doorway. Further afield, a circular walk along the south bank of the Tweed from Norham's castle to its Dene remains a walk through a history which feels all too immanent.

Most named characters in 'The Wicked Of The Earth' are historically documented, drawn from sources such as the Newcastle guild lists; corporation records; the regimental rolls of both the New Model Army and Royalist feudal levies; from petitions to Parliament and from other contemporaneous commentaries. The principal characters, James and Meg Archer, are entirely fictitious, as is Ephraim Ord.

The engineer's work is based upon real technologies associated with the contemporary coal and lead mining industries. Deep mining, located further away from ready water transport, had become common across England by the 1630s, necessitating research into engineering solutions such as water pumps and wooden wagonways. The first effective safety lamps were not introduced commercially into the Northumberland and Durham coalfields until the mid-eighteenth century, but an engineer like Ord, based in an expanding trading town such as Newcastle, would have had access to continental lamp engine designs. Large, crude safety lamps, such as the piece he shows to Archer, were at this time already in use in Scandinavia and the German states.

The needs of a fictional narrative have taken precedence over documented history in two further instances. Janet Martin, being from Morpeth, in the jurisdiction of the county of Northumberland, was held in Newcastle Castle, rather than in Newgate Prison, before being led to her execution alongside the others on the Town Moor. Archer's encounters in the Castle being focused upon Captain Draper, Sir Arthur Heselrigg and William Blackett, along with the discovery of Matthew Bulmer / Bonner's torture chamber, Janet's incarceration has here been relocated to Newgate. Similarly, there is no historical evidence to suggest Elinor Loumsdale's loss of reason, which is imagined for dramatic purpose.

The breek is a real, but undocumented, phenomenon. The term, possibly a corruption of 'breach', or alternatively a derivation from 'reek', was in use among telephone engineers working in manholes on Newcastle's quayside in the late 1940s. My father, an apprentice cable jointer at that time, experienced the rush of the breek, barely escaping from a manhole before one of its foul explosions. He spoke also of an older colleague having drowned due to being overcome by its fumes. The breek's inclusion is in tribute to my

Dad, a true Novocastrian who loved Newcastle and its stories.

Northumbrian hill-shepherds and lead miners are recorded as speaking a variant of Welsh well into the nineteenth century. A glance at a map reveals the extent to which place names in the old language dominate the Northumberland high lands. Elinor's few words are delivered in modern Welsh, since it would add nothing to the story to attempt to recreate such a lost dialect.

Finally, all dates are in old form, according to the Julian calendar. England did not migrate to the Gregorian calendar then in use in Central and Western Europe, and by which we reckon today, until September 1752.

ACKNOWLEDGEMENTS

To begin, as everyone should, at the beginning, first thanks must go to my late parents, not least for the many childhood days spent playing French Cricket in Warkworth moat, or fighting through a salt wind towards the low bulk of Dunstanburgh Castle. A love of history, of story and of place seems to have stuck. Thanks Mum and Dad.

My family have had to keep long company with Archer, Elizabeth and Wicked's wider cast of characters. Your love and support has always meant so much. Special gratitude is also owed to Mark Barnard, a great reader full of insight and enthusiasm, and Brian Nobile, who was unafraid to offer detailed criticism where it was unquestionably due.

I was fortunate enough to be selected for Curtis Brown Creative's comprehensive novel editing course, which I cannot recommend highly enough. All of the course staff offered tremendous support and challenge, but particular thanks belong to Jennifer Kerslake and to my fellow writers, most especially Joan Forbes for her meticulous reading, consistently sound advice and detailed coaching on Ayrshire dialect.

Finally, with love, to the late Sheila Patricia Bilbao, who first believed.

FIND US ON SOCIAL MEDIA

Facebook: @northodoxpress

Instagram: @northodoxpressofficial

Twitter: @northodoxpress

TikTok: @northodoxpress

www.northodox.co.uk

NORTHODOX PRESS

SUBMISSIONS

CONTEMPORARY
CRIME & THRILLER
FANTASY
LGBTQ+
ROMANCE
YOUNG ADULT
SCI-FI & HORROR
HISTORICAL
LITERARY

SUBMISSIONS@NORTHODOX.CO.UK

SUBMISSIONS

CALLING ALL NORTHERN AUTHORS!

Q Northodox.co.uk

DO YOU LIVE IN OR COME FROM NORTHERN ENGLAND?

DO YOU HAVE AN INTERESTING STORY TO TELL?

Email *submissions@northodox.co.uk*

- [ ] The first 3 chapters OR 5,000 words
- [ ] *1 page synopsis*
- [ ] *Author bio (tell us where you're based)*

* No non-fiction, poetry, or memoirs

OUT OF HUMAN SIGHT

A HISTORICAL MYSTERY

SOPHIE PARKES

Sometimes doing the right thing is the greatest mistake of all.

PAUL D COOMBS

THE GREAT ORME

ABRAXUS ELIJAH HONEY

ELLA RUBY SELF

Milton Keynes UK
Ingram Content Group UK Ltd.
UKHW042133211124
451468UK00004B/58